10-02

DATE DUE			
JUL 30 2006		NOV 27 2006	
OCT 0 7 2011		DEC 1 9 2006	
DISCARDED BY THE			
URBANA FREE LIBRARY			

The Mermaid
THAT CAME BETWEEN THEM

The Mermaid
THAT CAME BETWEEN THEM

by Carol Ann Sima

COFFEE HOUSE PRESS :: MINNEAPOLIS

This book is dedicated to
Selma and Morris
Diane and Mark
Hollie
Marla and Nicholas
Susan and Luke

Coffee House Press is an independent nonprofit literary publisher sup-
ported in part by a grant provided by the Minnesota State Arts Board,
through an appropriation by the Minnesota State Legislature, and in
part by a grant from the National Endowment for the Arts. Significant
support for this project came from the Jerome Foundation. Support
has also been provided by Athwin Foundation; the Bush Foundation;
Elmer L. & Eleanor J. Andersen Foundation; Honeywell Foundation;
James R. Thorpe Foundation; McKnight Foundation; Patrick and
Aimee Butler Family Foundation; Pentair, Inc.; The St. Paul
Companies Foundation, Inc.; the law firm of Schwegman, Lundberg,
Woessner & Kluth, P.A.; Star Tribune Foundation; the Target
Foundation; West Group; Woessner-Freeman Family Foundation; and
many individual donors. To you and our many readers across the
country, we send our thanks for your continuing support.

Coffee House Press books are available to the trade through our primary distributor, Consortium Book Sales & Distribution, 1045
Westgate Drive, Saint Paul, MN 55114. For personal orders, catalogs,
or other information, write to: Coffee House Press, 27 North Fourth
Street, Suite 400, Minneapolis, MN 55401.

Information on Volvos comes from "A Dream Car Doubles As a Guardian
Angel," by James G. Cobb, *The New York Times,* March 23, 2001.

LIBRARY OF CONGRESS CATALOGING-IN-PUBLICATION DATA

Sima, Carol Ann,
The mermaid that came between them : a novel / by Carol Ann Sima
p. cm.
ISBN 1-56689-124-8 (alk. paper)
1. Triangles (Interpersonal relations)—Fiction. 2. Fathers and sons—
Fiction. 3. Seaside resorts—Fiction. 4. Authorship—Fiction. 5.
Mermaids—Fiction. 1 Title

PS3569.I472353 M47 2002
813'.54—DC21   2001052944

1 3 5 7 9 10 8 6 4 2

PRINTED IN THE UNITED STATES

ACKNOWLEDGMENTS:

Ben Camardi, gallant knight, the man on the white horse, the slayer of dragons,
the doer of kind deeds. To Sir, with love. I thank you.

My publisher, Allan Kornblum, is a knockout editor. He really gets in there. Then he writes it
all up in such a masterly, diplomatic, positive way that even when I can't do a single drop more,
I'm suddenly thinking, Whole new chapters? No problem.

Family, who are also treasured friends: Blanche, Ida, Aaron, Edythe, Ken, Betsy.

In remembrance: Bubbe and Aunt Beaty.

The kids I love. On my best day, I was never this good:
Drew, Lauren, Tiffany, Matthew, Joey.

My second family, hearth of my soul:
Yolanda and Al, Chris and David, Howard, and Debbie.

More friends, the all-for-one, one-for-all kind: Jane, Natalie, Arnold,
Brian, Pamela, Edward, Mary, Joan, Pam, Llewellyn, Jerry, Jill, Sharon.

Saul: All of the above, and more.

My mother nurtures the daydreams.

My father understands the kid in the adult.

My sister is my guardian angel, my confidante. She illuminates and sustains me.

Mark is my great, enduring helpmate.

Hollie lightens my heart and captivates me with her imagination and wit.

Without Marla's approval, I would never have forged ahead. Her insights were the scaffolding
upon which I built my characters.

Nicholas, who sweetens all our days.

Years and years of reading my work, back and forth phone calls, two and three and four A.M.—
everything is better because of Susan's ingenuity and creativity. She's a kindred soul.
She does friendship and unconditional love like no one I know.

Luke never wavered in his faith. From the moment we met,
I just knew he'd be a major influence.

The Mermaid

THAT CAME BETWEEN THEM

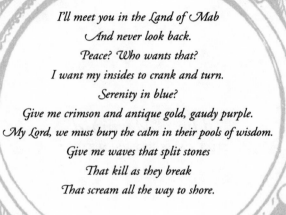

I'll meet you in the Land of Mab
And never look back.
Peace? Who wants that?
I want my insides to crank and turn.
Serenity in blue?
Give me crimson and antique gold, gaudy purple.
My Lord, we must bury the calm in their pools of wisdom.
Give me waves that split stones
That kill as they break
That scream all the way to shore.

—ROBIN DORMAN

Prologue

At the ripe old age of five years and four days, Jacob Koleman was about to fall in love. It was the start of summer, on a desolate strip of Southampton sand. Reared on Grandpa Marshall's stories of treasures buried at sea and sunken ships, he was especially fond of the Old Man of the Sea, royal ruler, king of jeweled castles and skyscraper cities, surfing the waves in a chariot drawn by six giant squid.

"The Old Man of the Sea has grandchildren, scores," Grandpa said, "some your age." Dozing off in the shade of a striped beach umbrella, perpetually tilted to one side no matter how deeply wedged in, Grandpa gave orders for Jacob to take the first watch. "Keep your eyes open, Mate. The Old Man's closer than you think."

Jacob put the finishing touches on his sand castle. He patrolled the shore, careful to stay within shouting distance, even though Grandpa was so hard of hearing, everything you said had to be repeated. Sometimes you had to act it out like you were playing charades.

When three barechested girls surfaced just offshore, Jacob wasn't startled. Standing at the water's edge, he asked, "Is the Old Man of the Sea your granddaddy?"

"Sure," they said. "Want to meet him?"

Jacob was not a willful child. Fooling around with matches was unthinkable. He ate his spinach without complaint. Each and every Sunday, without fail, he dropped ten of his pennies in the poor box for the starving children of India. He obeyed the rules.

One rule was, if Grandpa's napping, go up to your ankles. No farther.

The girls smiled, their two front teeth missing, same as his. Boys aren't supposed to stare at titties, so he didn't.

"Follow us," they said. Hurry.

He waded in. Ankles, calves . . .

"Now or never," they said.

. . . knees, waist. He was in, all the way. He clutched their hands, holding tight like Mama said to do crossing the street. He thought of Grandpa Marshall, snoring up a bee storm, opening one eye, then two, seeing the castle Jacob carved. But no Jacob. Grandpa Marshall would search the Ark, a real live, old-as-Grandpa ship turned beach house. Still no Jacob. Grandpa might release the Ark's grips, put his shoulder to the Arkhouse, slide it back into the water, and set sail. Only nowadays, Grandpa couldn't stand too well and the decks of the Arkhouse creaked, the roof leaked, the masts swayed in the wind—the sea might swallow them up. And Mama would weep.

He squirmed. He tried letting go, but it was three against one. He was seized, netted, and towed. In the struggle, he saw the girls were bare down there too. But they didn't have legs. They were fishtailed.

Dragged kicking and screaming, Jacob Koleman had every reason in the world not to fall in love. Yet far more wondrous than the Old Man in his kingdom at sea, Jacob was moments away from catching a glimpse of an altogether different kind of kingdom.

They were under an abandoned wharf. The shallow water was lukewarm. Small as the holes in the netting were, they couldn't keep his skinny arms from sticking out. The three girls nipped before he could swat them. The stings stopped him cold. Freed from the netting, he went limp. The girls sang. "Oh Still-Waters-Running-Deep, wise and ancient waters of life, do not forsake your Daughters of the Sea. May this be the day we spawn."

They shivered, they got goosebumpy. They made baby sounds like the newborn kittens belonging to Jacob's neighbor. He got goose-bumpy too. His arms burned where he'd been bit. His head felt fuzzy like it had bubbles.

The girls rubbed his thighs, he didn't push away. Their hands on his chest weren't anything like Mama's fingers patting him when he had a fever.

It was at that instant that he decided to take a good, long look at their titties. Just what he'd been taught not to do. Mama's Little Prince, behaving just like a pirate.

Suddenly, his pee-pee swung out. He pushed it down. It wouldn't stay. He escaped and darted wildly away. The girls looked like their feelings were hurt. They were stuck in the mud like somebody glued them in. Their faces got spotty red. They bit their nails. As he ran across the muddy banks, he could feel their pretty-please-don't-leave-us stares. The two diddies on his chest were pebble hard. Pressure in his groin swelled him up.

Sprinting past Granddaddy, still sound asleep, Marshall's tummy the shape of a basketball, legs thin as the letter I, the bulge in Jacob's bathing suit pointed him straight thataway. Leaving a muddy trail of footprints, he barely reached the Johnny in time. He relieved himself, the most he ever peed. Rain buckets. At least it wasn't stiff and sore anymore.

❦

Many things were beyond his understanding, but this he knew: Never tell a soul who dragged you off. Keep it to yourself. You aren't a single drop sorry where your eyes went (almost stayed, too). They'd send him away to summer camp, wash his mouth out with soap, say he was girl crazy when it wasn't girls he was zippo over.

Nothing but questions remained.

Did mermaids do sleepovers?

Were their titties magnets?

Would they let him touch?

Most of all, would he ever tell Mama her perfect Prince was, once upon a time, a Naughty Boy.

AUGUST, 1963

Smitten for the second time, the circumstances were entirely different. Jacob had been hired to write a brochure for a New York City public school. He visited the site. This was in the era before security guards and metal detectors. All the same, one couldn't just roam at will. There were procedures.

He went to the main office where he was name-tagged. The guide assigned to him was soft-spoken. When she asked him about himself, she listened to his answers. He liked that she wasn't too inquisitive. She didn't toss quips like horseshoes. She wasn't put off by his awkwardness or how his voice sometimes broke out like he was still stuck in puberty. Baby pink ribbons adorned her hair. Another time, another place, she might have carried a parasol. She would, perhaps, have looked after orphans and strays. Her eyes were green—almost sea green—but with none of the sea's turbulence. They were serene as cathedral glass. Her curves were female. There was nothing not to like.

A year later, they married.

Not until they were legal did his pee-pee make the acquaintance of her sugar cube. The whole time, he kept his eyes shut.

They honeymooned at the Ark. He scanned the ocean. He didn't tell her what for. Every mermaid sighting turned out to be dolphins. Just as well. The second time one falls in love, one ought to be able to look back on First Love like it isn't even a close second.

$\mathcal{O}ne$

In which Jacob discusses his divorce with his ex,
attends an art opening, offends his son's girlfriend,
and meets Kate Vestor, Conflict Counselor.

AUGUST, 1997

The keys were a hurdle. The lawyers handling the divorce gave the Kolemans rave reviews, lavishing the kind of unqualified praise that Jacob's novels, well-received as they were, could only aspire to. Phrases like, "best in decades," "if only they were all like this" and—Jacob was especially partial to this one—"restores our faith in the benevolence of mankind." But usage of keys was, of course, restricted. He may not barge in uninvited. He may not let himself in, even when invited. They were strictly for emergency purposes only.

Cheryl called, mother of his child, executive in charge of keys (not by word of mouth, in the divorce decree, printed large enough so you didn't have to squint). He nodded into the phone. Yes, be right over, Mac's room? last lingering looks before we ship him off to college? Cheryl asked for verbal confirmation. He forgot she couldn't see him nod, wasn't there in the room, didn't physically share the same space. "On my way," he said.

The keys in his pocket felt like paperweights. But standing outside the door to her brownstone, he was honorbound.

It was August. Sweltering, unbearable . . . naked in New York City, and you'd still be overdressed. His earlobes were growing slacker by the minute, practically grazing his shoulders. Prior to the inexorable wait to be buzzed in, they were nowhere near swinging, cheesy pendulums. Killer humidity, gravity using him for target practice—if not now, when?

"When I key in on why Cheryl divorced me, that's when," he thought. "Saying she doesn't know the reason is not the same as saying she doesn't have one. Once I have the passkey to that, there's no door in the world that can keep us apart."

The brownstone's owner had never installed a security camera. No one would be the wiser. After all, puddles were forming at his feet. "She dumped me without any probable cause whatsoever. Thirty-three years, our voices were never raised." Under his watchband, things were getting squishy.

He held out, dug in, kept his itchy trigger finger off the keychain, observed protocol, did it by the handbook, like his laudable driving record—only one traffic violation, period. Marital record exemplary. Lusting after no other nonamphibians except his wife . . . and Marilyn Monroe. (His feelings for Marilyn weren't chaste—whose were?—but at no time had he ever maxed out on masturbation.) The marriage exemplified fidelity, not sainthood. (His pursuit of mermaids didn't mean he loved Cheryl any less. Or them more. Rowing and swimming in the Atlantic is the lowest of low-rung surveillance. Exercise is cardiovascular. Can't a man have a pastime? Be nostalgic? Stretch his legs? Study footprints in the sand to see if any are tailprints?)

Just when the squish under his watchband began rolling down his fingers, she buzzed. The door clicked open. Borne by love, his legs sprang to life.

Cheryl, my land Goddess, won't you please take me back?

THE MERMAID THAT CAME BETWEEN THEM

The points of her elbows were snub-nosed.

She stood in the doorway, left arm folded vertically. Her hankie, cradled in her palm, was trimmed in lace, like a wedding veil. Blotting is for ink; her tears were dabbed. A documentary he once saw on art restoration showed the same tender ministrations. Not seeing the wedding band on her third finger, only a ghostly band of pale skin, he compared it to the time before. His little ritual: take readings of the fading outline, like you do a barometer. He set a tentative date, sort of a deadline: the day the mark would be no more—early fall was his estimate—by then, she'd change her mind. Hopefully. Because love lives on. Because she treasures him.

Cheryl's air kisses were plentiful, released in threes and fours like doves set free at a peace rally. "Soon as the packing crates came, I started blinking back tears of happiness." Pivoting with grace, she started for Mac's room. After years of ballet classes, she was sea foam.

"Mac's over at the gallery," she explained. "Intellectually, he recognized how meaningful it was for you and I to mark this auspicious occasion. All those touch-and-go years—the crisis over college applications—how can we be matter-of-fact now? Our boy's going away. The stuffed owls are going into storage, even Mr. Gerbil's corpse is going beddy-bye."

En route, they passed the living room, nearly identical to the one he went home to nightly. His re-creation of the original was an homage to enduring love. Carpet, gray with blue overtones, the color of winter ocean. The wooden tips of the chairs and divan seemed squiggly one day, wavy the next.

Arriving first, she graciously waited. Her emerald green sleeveless silk was more muted than neon. Cheryl didn't jar the eye. She was that other kind of eye candy. Quiet elegance. Delicate slithers of gold graced her wrist, bangles one could wear with assurance to the theater. Her poise made him stand up straighter.

"The confined space may have prompted Mac's absence." Her voice precisely the tone of warmth and concern you'd want of someone delivering a eulogy over your casket. "We know exactly where we stand in relation to each other: friends forever, but husband and wife, never again. However, within the narrow confines of his room, the three of us in close quarters—you on one side of him, me on the other, Mac in the middle, enveloped in close family bonds and no hard feelings—seeing it through the eyes of a child, it's a challenging setting. By fleeing to the art gallery, he's telling us he's not emotionally up to the challenge."

Jacob could identify with that. What kind of divorce is it when two people get along so well? Alarm bells went off in his head. In a misguided attempt to reduce Mac's alleged confusion, might Cheryl have deliberately distanced herself? Found another friend to confide in? Worst scenario, she would begin leading the life of a single woman. She'd date, she'd expose Mac to tall, dark, handsome strangers who'd wine and dine her. She and the tallest, darkest, handsomest might ride off into the sunset. Somehow, he would have to find the words to preserve their close-knit happy home.

"We pep-talked him through the choppy waters of high school," he agreed. "We'll continue to toss him lifelines, and he'll catch them. Six years from now, after the bar exam, he can study taxidermy to his heart's content. I'm confident, trust me on this: Seeing us together, regardless of the size of the room, provides the kind of solidarity he can draw strength from."

She smiled appreciatively. He felt as if his tummy had been rubbed. She wouldn't enter the room ahead of him. Her consideration wasn't just window-dressing; she sincerely wanted a simultaneous entrance. He obliged by aligning himself shoulder to shoulder. They crossed the threshold. To his right was a mirror. The short guy with the close-cut, thinning gray hair looked played out. The sack on this kangaroo wasn't empty. Attached to his abdomen was a ten-pound lump of fat. The rest of him was slim. Muscles indecipherable, like the fine print you need a magnifying glass to read. His dockers looked blah.

They sat on Mac's trundle bed.

"It's been such a long haul. His journey from preemie to pre-law placed so many demands on us," she sighed, crossing her legs, barely disturbing the air. "Had I known then what I know now, I wouldn't have been so indulgent. Spending that year volunteering in P.S. 12's gifted and talented program was instrumental in predisposing me to bright kids pursuing eclectic interests."

"I, on the other hand, was the stay-at-home dad, the reins were mine to pull as well. Does stifling a kid's hobbies stifle his creativity? I didn't have it in me then, and I don't have it in me now."

The gold standard of most green-eyed beauties was not in her arsenal. Her eyes didn't spit fire. They could, however, narrow to slits . . . tender drops of tears peeking out the corners like pristine petticoats. "These are still his formative years. We are his reality checks," she explained, gesturing toward the walls. "In other words, the worship of a dead icon is not what a woman looks for in a companion. Man-to-man, you've got to tell him to lay off Marilyn."

Posters of Marilyn Monroe peered down on them from the ceiling. Every inch of wall space belonged to her too, even the inside of Mac's closet.

"There's never been a bone of contention between you and me," he offered, buying time, arranging the words in his head.

"Hardly ever."

"He's a late bloomer, eventually he'll get off the ground," he tried to take the heat off Mac.

"No, the spell must be broken. Eighteen dateless years? Marilyn's marginalizing our boy."

Drawing himself up to his full five feet seven, pulling his stomach in, he stood with the dignity of a patriot singing the national anthem. "Marilyn Monroe *is* an intrinsic part of the American landscape. Generations of boys owe her. She is the male fantasy. Crossreference *that* with your shrink. Life without fantasy is a harsh reality. To live in the real world, both feet on solid land, earth between your toes, floor beneath your feet, reality *must* occasionally be checked at the door." Hand over his heart. "When it comes to accepting our lot in life, the path would be rockier without her."

"Mac's a diehard, he's hooked."

"Point well-taken. But not tonight. Not yet. It's the stuff of turning points."

She toured the room, fingers to lips, puckering, kissing, touching the furniture like sacred relics, bestowing canoodles of kisses more substantive than the air-filled ones she greeted *him* with. It broke his heart. He wanted to put his head on her chest and cry, *Take me back, I'll do anything.* He embarked on a different tack.

"This mutual admiration society of ours isn't getting us anywhere. Suppose we turn up the static. I'm not advocating slinging mud or tongue-lashing—more along the lines of a heated exchange. People in the heat of the moment stand a better chance of inadvertently saying things they never would otherwise."

Her hands, only seconds earlier fluttering like the wings of angels, dropped to her sides. She came toward him, gliding like a heron making a water landing. She requested a moment to collect her thoughts, ended up taking several. Then her words took flight.

"Much as I told myself this day might come, there's really no preparing. Go ahead and have your outburst. But first hear me out. It's my hope our divorce will be every bit as successful as our marriage. You always brought out the best in me. But I can't tell you what I don't know. One bright spot—it's not as uncommon as you think. Getting divorced under a cloud of mystery surrounding my motivation, though frustrating, doesn't mean I'm mental. In Finkle's experience, rushing to judgment leaves one with more questions than answers. Arriving at an all-conclusive universal takes time. And even then, Finkle's seeing a trend toward flip-flop. Complete switcheroos. The definitive answer (derived under proper supervision) often backslides into hypotheticals. What you have left is . . . square one."

His voice was level, like train tracks across Kansas. He couldn't spook an old lady on a dark, dead-end street. The furrow of his brow lacked hump. "I demand an answer, I don't give a damn what that cockamamie radio jock pseudo-shrink says. That's *my* outburst, and I stand by it."

"You wonderful man, you. There's nothing about you I don't admire. Kind, courteous, patient, loyal, faithful, principled, smart, attentive. Your nurturance—innate to you—has no rival. None. My Prince."

Writing of knaves and cutthroats who get away with murder, manipulative, blackhearted pirates of the high seas, was how he earned his living. But the Prince's Code of Conduct was how he lived. During his outburst—brief as it was—he felt his entire Princehood at risk.

"Yet somewhere along the line, I . . . the Prince . . . fell out of favor. It's Mac, isn't it? While you were knocking yourself out raising private funds for public education, I was the primary caregiver. It was at my breast he first developed an interest in gerbils, hamsters, and whatnot. I introduced him to Marilyn. Me. Me. Before he lost his first tooth, he was watching Marilyn flicks."

"A boy couldn't wish for a better father," she consoled. "Whatever the inexplicable rationale that's compelled me not to grow old with you, the quality of your parenting isn't it. Dr. Finkle and I are constantly dialoguing. Anything even remotely resembling an approximate answer would be a start." Her lower lip trembled. Her voice quivered.

"Do you really think I relish feeling like mystery meat?"

Under Marilyn's glare, they resumed sitting on the bed. Achingly close. The scent on her skin was arousing. He didn't have on any after-shave, not that it would do any good. Marilyn was available. They'd done it before. Now and then. Never in Cheryl's presence, that would be a cheat. The divorce didn't kill it for him and Marilyn . . . but something had been lost in the transition.

Tomorrow night he'd be at the Ark.

Oh Daughters of the Sea, you got there first . . . nobody ever forgets his first time. But I can't help who I really am.

❀

The title of the show was *Dickheads,* something he and Cheryl found out when they got there. Jacob read from the flier. "Maya Evans's exploratory range has been called defiantly delicious. Looking at her portraits, the viewer looks in vain for faces. Maya's globes—males turning their backs to the camera—is a back-of-the-head striptease. Not content to just let the lads' posterior heads flaunt the phallic, she delves deep into the erotic. In the tradition of Georgia O'Keeffe's sexed-up flowers, Ms. Evans's cranial photos are imbued with sensuality and vulnerability. In the best sense of the word, the back of these heads are two-faced. *Dickheads* will be shown through Labor Day, part of our Discovery Showcase, sponsored by EYE PRIDE."

They hadn't spotted Mac yet. The gallery was on two levels. Just inside the entrance was a wet bar.

Glass in hand, Cheryl said, "If this isn't one big divorce backlash, then what is? Three months go by. The crucial three. Each session with Finkle, I report there's nothing to report. Mac doesn't act out, the moods don't swing. Now that his delayed reaction is finally here, it's like nothing I expected."

"The important thing is, we aren't floored *individually*. We live apart, but we unite to floor together."

"Three months of anticipating God-knows-what. He doesn't give us the finger, no fresh batch of cadavers, no spending spree on replicas of Marilyn. Instead he gives us . . . penishead." Clinking her glass forcefully against his. Had his glass been filled to the rim, his sandals wouldn't have walked away unscathed. "Granted, it's artsy-fartsy, but any way his teenage sexuality comes, I'll take it. He's broadcasting loud and clear: Look Ma, I'm a boy."

Over his dead body would divorce get all the credit. "And you attribute this to breaking up?"

"Finkle says all children of divorce backlash."

"For all you know, Mac's first baby steps into teenage sexuality could be connected to Marilyn." Momentarily dropping his eyes to his groin. "Suppose Mac went into overdrive, patting himself while gazing at her. What's he really broadcasting? *Look Dad, Marilyn's finally made a man of me?*" Eyebrows arched to his hairline. "Understand, I'm not being belligerent, there isn't a belligerent bone in my body. But I strongly caution against snap rulings."

She mulled it over. "My magnificent Prince. Always encouraging me to give all sides a fair hearing. First chance we get, we'll ask Mac directly."

They started through the crowd, four deep in front of the photos, backs of heads obscuring their view of pictures of backs of heads.

Finally, they spotted Mac. Hanging on his arm, another arm. A female, old enough to be his mother, red nails sharp as talons.

🍥

Mac and Cheryl nuzzled. They hugged. They kissed, five consecutive, nonincestuous thirst quenches. A miserly chickenscratch peck for Jacob. Boys will be boys.

"Mom, Dad, I'd like you to meet Maya Evans."

Cheryl gave her proper first name: Cheryl. She gave Jacob's too, first and last: Jacob Koleman. Maya thrust her hand into his, a handshake like a gladiator.

Hands off my son. Rumors of my open-minded/sissy-liberal-pacifist peace-on-earth reputation have been greatly exaggerated. I am a strict/no-nonsense/authoritative/patriarchal/neck-wrenching despot. Mean streak miles long. Raw meat for breakfast. One bad ass. Right before bed, bacon rinds. Don't go by my grip, go by my clenched eyebrows.

Unflaggingly cordial, Cheryl made Maya feel welcome. "A portion of the annual monies I raise for public education goes to the arts." Then she consumed the rest of the wine. Half a glass, down the gullet.

Even from the front, the back of Maya's head loomed large. Her hair was a curly red blaze that wouldn't go out. Her perfume was citrus. In keeping with her age—forty if she were a day—the face was lined here and there, not running riot, but gearing up. Her T-shirt, the color of Milk of Magnesia. Jeans tight enough to cut off circulation. "The camera loves the back of Mac's head. I could just sink my teeth into his neck, it's so tender. And the skull," palm stretched out over Mac's head, making a saucer landing, "so childlike, on the verge of manhood. What baby-fine hair, what ears—they are his crowning glory. His cherubesque ears."

Cheryl and Jacob mobilized, voices colliding, Jacob's deferring, Cheryl insisting he talk, without delay, say something.

"Great turnout," he said. "Kids, parents, family branches. The controversial nature of your work, it goes without saying . . . jumping to conclusions, you must get alotta that. I write. Mac musta told you, how could he not have? Same in literature. Write a certain way, people get the wrong idea. They think it's you on the page. But who knows you better than you?"

August heat. Mac wore a white shirt and black leather jacket from his junior high days. The shooting-up-overnight stage—boys growing out of their clothes by morning—had skipped him.

"Perhaps I was being too abstruse," Jacob said. "Do you see your work as *self-expression* of the true self or the *opposite* of self?"

The pup zipped his jacket. "Maya's a babe," Mac said. "Now you know." He stood with legs apart, like a gunslinger.

Slender and featherweight, delicate as froth, Cheryl hardly tipped the scales. Meringue as pie filling. Helium light. Noncorporeal. But with the deftness of a samurai, she severed the connection between Maya and Mac, inserting herself between them. Not pausing to rest on her laurels, she said to Maya and Jacob, "Mac's going to give me the grand tour. We'll leave you two to get better acquainted."

Off they went.

Could this be his son? The razorcut on the rear end of his head was a tiny likeness of Maya.

"Ask away," Maya said.

"How serious is it?"

"Semiplatonic. We hold hands. We kiss, mouths shut. We don't feel each other up below the waist. I've got an instinct for cuntteasers, groupies, and fortune hunters. Your son doesn't meet the criteria. Let's just say he's curious and leave it at that."

A moment ago, it was "ask away," now it was "leave it at that." Two riddles too many. An unsolved divorce wasn't like driving yourself crazy looking under the couch cushions for reading glasses. The mental antics, wrestling, self-recriminations, chasing after your own tail, investigating, pouring over testimony—what Prince wouldn't be stretched thin?

"Have a heart. Don't leave me hanging. I throw myself on your mercy. There are things you aren't telling me." His whole body went slack.

"Don't start in on tears. It doesn't warrant tears. Mac's just passing through. End of story."

"Done?" he asked.

"In your dreams," she snapped. "I'm good company, damn good.

Dynamic. Interactive. I give off. Mac may be passing through, but while he's here, it's never been better. He's one hell of a soulful kid."

Not far-fetched at all. Mac's touched her tender spot. She admits it's going nowhere. But she's melancholy, disappointed, lonely, lost. His tender spot had a sudden urge to comfort hers.

"In fact," he offered, "I see what he sees in you. If I may say so, one feeling person to another, you are special."

Three inches taller, she didn't have to stand on tippytoes. She fastened on. Her palm to his cranium. She traced his lumps and bumps. She studied him from behind. "He gets it from you. I sense it, you sense it, don't bother denying it. You're some kind of special yourself. We should put our heads together. Meet me later for a drink. If anything comes of it, I'm sure the three of us can work out an . . . arrangement."

A string of stunning blows, now another stunner. Ambushed by mermaids precipitated decades of celibacy. He married for second love. He fell for Monroe (more unrequited love). The one and only fully consummated love of his life divorced him. Plus bringing a child up properly is no picnic. Now Maya wants what she can't have. Sharing a woman is as taboo as it gets. He wanted to say, Forget it Lady, the Kolemans will never join a harem. What he actually said was, "Thank you, no."

"Dickhead," she gave him the middle joint. "I'm gunna tell," vanishing into the crowd.

Imperative he find Mac before Maya wreaked havoc. A man of Jacob's character doesn't make moves on his son's babe. His word against hers. Yet she had the advantage. His son held her hand. Kissing took place. No one ever forgets his first time. He yanked his cell phone, frantically trying to raise Cheryl. No margin for error. Always a first time for everything—so the proverb goes. Anything at anytime. A loophole through which sons and dads become estranged over something that did not, could not, wouldn't in a million years take place: threeways, ménages-à-trois, love triangles, father and son vying for the same woman. The Kolemans would roll over in their graves. These are not the ways of Princes and their descendants.

"What's your present location?" he said after Cheryl picked up.

"Restroom, second floor. Make an immediate left."

"And Mac?"

"Waiting outside. I'll be a while, it's only a two-stall."

He delayed for an instant to do what people in foxholes do. I'm not a man of any faith in any heavenly being, but God in heaven, could You use Your influence with Maya? Distract her, detain her. A Koleman father/son talk is boys only. I talk, Mac listens. Give and take: Mac talks, I listen. I set the tone. I lead. Mac is free to agree or disagree. Then I take him by the hand.

The system had been put to the test many times: bedtime, doing homework, weekly allowance, watching television, curfews, flossing. There were bugs. Mac overdid Marilyn, Mac's longstanding interest in the taxidermical was cause for concern. Thanks to their talks, however, it was determined that Mac's interest in death wasn't pathological. The boy merely wished to give new life to dead things. Restoration. The dead aren't dead and gone. A pet gerbil is rendered lifelike. Death and life in peaceful coexistence.

He squeezed through the crowd, he struggled up the steps, he speeded up. Still time. Mac was by himself.

"Sorry for springing her on you." The leather jacket was perched on his shoulder. Even if he had not had the good sense to take it off, Jacob wouldn't have automatically thought "impaired judgment." Fashion has its own dictates. "I would've told you guys in advance, but everything happened so fast. Two hours ago, she was somebody else's babe.

Mom will fill you in. No more lectures. We pretty much nailed recreational sex with women on the rebound."

These days Mac was clean-shaven. Facial hair had only made infrequent appearances, like relatives you hear from only on holidays. As a baby he didn't carry much extra weight. Even now, the wind could play catch with him. "So what did you think of her?" The hand in his pocket shot out and squeezed Jacob's arm.

"The shock you're about to receive is for your benefit. Whatever stings you, stings me tenfold." Setting tone, paving the way. "She isn't the one, beyond a shadow of a doubt . . . she doesn't do much for me." His eyes like kites ready to jettison into the wild blue yonder. "My heart goes out to you, Mac. God should strike me dead, I would never lie. The son wasn't enough. She wants the father too."

God, don't strike me dead for my disbelief in You or invoking You at my convenience.

Mac took a step back.

Jacob curved like a parenthesis. "You touched her in her tender spot. She speaks well of you. She cares. Soulful was how she described you. But her expectations for the future of the relationship—as she put it, 'Mac's passing through'—attests to the transitory."

On. The leather jacket, in a hurry, zipped. Lock' n' load over the rib-riddled chest, like the metal rungs were greased.

Rubble on top of rubble. "I simply told her what I saw in her, to comfort her, to aid her in her time of need, to tide her over till she gets over you. The long of and short of it: She's special. As are we all. In the eyes of the Almighty, we give off."

Up. Mac flipping the collar. Too noisy in the gallery for the snap of leather to reverberate. But Jacob caught it. Like the lash of a whip.

"She responded by offering to meet me for a drink, with other sordid interrelations to follow, i.e., going from one to the other, father and son taking turns, getting herself passed back and forth between us like a canapé tray."

"Some Prince you are," Mack finally erupted. "Poured on the charm, and she went for it. Muscled right in. Well, I've got news for you. You aren't the only one on a divorce backlash alert. I've been watching you. Mom and you both. Under your eyes, Bag City. She sleeps with the light on. You live with copycat furniture. Her tears can't all be tears of joy. More has to be on the way. I wasn't born yesterday. I've caught her fussing with her hair. One of these days she'll restyle, maybe change her color. You'll join a gym, tighten the abs, occasionally get your head out of the books. Whenever I tried picturing the two of you in the dating scene, I never put us all in the same scene, everything popping at once." He motioned with his chin. "Before you look over your shoulder and see what I see, remember she's a free woman. Her charm is hers to turn on." The sob had a jagged edge. "Christ, Dad. I'd never poach on you. Get your own babe."

Forcing himself not to turn around, first priority is Mac. "Stay, we'll thrash it out."

"So you can bend my will to yours?" Point-blank range. The same mouth that used to suckle at his dry teat went rat-a-tat-tat. "Divorce is making you nuts. Mom owes you an explanation. Big time. In the meantime, seek help. Until further notice, I'm going to crash on Maya's couch. Don't look me up. Don't trespass. I'm not unraveling. My head's never been in a better place."

Mac sped away.

Jacob called after him. "Her title, *Dickheads,* didn't just happen. A world of titles to choose from, she picks a classic putdown. Hands down, your babe's latent."

Too little, too late. Who but Cheryl to turn to?

Turn and see what?

I can chat up my own ex, can't I? As the recipient of her love and devotion, her admiration, her goodwill, I can turn at will. No reason not to expect a pleasant reception. Why think twice? I come in peace. No latent anything. Up front as they come.

To turn or not to turn?

If she's doing what I think she's doing, she may need a sounding board. I know I do.

To turn or not to turn?

Our son's taken a turn for the worse.

To turn or not to turn?

For the welfare of our son—nothing to do with who Cheryl may be carrying on with—I turn.

She'd never turn me away. As the world turns . . . she's a Princess.

"It is with pleasure I present Mr. Scott Kelsco, Vice President of Kelsco Textiles, on the Board of Directors of Santa Claus Enterprises, and the architect of Weave-It Leave-It, a local chapter of Welcome Mats For The Elderly."

Jacob would have to be from another planet to miss the telltale signpost. Lobbyist at work.

Cheryl netted a cool half mil annually. Trained to see dollar signs, she didn't hit and run. Her solicitations were closer to hospitality visits. She brought sipping port and pitchers of tea made aromatic by herbs grown in the rain forest. He was introduced with meet-the-somebody pride. "Jacob Koleman, author of the Pirate Cassidy series."

"Two of you married?"

"Used to be, not anymore," she said.

Scott lifted Cheryl's hand to his lips. Four Jacobs could fit inside the tan shirt and slacks. Despite the portliness, his features were sharp. Press them against anything fragile—the skin of womankind, Italian leather, wet clay—there would be markings.

Jacob weighed the pluses and minuses. The demand for textbooks in public schools exceeded the supply, never enough computers to go around, too much empty shelf space in the library. He knew just where Cheryl drew the line. No peddling of flesh here. Benefactors may look, but they can't touch.

"Mr. Kelsco's committed five thousand dollars. We're working out the details." Gushing with gratitude, as if four digits were a princely sum.

"It's urgent I speak with you," Jacob said. "A family matter."

Scott straightened up. The kiss mark on her hand was overtly moist. Although the skin wasn't broken, her knuckles were wet as if a dog had slurped all over them. A Band-Aid wouldn't have adhered. He put a monocle in his eye, stepped away and clicked his heels. "Ten A.M. tomorrow, my chauffeur will pick you up. Now if you will excuse me."

When he was well out of earshot, she said, "Ugh." She wiped the mess off her hand, crumpling the hankie afterward.

"I didn't manufacture the family matter. I have too much respect for the work you do."

"Not for one minute did I suspect you of duplicity. The thought wouldn't cross my mind. That it should cross *yours* that it *might* cross mine, instead of being the furthest thing from it, suggests a lack of trust. Oh Jacob, I have been and always will be forthcoming with you."

His face was as crumpled as her hankie. "Mac's under the impression I flirted with Maya. In retrospect, I can see how her wires came to be crossed. My sympathetic ear isn't totally wet behind the ears. A radar tune-up is what I need, some kind of early warning screening process. She wasn't right in the head. Here on in, sympathy from my heart only makes it out through my mouth when the object of my sympathy is socially appropriate. Father and son, alternate days, both on the same day—can you imagine?"

"Where's Mac?"

"In the clutches of her couch. He left strict instructions. We are not to intrude."

"How can we not?"

"He's turned the tables on us. In light of the divorce, our actions aren't going to be seen in any other light. It's like one big smear campaign. Just like that, he declares divorce fallout is at our door. We are, in effect, living under a shadow of suspicion. He anticipates lapses. Metaphorically, he's called into question the competency of the governing body. He thinks we can't uphold the highest laws of the land."

Cheryl uncrumpled her hankie. She bent her arm, the point of her elbow a smooth slope. You couldn't cut butter with it, it couldn't mash a fly. "Yet there is a kernel of truth to what he says." Suspended in space, the hankie lingered between his eyes and hers. She held it steady. "After all, two unmarried, eligible adult entities at loose ends . . ."

Borrowing his son's expression, he said, "I wasn't born yesterday. Lord knows my abs could use work. Feel free to go blonde, cut bangs, perm. Nothing drastic, I hope."

"You want me to be absolutely forthcoming, right?"

"Or sleep on it, see what the morning brings."

"I would like the housekeys returned."

His eyes watering, orbs trying to float away. His tears sprayed. Hers were more like Olympic divers hitting the hankie dead on.

"At least let me see you home," he said.

They weighed it, then agreed. Mac was to be given a two-day cooling off period. Next Thursday was Mac's official college moving-in day, a whole nuclear family event. He offered to cancel his four-day trip to the Arkhouse, bump the departure date up from tomorrow to the weekend, any or all of the above. She said, "Let's play it by ear."

At the brownstone door, she put her palm out.

He looked down at his sandals and murmured, barely audible, throat stoppered up. She stooped to hear him. "No divorce is hassle free. You're not getting off so easy." Taken in context, it wasn't a threat. It was a cry for help. "I like having the keys in my safekeeping. Keys represent significance, something akin to the keys to the Kingdom. Last chance."

His voice dropping to the cheep of a baby sparrow taking in the wide expanse of sky, thinking, No way, you gotta be kidding. "I am this far from balking."

"My Prince, my moral, ethical, hero. You're an impossible act to follow."

"And don't you forget it."

As per her request, he handed over the keys. He walked down the stoop. The door was almost closed. He reversed, taking the steps two at a time. "This is where I put my foot down. Keep my set of keys. You'll always have a place to hang your hat. They're nonrefundable."

She didn't argue.

Coincidentally, just as he arrived at the door to his brownstone (conveniently located just around the corner) the empty space where her keys used to be began burning a hole in his pocket. He couldn't look his own pair in the face. He dialed her from the nearest pub. "No hidden agendas, no latent motives, what would you say if I said, I'm feeling sorry for myself? There, I've said it."

"Your openness does honor to us both. I take you at your word. Your face value is beyond reproach. The 'you-ness' of you isn't anyone else's but yours."

He didn't want to hang up.

She expelled a lengthy string of kisses. "Before you know it, some girl will snatch you up."

Should he deny his availability, it wouldn't be the whole truth and nothing but.

Daughters of the Sea, one's all I ask. Make us compatible. Two hearts beating as one. Continuing as one. Continuity's what I seek. No abrupt adieu thirty-three years later. And if it's not too much trouble . . . stand-out tits.

"Good luck with Scott tomorrow. Mac calls, don't hesitate."

Exchanging vows of love, they hung up.

"What'll it be?" the bartender asked.

"Brine," he said.

The head on the beer was three inches of mouth mustache just waiting to happen. Many times over he witnessed men using the back of their hands. It suited them. But it didn't suit him before the divorce, and it wouldn't suit him during. Cocktail napkins were more his speed. Yet it would be foolhardy to declare himself impervious to change.

Cheryl ended the marriage.

Cheryl demanded the keys back.

Cheryl is a divorcée.

Does it not follow then, a bachelor Prince is free to acquire a consort?

"Want a second?" The bartender used a dishrag to swab the drips and drabs sliding down his mug.

"Sure," he said.

Narrow it to mermaids, and the pickings were slim indeed. No mermaid had ever emerged again. If one had, and he had seen her and he had been married at the time, his course of action would've been wise and just. A Prince does not think with his pee-pee.

Yet First Love is heady waters.

He picked up his beer glass and brought it down with a bang. Jacob Koleman doesn't swim in muddy waters. But unlikely things occur.

Being divorced for no discernible reason was a watershed. Therefore, the Prince (currently unmarried) could not rule out taking a consort. She should be fair in form, easy on the eyes as Marilyn, unspoiled, fresh as springwater, a law-abiding citizen, in every way a feast fit for a Prince. Or she could go back under the rock she crawled out of. Case closed.

The consort hasn't been born yet who can lead me to mudcaked waters and make me drink, he thought. Wet my lips . . . maybe. Swallow mud? . . . fuck no. No stain on my record. I don't carouse. The ways of the wise and just are my ways. A Prince isn't a commoner. But can't a Prince have any fun?

He hoisted his beer. He stood on the stool's rim. Here's to me and a mermaid's bosom.

The stool's rim almost gave way. He grabbed onto the bar, extra anchor insurance.

"Mud in my eye," he muttered. "Here's to kissing and making up."

Then the world toppled sideways.

A young woman broke his fall.

"May I buy you a drink," he asked, "to show my gratitude?"

"On one condition." She was in a business suit. Next to her was an attaché case stuffed to splitsville. "Twelve minutes flat, I'm outta here. Any problem with that?"

"None that I can foresee."

"The meter's running," she said. "You are?"

"Jacob Koleman."

"Kate Vestor. Your occupation?"

"Writer."

"What of?"

"Swashbuckling nautical adventures. Your field is?"

"Conflict Counseling. I'm almost finished with my degree. Where there's peace there's prosperity. I can't believe I get paid for making peace.

I'd do it for free. I'm also cool with conflict preservation. Conflicts shouldn't be put out indiscriminately. They aren't bushfires. Where would passion be without conflict? The battle of the sexes—where would that be? But if you're going to ask me if I'm a success story, do I live by what I preach, save your breath. It's privileged info. Marital status?"

"Divorced."

"As of when?"

"Recently."

"I'm just out of a relationship myself."

While Jacob fished for something to say, she continued.

"He's deceased."

"My condolences." Jacob was no yokel. Hold your sympathy in abeyance till you determine whether Kate Vestor is or isn't missing a screw.

"Maurice didn't rock my world. He was, however, my first brush with death. I try not to dwell on it. Life is for the living. When you raised your glass you seemed in high spirits."

The moment of truth.

"Just how good a problem solver are you?" he asked.

"Try me."

"A guy walks into a bar. He's a good guy. He doesn't have a dark side to his name. Latent nothing. What you see is what you get. He meets this woman. She's half his age, dark sultry eyes, black hair, plump lips. Her lipstick leaves fingerprints on her glass." He fiddled with his cocktail napkin. He folded it into a fan, holding it to his face like a geisha.

"And you'd like to be that glass, wouldn't you" she smiled, tapping the glass like a woodpecker at a telephone pole.

He had no repartée. But he had conflict. "The red-lipped young lady asks if he's in high spirits. It's on the basis of that first impression that she will reach a verdict. Not every single first impression is do or die, but enough are. Basically, there's no impression like the first. First impressions tend to stick forever. But I digress. My conflict is as follows: High Spirits is a crowd pleaser. She works with those who are in turmoil. On a personal level, wellness is probably what she looks for. She finds the mentally healthy in high spirits more appetizing than the mentally healthy who are brooding."

"Safe to say, you aren't in high spirits."

"I wouldn't want to pass myself off as someone I'm not."

"You always talk like this?" She dropped her card on the bar. "You've initiated a conflict inside me. I like that in a man. Obviously you need guidance. You don't have your basics. But I don't have a year-and-a-day." Walking away with a wiggle, her attaché case bounced against her hip like a tambourine.

He left a short time later. No quandary at all. Tomorrow he'd phone Kate Vestor, Conflict Counselor. If the shoe were on the other foot, he'd want her to return the courtesy. He'll explain the purpose of the call is to say there will be no further calls. He will never darken her door. She will never hear from him again. Nothing to do with the impression she made (which was nothing if not spectacular). He just couldn't bring himself to consort with the opposite sex.

Like a kid tying laces for the first time, he fumbled with his keys. His blood alcohol level was a secondary factor. Being stripped of the keys to his former residence was the equivalent of being stripped of rank. The apartment wasn't the same floorplan as his real home and hearth. The bathroom was right off a sprawling living room. The bedroom was in the wrong place too, almost joined at the hip to the kitchen. Cloned furniture was supposed to give the illusion he'd never left, but his kind of homesickness was different from sleepaway camp. The pictures on the night tables were of Cheryl and Mac. They covered a thirty-year span. Opposite on the wall, an enlarged photo of Marilyn. He readied himself for her.

Do with me what you will. The limit's two minutes.

It felt forced like the ahh you give your dentist.

When the deed was done, Marilyn scolded him. *Princey's such a spoilsport. Your heart's not in it.* He pressed a pillow to his chest. His boxer shorts were from last Father's Day. Mac to him, the message inscribed for life in red stitching: World's Greatest Dad.

Cheryl was on his speed dial. I am not a phone stalker. I won't call her. The pillow muffled his sobs. Call me, call me.

Two

In which Jacob suffers the advice of Yondle Carr, (assistant to his agent), receives disappointing news from his agent, Finch, reconciles with his son, hears his ex-wife's R-rated confession, seeks emergency conflict counseling, checks in and out of a clinic for diseased books, and gets fondled by a wet stranger.

His A.M. phone query caught her just as she was leaving. "Mac call yet? I don't have to go to the Arkhouse. Finch isn't my only means of transportation. I can rent from Avis, just say the word. I'll come over in person, pack a bag for Mac. If the kid's a runaway he should have fresh underwear."

She invoked Finkle. "Finkle thinks otherwise. Don't crash Mac's party, especially not when he's mainstreaming, right where he should be on the bell curve. Offspring of the newly divorced who *aren't* touchy, aren't *normal*. Check with me later. I should be through with Kelsco's Textiles anywhere between twelve and one. In the meantime, pick the car up from Finch as planned."

He went through the motions: shaved, missed a spot under his chin, spilled instant coffee grounds on the floor. The milk was sour; he drank it black. He dressed, buttoned his shirt wrong, fixed the shirt, a button rolled, dustballs under the bed ate it. Nose runny, eyes red from the night before (fucked up worse by dust bunnies as big as Marilyn's

41

breasts) he undressed to shower—which he should have done in the first place, but he forgot. He freshened up. Extra strength every-thing—deodorant, mouthwash, foot powder.

The new diet: Sweat to within an inch of your life. He walked the twenty blocks to his agent's office. His open fly escaped notice till Yondle, Finch's secretary said, "I'm expecting him any minute. What's that on your underwear? World's Greatest Da—?"

He zipped up.

"Your eyes are shot to hell. Walk around like that, you'll make babies cry." Yondle was multitasking, her desk a command center. Writers seeking Finch's representation had to make it past her. Dozens of boxes were opened. She was logging in manuscripts, sorting corre-spondence, and speed-reading, while giving him the once-over.

"I had a run-in with indoor dust. Your eyes would look like this if you saw what I saw under my bed. Finch leave the car keys by any chance?"

Yondle's hair was an enlargement, a plethora of plaited extensions, a potted plant of symmetrical, hemplike vines dangling upside down. When the winds were right, they were aerodynamic. Generating addi-tional breezes as she rushed out of her chair to Finch's office, the plaits winged out. Jacob detected a faint rustling like cows grazing in the field. Anticipating she'd be back with the keys, he planned ahead: Find out where in self-park the Ford Escort was, then leave a message for Finch, something along the lines of a gentle nudge: *Would like your take on* Pirate Cassidy and the Sea Witch. *Did you finish yet?*

Return flight, hair streaming. She held out a plate of cookies. "Baked 'em myself. Finch has the keys, and he's on his way."

It wasn't as if he couldn't come back later, but there was no place really he had to be. Yondle, unlike her predecessor, cosseted authors, but the cookies and cosseting came with a price. He'd have to listen (yet again) to what a hard time Yondle had accepting his divorce.

He plopped on the two-seater couch, the only furniture besides her enormous wraparound desk. She sat too, the tips of her hair fidgeting. She chewed and talked at the same time. "You had a little fan club in me. The two lovebirds, goo-goo eyes, blissful sighs, always with the tiny kisses. The longest-running honeymoon I ever saw." Scrunching her face, a pained expression, put there by his ex-honeymoon. In the eleven years he knew her, she was either bottomheavy or top, one or the other, but never one and the same. Between the chubette and the hyper hair, her face could have been lost in the shuffle, though it was not a face easily dismissed. Her skin was flawless. No amount of scrunching could make her unsightly. "And now I'm crushed. It wasn't only you she left high and dry, she also burst *my* bubble."

"Cheryl's suffering too, believe you me."

"I tried not to take sides. As an outsider, I don't have all the facts at my disposal. Perhaps she was provoked. Not by you. You couldn't get a mosquito to bite."

"She asked for the return of the housekeys. I'm permanently barred."

"No." Her mouth drawing it out. Nooo.

"Mac's stressed, he picked a fight with me. I went for a drink last night, nowhere you'd know. A comely female gave me her number. But no, I'm going to call her to explain why I won't be calling."

"My group's women only, but from time to time we allow male guests. Why don'cha?"

"What's the use? Cheryl's spoiled me for *other women.*"

Repossessing his cookie, she tossed it into the wastebasket, scoring a hole in one. "Woman basher." There was a grrr in her voice. "Nobody slanders the sisters. How would you like to be lumped together with *other men?* Woe to you, Jacob Koleman. Bite your tongue. While I do not endorse pussyhood, tramphood, or feminist terrorism, I defend with my life the full flower of womanhood. Whatever it may be."

"All I'm saying—"

"Although at times I'm tempted to wipe the floor with certain male lowlifes, I'm ultimately committed to the survival of the male species in all its subspecies and subsets."

"No insult intended," his mouth went dry.

"What is it about edgy, sullen loners, the undomesticated, untamed, unbound, badboy manchild?" Yondle pondered.

"Now that you ask—"

"Shut up." She tugged a braid. It came out like a loose tooth. "I say this merely for your benefit. Not mine. Phewy on the male shrew. Let him take his wild streak and shove it."

Since he wasn't, hadn't, never would be a shrew and/or in possession of a wild streak, her phewy—unless she was a minority of one (highly unlikely)—put him in the running. Way to go.

She stood. She tousled her hair. The braids snaked through her fingers. "I go weak for a wild streak. Guys give me a hard time, who am I to whine?"

Uh-oh. Since he wasn't, hadn't been, would never be a shrew and/or in possession of a wild streak, it disheartened him to no end to know he was out of the running. One less A-list; how many more to follow?

"What portion of the sisters do you see yourself representing?" he asked.

"I'm thirty-eight years old. Ms. Lonelyhearts never had it so good. You'd think by now my preferences would be set in stone. I'm a woman of discriminating tastes. Picky, picky, picky. Yet I'll be damned if I'm going to let a little thing like good taste stop me."

"I get it. A *no* can still mean *maybe*. Thanks for the tip."

"Think harder."

"A definite yes is indefinite?"

"Harder still. If it happens to me, it can happen to anyone."

Finch walked in. "Come to my office," he said. They both started forward. "Not you," he said to Yondle. To Jacob he said, "We've got to talk."

"Mark my words, Jacob Koleman," Yondle declared as he followed Finch, her words tumbling out faster, decapitating the cookie in her mouth. "You're more of a work-in-progress than you give yourself credit for. You may surprise yourself yet."

His mind was elsewhere. Got to talk? It didn't look promising. A writer hears got-to-talk from his agent, he thinks ohmygod, the book stinks. He turned to close the door. Yondle, behind her desk, was jet-propelled, typing, answering phones, thumbing through papers. The braids were crossed for him, like fingers for luck.

There were no windows. Floor to ceiling bookshelves covered the walls. Finch walked rapidly to his desk, a slab of wood bridging two waist-high filing cabinets. His suits cost a pretty penny but never looked it. He dressed like he couldn't be bothered checking himself out in a full-length mirror. Everything was slightly off-kilter. The pocket flaps on his sports jacket were tucked in, the knot in his tie bulged like a lumpy cheeseball, his loafers were scuffed. Even his face looked like a rush job, arranged with little regard to proportion. A too fleshy nose paired up with small squinty eyes. His upper and lower lips were a color clash. His ears didn't match up.

"The divorce attorney I set you up with didn't cost an arm and a leg. I've been your agent from day one, since the lean years. There for you then, here for you now, all my resources. Mac's stuffed squirrels will outlive me. Every summer I put them in fur storage, nothing's spared. The care I lavish on them, I don't lavish on myself. I ask you, is this the picture of someone in it merely for commission?"

"Any changes you want in *Pirate Cassidy and the Sea Witch,* consider it done. Give me notes, I'll take it from there."

Finch didn't have to leap from his seat. He never got around to sitting down. He skittered out from behind his desk, hunched over like a small rabbit too quick to be cornered. "Your book's the first thing I see in the morning, last thing before going to bed. It sleeps on the pillow beside me. A book's a companion. But no matter how hard I try, we don't connect."

Feeling like his whole life was passing in front of his sweat-clogged pores, he asked "Could you be more specific?"

"Four hundred thirty-two pages, only one single cloud on the horizon. No stretch to say your plot doesn't thicken. The Sea Witch Cassidy marries—we'll get to that next—makes no apology for her fellow sea witches stalking young, thumbsucking males. There's no nice way to put child molestation. This you call the foundation for Cassidy's lifelong crush on sea witches?" He loosened his tie as if he'd had a noose around his neck. "I think not. Get real. Five-year-olds are crybabies. By rights, Cassidy the child should have called for Mama. You tell me what I'm missing."

Jacob couldn't use himself as an example. In the first place, most people didn't believe in mermaids. Secondly, as a writer of fiction, he wanted to maintain the fiction that nothing he wrote was autobiographical. "The Sea Witch fired up his imagination. Love and sex all in one package. Raw and primitive. Counter to everything the child knew. He grew up in a home where even the garret was cozy. Happens to kids all the time, they get strange sensations."

"Moving right along. He *marries* the Sea Witch, they butter each other's toast." Finch was incredulous, "Years of domestic bliss do not an adventure at sea make."

"I wrote from the heart."

"Nobody's faulting you for heart, but you let your life leak onto the page. In an effort to preserve the epic serenity of your marriage to

Cheryl—definitely one for the books—you shifted it almost verbatim onto the page. Pirate Cassidy became Jacob the Pussycat."

The one time he doesn't write pee-pee driven plotlines, suddenly it's not a good read? "Can't a pirate get lucky? Where is it written a pirate can't settle down?"

Finch handed him the carkeys. "Level H. The garage is being remodeled. Take the elevator to J and walk down. Nobody's twisting your arm. I sent a copy to Berry. He's on the Hampton route. Stop in, he's expecting you."

"Book Doctor Berry?"

Finch caressed his arm like Jacob was a bird with a broken wing. "Probably I shouldn't bring it up, your life's in the hole enough as is. But maybe the book's not the only one who needs a doctor."

Surprised at first, he suddenly went from not seeing Kate Vestor in his future, to seeing her in a prominent role. "I'm going to engage the services of a conflict counselor," he said.

Finch clapped him on the back. "Couldn't happen to a nicer guy."

Picking the car up, setting up an appointment with Kate—everything would have to be put on hold. Finch was somebody whose opinion he respected. Cooly, calmly, objectively, dispassion-ately, impersonally, intelligently, logically—he'd put this Berry idea to bed. Fair hearing to one and all was a veritable Princely hallmark, but a book doctor? What the fuck for? Obviously, Finch (without peer in the annals of agenting) had a blindspot. A Sea Witch with designs on young boys isn't a shark in the water. She's an inspiration. Titties plus bites plus goosebumps equals quite a chunk of change, coins in the piggybank of inspiration. Who is Finch to say what love is and isn't?

Book doctor? That'll be the day when somebody puts words in my mouth.

The twenty-block walk back to his place really winded him. He opened the door to his apartment. Mac flew into his arms. The break he needed, a chance to live up to his underwear: World's Greatest Dad.

"Scream at me," Mac moaned, "I deserve it. First-class schmuck. You should have knocked me on my ass."

"You aren't the only one who ever gave his parents a hard time. My own mother—may she rest in peace—pissed me off. Just once. I was seven. I felt a rumble. Grandpa yelled for me to get to the attic of the Arkhouse. I peeked down. The Arkhouse bucked like a stallion. Grandpa's skull was cracked. He went into a coma and died. My mother said I dreamed it up. I told her to eat doo-doo."

"Houses don't kill."

"This one did. A teaspoon of castor oil was my reward for telling the unvarnished truth. I have no problem with parental discipline if and when appropriate. Maya was way offbase, but my signals may have been misleading. I was keen to offer empathy. Let this be a lesson to you—there's a lot riding on first impressions. They can shake you up so you don't know whether you're coming or going. They can light your circuits and fan the flames of your imagination till death do you part."

"Maya swapped me for the guy down the hall."

"I'm almost afraid to ask."

"It wasn't First Love."

"No giant wave?"

"Nothing like that."

"Your brain chemistry didn't go zippo? You didn't feel ignited in the urination region? Notice any creative impulses, did you draw or compose music?"

"She didn't send me over the waterfall, but I'll be straight with you. She threw a scare into me. What if we meet somebody who attracts us both?"

"We make a pact. Repeat after me: Any woman does anything to come between us, she gets thumbs down. The bonds between father and sonny boy supersede libido, loins, the entire pee-pee gestalt. Muses are no exception to the Pact."

Mac began taking the oath, Jacob interrupted.

"Time out. On the outside chance we really fall hard, no father and son competition. Three's a crowd. She chooses. Nobody behaves latently. Duels are not an option. Father and son are blood brothers."

Mac bowed deferentially. "You want her, take her."

Answering in kind, "Be my guest."

"Nope."

"Where does she get off messing with us?"

They sealed the Pact with manly high fives.

"Your mother will be thrilled."

"Be my spokesperson, I've got freshman orientation. And put in a good word for Marilyn. Mom doesn't get her like we get her."

Jacob read something additional in Mac's eyes. "You're leaving something unsaid. I'm not made of cookie crust. Shoot."

"Mom didn't make any formal announcements, nothing like that. I just have this gut feeling she's going to do more than change her hair."

"Your mother asked for the keys."

"Right," Mac said, "I don't know it for a fact. More like a sense of things to come. But I think she may begin . . . *dating.*"

Jacob went on automatic pilot. "I'm not exactly a social recluse myself. Just last night I had social intercourse at a pub. Naturally you're upset, it would be unnatural not to be. How upset are you?"

"The two of you have bent over backward to make me feel I don't come from a broken home. I'm not over the hump, but I would never stand in your way," Mac said, slyly, "like *some* people I know who tried to block me from taxidermy." Mac put his hand on the doorknob.

Jacob asked, "A minute of your time?"

"Don't ask me to spy. We're clear on that. No watching over anybody's shoulder."

(Why couldn't she spend the rest of her life in a convent? A convent in an isolated mountainous region.)

"Are we clear on taxidermy? We want you to be happy. You can demonstrate your love of animals without stuffing them. In a legal court of law you could defend the creatures of the lower kingdom from getting persecuted to death." (Dying before your time is tragic. Cheryl's dating would take years off his life. Cheryl in a convent would extend his life expectancy.) "In some respects, morticians and taxidermists overlap. Girls might not catch on to the nuances, they might conclude you have a morbid fascination with death. Girls you might love, who might love you back, might be put off. Taxidermy could send them screaming into the night, giving them the heebie-jeebies."

"I'm not that much of a killjoy," Mac protested.

(A convent where the only dates are with God and the Good Book.)

"Anyway, right now I'm not thinking about girls. I signed up for pre-law, and I'll see it through. By the terms of our Career Pact, after the bar exam, I'm my own man."

"Enough said. On a totally unrelated subject, I'd like your assistance on a literary matter."

"Shoot."

"It's a Cassidy plot, the early years. Five-year-old boy. Trio of rowdy little girl sea witches. He's netted and bitten. Their saliva's some kind of intoxicant. He's aroused, transfixed by their . . . uh . . . nipples. His emotions escalate. He's zippo infatuated to the hilt. Attraction overrides terror. Pee-pee's a player. But pee-pee isn't the epicenter. His imagination's gripped." (Cheryl, convent-supervised by the Mother Superior, and to top it all off—a chastity belt for all eternity.)

"Five years old?"

"Age is irrelevant."

"Ask around, what does Finch say?"

"He doesn't buy the stirring of imagination. In his eyes, the child was molested."

"Run it by Mom." Then Mac presented him with a short kiss on the cheek. The duration wasn't sheer heaven, but the contact was. Jacob reminded him not to talk to strangers.

"Knock it off, Dad."

No sooner did the door close than Jacob rushed to the window. Mac didn't jaywalk. He crossed on the green. He didn't dawdle in the intersection. Satisfied that Mac was safe (for the time being) he hurried to see Cheryl. Her safety also paramount. How safe is it to date someone you don't know for thirty-three years?

Odds are the only joining she'll do won't be a convent—it'll be a health club. This ex-husband doesn't want to know from his ex-wife's dating debut. But this ex-husband can't help himself. They'll be scraping me off the sidewalk if I don't ask a few thousand leading questions: What's up? Any men in your life? Who is he? What are your intentions? His? See yourself spending the next thirty-three years together? Don't you think you should run a background check? What you don't know *can* hurt. Not everyone's a Prince. Don't do anything I wouldn't do. Know what I'd do?—I'd join a convent. I'd wear a chastity belt. I'd date only God and the Good Book. Don't like that? Go join a secular club like bridge, gardening, nothing too social . . . unless it's with other women. Better safe than sorry.

Cheryl wasn't in. He wiled away the time at the florist. Ribboned box tucked under his arm, he proceeded to her front stoop. These steps and I go way back. I lost a wheel on Mac's bike on these steps. These were steps we all hung out on. Cheryl discovered him staring at the steps. He explained. "The steps over at my new digs are older. But to me they'll always feel new."

She was a vision in vanilla: white suit, white pearls, white T-strap heels.

Fearing she'd evict him from the steps on a flimsy premise like Don't-you-have-anything-better-to-do-than-haunt-my-steps, he stated his business. "Mac stopped by. We patched it up. We made a pact. He nominated me to tell you. He and Maya are no longer a twosome."

"Let's go upstairs to my place," she said.

Following her to *her* place, standing in *her* living room, he presented *his* left cheek, ready to receive *his* customary kiss.

No kiss. No takers for the flowers.

He walked to the couch and sat with the box on his knees.

She slumped down next to him, legs apart, her stuff open for all the world to see. "I'm a tormented soul, will the torment never end?"

Hens would take him for one of their own. His tongue clucked sympathetically. Her plight was his plight. He drew closer.

"Invest in public education, you invest in the future. There I was in the executive suites of Kelsco Textiles when Something-I-Have-No-Name-For possessed me." Her face was pressed up against his, all but the lips, which yapped away. "You should have seen the Something-That-Possessed-Me in action. It was not to be believed. I was present, but I still cannot believe the antics."

"Possessed? . . . As in alien takeover?"

"I'm not a party animal."

"Course not." The sweat he broke out in was so all-encompassing, the insides of his shoes were slick. "Possessed as in needing an exorcist?"

"I've *got* a lot to flaunt, I just *don't* flaunt."

"As in split personality?"

"That-Which-Possessed-Me parked me in Scott Kelsco's lap. Horsey up, horsey down."

"Humped him?"

"Said the Something-Or-Other to Scott: 'Don't flatter yourself.' Then my hand, possessed by God-Knows-What, unzipped his whatsit and jiggled his whoseit."

"A hand job in broad daylight?"

"I can't dignify that with an answer."

"Then dignify this—yesterday you went Ugh."

"Don't use that tone with me."

"Tone? Tone? Feathers fall with bigger bangs. Mice are louder. Any more toned down, you'd have to read my lips."

She put a finger to each temple. "I am not mystery meat. I am not impenetrable. Knock on the door to my psyche, cupboards fly open. As light passes through cracks, I will illuminate the narrowest confines of my nooks and crannies. Hear my countdown."

Counting backward from a hundred.

The box of flowers, unable to withstand the pressure of his hands, detonated.

At the conclusion of the second countdown her fingers dropped from her temples. She drumrolled her kneecaps. The rise and fall of her chest didn't look promising. Her sighs were not how you'd aloha a setting sun aglow with Nature's bounty.

Her mouth went to his ear. "You're the soul of discretion."

"Yes I am."

"Promise you won't tell Mac. I'd rather he hear it from me."

Warm woman breath, the heat of tropical nights blowing into his ear. "Take the shirt off my back," he said.

"It was an inside job. The brains behind the possession was me."

Palm clapping his forehead forcefully, hard enough to sound like a tennis ball hitting a racket. Head reeling, "Sold your soul to the devil? Tell me it isn't so. Sex for a charitable contribution to public education? If Finkle were here, he'd forbid you to bare your soul to Mac."

She bristled. "There is a bright side. Speaking in my own defense, I didn't sell out. Guess who isn't a cold, calculating she-bitch mercenary?"

"Rhetorical, right?"

"Next time—if there is a next time—if the occasion should arise—it could be sooner than you think . . ." She covered her face. "I'm so torn. I gave it away for free."

His jaw went slack.

"Say something constructive," she said.

The Prince used to be a Boy Scout. His emergency first-aid kit was well-stocked, but not with platitudes. It was a point of honor with him. Speak as you would write. From the heart.

"If it's any consolation, Yondle predicts surprise is in the offing. Jolts to the system. In other words, coming undone is apparently how some do it. It could be I myself am a work-in-progress, systems being what they are . . ." At his disposal, a ton of Boy Scout *Thou Shalt Nots*. Thou shalt not overtax the system; stay with low-end voltage; one's close calls should never be too close for comfort. Thou shalt not court danger. He wanted to hear her say she'd never do it again. "Somehow I can't picture you going horsey up, horsey down on the lap of a person you barely know."

He wasn't a tit-for-tatter. Speaking not from the need to keep up, but simply to show her the light, he said, "If I found myself in a compromising position—I assure you it could happen—I would take the necessary steps so it wouldn't happen twice."

She got to her feet, hauling him up with her. "Nonsense. Like Yondle's the best judge. Her eleven years to my more than thirty. My money's on you living up to your title."

It was his sneaking suspicion too. Once a Prince, always a Prince. But did she have to rub it in? "That's it! I'm delaying the trip to the Hamptons."

"Don't stay on my account. Starting one hour from now, I'll be away."

"Where to?"

"Scott's weekend retreat. The man disgusts me, yet it's too much to go through what I've gone through and walk. My very first landmark, milestone, groundbreaking close call with scandalous cocky behavior, how could I not come back for a closer look?" She grabbed him by the shoulders and shook. "Yes, yes, yes."

"No, no, no Hamptons for me until you make a pact. No more horsey."

"See you Thursday, Mac's moving day." She hustled him out the door, not like a bouncer would, like a lady who had a legal right to *her* place. "Sixty minutes from now, I'll be . . . inching up to Scott for a closer look."

Behind his eyeballs, rubber bands were drawn back like archer bows. The rubber bands snapped. The momentum slingshot him down the hall—

"Sweet, helpful Prince," Cheryl stood in the doorway, "good-bye my good guy supreme."

—down the steps and into a cab. He pulled out Kate Vestor's business card. "East Fifty-Third," he said. "Step on it."

۞

Hard body in all the right places. The doorman's baldness looked like a life choice. When your head's a massive bowling ball and you've got humongous neck muscles to keep it from crashing to earth, you can afford to be cavalier about hair.

"Jacob Koleman for Kate Vestor."

The doorman let his thumbs do the talking. They were grossly callused, but not disfigured. Push-ups might cross your mind, two thumbs doing the workload of whole hands. The doorman wasn't steering him toward the lobby phones out of the goodness of his heart. Three times, Jacob had phoned from the cab. She could've been out but he had the feeling she was deliberating. Now that she was going to pick up, he didn't want to repeat every word. Three messages to pare down.

Message one: All due respect, sorry for the intrusion, happened-to-be-in-the-neighborhood, won't take up too much of your time, gladly compensate, you hungry? We could eat, drink, munch, snack. You name it. Message two: I didn't casually wander over, your residence isn't local, retract the happen-to-be-in-the-vicinity. Allow me to pick your brain. Message three: The nature of my conflict is confidential. More than that I cannot say till we meet face to face.

The house phone was within visual range of the doorman. Cupping the receiver, Jacob cut the fat. "I'm the man from last night. In the pub. You gave me your card."

She breathed like someone just off the treadmill. "My services would be gratis. Give your informed consent, I'm yours. Case studies are a requirement for graduation. You'd be disguised, your own mother wouldn't recognize you. But know in advance, when I gave you my card, I wasn't soliciting a client. My interest's personal. Any conflict mixing business with pleasure? Just say what's on your mind, Jako."

"Jacob. Friends call me Jacob. I don't date."

"My companion, the gentleman who died, was a much older man. Since his demise, my appetite for dating has greatly diminished. In some ways, you remind me of Maurice. He had to be coaxed into taking his socks off in bed. Can you live with that, Jako?"

"The name's Jacob. When I do date, you'll be the first to know. I'm a work-in-progress."

"And I'm an innovative venter. Apartment 6E, third on the right."

"A what?"

She clicked off.

Nod from the doorman officially clearing him for takeoff. No socks in bed is nothing. Piece-a-cake. She wants my pee-pee to make a public appearance, *that* is everything.

❀

"In here."

Walking through the living room, he had only his own two feet to trip over. All the furniture was pushed to one side and stacked. The rug was rolled and set against the couch. Two guys could've done it with one hand tied behind their backs. But the rest, a job for a moving crew. Men to lift the loot, an engineer to prop it and keep it stable. It was that high a pile. Home base: couch, topped by four large recliner chairs, glass coffee table, two televisions, magazine rack, coat rack, CD player, CDs, books, and two floor lamps, one on each side.

He entered a small room, dimly lit.

"Welcome to the think tank."

Twin chairs, low to the ground like tree stumps. They were more accessible than they looked. Sinking in, his legs didn't lose a minute nosing out, like somebody was on the other end pulling. Kate's legs, going in the opposite direction, were bare. He glimpsed the back of her knees. Toned and chicken-on-a-spit tanned.

"Unlace." She didn't wait. She relieved him of his shoes. The socks remained intact. He scarcely saw her hands move. It could have been the lighting.

"Are you redecorating?" Pointing over his shoulder at the living room.

"Oh that." Her midriff was unclothed. The halter top, closer to an ace bandage. Her cleavage was deep enough to conceal several pads of Post-Its. "Resistance helps with stress. I like something to push against. Innovative venting's my own little quick picker-upper. The last vent was the most benign of confrontations. I stacked like I was handling the bones of a dearly departed loved one. Now that he's gone, Maurice means so much more dead than alive. I vent to shake him off, to shake myself up. When I'm not venting to kick ass, I do it to burn calories." She hiked up her skirt. "Let's get to work. Describe the nature of your conflict."

He rolled up his sleeves.

"My ex-wife's evolving. Aren't we all? Start out at A, end up at Z. We were married for more than three decades. On her, inner beauty is outside too. Godspeed to the postdivorce evolutionary process. I look forward to the day—the moment, the very second—I too turn the corner. For I am no less divorced. No less progressive. No less the author of my next chapter." His mouth, hardly moving a muscle, stalled.

"Just a shot in the dark, but you strike me as someone who needs a crash course in speaking up. Raising one's voice is permissible."

He took out his handkerchief and blew his nose. "Cheryl's body is hers to do with as she will."

"Louder."

"People have genitals. Genitals need tending to."

"Can't hear you."

"I'm no enforcer. I just want what's best for her and her genitals."

"We'll have to work on self-awareness too. The resolution of conflict begins in communication . . . with yourself. Level with me. You're looking out for number one. Jako can't have her, no one can."

He drew his knees up so quickly they cracked like knuckles. "Does everything have to have hidden motives, doesn't your training make allowances for brother's keeper? I deplore base motives. I wouldn't stoop so low. What's latent in others *isn't* latent in me. I categorically refuse to own up to what I'm not."

"Been there, done that. I profited financially from Maurice's death. And though I wasn't his executioner, there are days it gets to me, when I'm my own naysayer." She rose. "Come this way. The

Spanish Inquisition abused the rack. But as a shortcut to crux, there's much to be said for physical torture."

She showed him to the bedroom. Everything was in its place.

"I've never piled furniture with a partner. Next to innovative venting, the standard smacking the daylights out of a pillow and primal screaming is pussy. Done my way, you get whupped, drained of all your defenses, vulnerable as you've never been before, exposed, naked, softened up for the ultimate crux of what's what." She put her shoulder to the bed. "The entire force of the universe squashing you like an ant, you're down to the wire, blowing bubbles with your saliva." She grunted. The bed flipped over on its side. "For sheer life and death eye-openers, why traipse all the way to Everest?"

She seemed lost in thought. As she righted the bed, the headboard clattered, pieces of floor tile were dislodged. She reclined on the mattress. "Maurice tried to be a tiger in bed." She parted her legs and arched. "Regrettably, he dropped dead before we could make beautiful conflict together. Are you able?"

Able?

Able?

"Fifty-four and still going strong," he said. "In my prime."

He asked to use the bathroom.

He left. Three blocks in his stocking feet, a dead run.

Able? Able? I'd stake my life on able. The Kolemans may curl up with a good book, but their pee-pees don't.

He went home, packed a bag, and picked up Finch's car.

The town isn't big enough for the both of us. If I gave Kate a second thought—and I'm not—I'd say, You sure know how to back a guy into a corner. Go manhandle somebody your own size. Able? Able? Do I look like a piece of furniture? Heap this on your junk pile: Living in a conflict-free zone far surpasses a war zone.

The radio in Finch's car was from the year one. He searched for the classical station.

Moreover, I don't spar. Haven't since I-can't-remember-when. Would if I had to. If the spirit moved me. In a pinch, where warranted, I'm confident I could dish. The chemistry would have to be just so. Ask anyone, even a five year old. Spice is nice. Spice is what they wash your mouth out with soap for. But dangling trumped-up spiceballs isn't the way to a man's heart.

Weaving in and out of traffic, racing the lights.

Head games from Finch's radio? Where the hell was the classical station? Getting a talk show . . .

The voice. He'd know that voice anywhere: Dr. Wallach Finkle. Radio celeb and newspaper columnist (Sundays only).

"Today's topic is Monday morning blues," Finkle said.

First time around, I didn't ask to be abducted. Abduction isn't kosher. But given half the chance, I'd do it again. Let the record read: At five years and four days old, Jacob Koleman made out like a . . . pirate.

Able?

Able?

Of course, he could put up with Finkle on the radio.

"Our guest today is Bo Keigle, author of *Monday Morning Blues*. With her lack of academic credits, this is the book that probably shouldn't have been published at all. Yet it's garnered national, even worldwide acclaim. *Monday Morning Blues* has won the blessing of the American Board of Psychiatrists. Voting is underway to confer formal status on the disorder, pervasive enough to be called epidemic. Yet just yesterday, Ms. Keigle formally petitioned the Board to shelve the vote. I begin today's interview by asking: *Why?*"

"If you take the blues out of work, you're restructuring the workplace. It's all the trend nowadays, isn't it? Employers installing gyms, scheduling nap breaks, offering lucrative stock options. The blues, however, persist. Regardless of income, whether or not job satisfaction is high, come Monday morning, the blues master the universe. I don't argue debilitating. In certain segments of the population—supermarket clerks, postal staff—the Monday morning blues are still going strong by Friday. But work isn't play, that's why they call it work. Do we really want shoe salesmen plotzing over their inventory, the man at the corner deli rapturous over making change? God save us all from a world where you can get service with a drug-induced smile. The tortured writer/artist never gets any heat for blues in perpetuity. I say what's good for me is good for all. Writing is tedious, solitary, lonely, backbreaking, ballbreaking, a real grind, mind numbing, a labor of love you hate, a chamber of horrors, a day-in-day-out bad hair day, a pound of flesh for every half-decent line. They can't pay me enough. And I'm one of the lucky ones. Think of the basketcases who never make it into pr—"

Jacob slammed the radio shut. Able? Able? I'm so able I can relate to what Little Bo Peep's saying even if she's got lousy taste in talk show hosts. Writer's blues *are* a shade deeper, writing is rough, getting the words right . . . which ones make the cut? . . . which words do you divorce? He exited the highway.

Just let Berry the book doctor try turning me away. I'm Finch's boy. Finch doesn't have children of his own. He sends somebody to a book doctor, it's not like a car going in for a tune-up. Pull Finch's authors back from the brink, you've saved his beloved Kinder.

Beds: In a neat row, lined up against a wall, five singles with metal frames. "You'll stay overnight." Berry wore doctor whites, the stethoscope around his neck was authentic. Listening to Jacob's lungs, he ordered him to take a breath, hold, cough. "You're in good hands. I've seen it all: writer's block, weak character development, redundancy,

wordiness, too many flashbacks, lack of definitive point-of-view, narration and more narration, dialogue you could puke from . . ."

It was all Jacob could do just to pull the covers up to his chin. His
teeth were chattering, the thermometer in his mouth was having a nico-
tine fit. "You sure I'm not putting you out? I could stay at a hotel in town."

"Writers are usually outpatients. Only the most critical get to use the
facilities. The rest of the beds won't be empty for long. Who doctors the
book doctors? My colleagues come here to recuperate. Doctoring is a
noble calling. We save the lives of books, midwife paragraphs, spoon-feed
writers. Curing literature isn't putting a splint on a broken leg. The bed
you're now in was last occupied by a book doctor who loved too much."
Berry's cheeks were dimpled, he had girth. The squareness of his body
was reassuring, as if he were more solid than mere flesh and blood.

He prescribed super strength Bayer. He mashed them. Jacob was
helped to a sitting position. As he swallowed, Berry told him where the
bedpan was.

"Eight A.M. tomorrow, be showered, be dressed, be just what the
doctor ordered. Don't give me your life story. No ego trips. Accord me
the same respect you do your physician. Now say, Yes sir."

"Yes sir."

Sometime during the night, Jacob was awakened by a high-pitched
voice funneled directly into the ear that wasn't buddied up to the pillow.

"I've been reading you all my life. When Cassidy killed the harlot
who poisoned him and her ghost cried out for vengeance the mix of
genres was a shift from your usual authorial voice."

The night-light was on.

Jacob turned over. "How old are you?"

"Old enough to know what I do and don't like. I see that book as
your most cinematic."

Jacob estimated eight years old.

"Your least successful was the third. Sunken treasure's been done to death. And I don't think you're a hack; if I did, I'd say so."

"Your father sent you, right? You're part of the treatment."

"When you were little did they ever get on your case for reading at the table?"

"Burying my head in a book? Yeah, I had a thing for *Treasure Island.*" The boy's pajamas were devil red.

"I'd rather go without food or air or the comforts of home than give up Harry Potter."

"Glad to hear it, a book person's enthusiasm is music to my ears. See you in the morning."

The boy carried a flashlight and a hardcover edition of Harry Potter. "Daddy's on a witch-hunt. He's got his wires crossed. Ever since he saw the *The Exorcist,* he's spooked. You ever read *Harry Potter and the Sorcerer's Stone?*"

"Can't say I have."

The child trembled. "Nobody comes between me and Harry. If they tried to take away *Treasure Island,* wouldn't you fight to the death? Much as I love Dad, he better back off. So I forget to floss. Harry's the best read of my life. Where he goes I go. He goes to Wizard School. Maybe I do spells, maybe I don't. It's not like warlocks can't be gainfully employed."

Diplomacy was called for. Jacob had no desire to give the child any ammunition. Yet he, of all people, connected to the power of the written word. "Harry's captured your imagination. To the end of your days, you'll be drawn back, as if he put a spell on you. But neglecting to floss is an extremely serious matter."

"Books are my friends, I don't screw friends." The child ran away. Jacob took a long time to fall asleep.

He overslept. Berry pulled the pillow out from under him.

"I'm not running a bed and breakfast. There'll be no sleeping in. Perhaps I didn't make myself clear. Book doctoring's a risky business. I could take sick from a run-on sentence. If the book doctor's not in the best of health, it's literature's loss."

Jacob had slept in his clothes. "I'll just go get changed."

Berry flipped up the sidebars. "Do not shirk responsibility. First and foremost, we must decide if the book deserves to live."

Jacob panicked. "Not everything's *War and Peace*. Escape literature is a legit form of entertainment."

Berry's square body cast a large shadow. "Books put ideas in people's heads. Will I be doing the public a disservice by assisting you?"

Jacob rattled the bars like a baby in his crib. "Please. Can we avoid going down that road? I'll watch over you. First sign of loving too much or turning yourself inside out, we'll take a break."

Berry fell backward into a bed. "The fuck you will. I've crawled all over *Cassidy and the Sea Witch*. It's a loser. I can't possibly be hooked by happily-ever-after ad nauseam. And yet I couldn't put it down. Absolutely nothing to recommend it. On no level do I buy nonstop mush." His dimpled cheeks deflated. He made the sign of the cross. "Go Jacob, leave this place while you still can. If you have an ounce of brains, you'll put the manuscript in the drawer and leave it there. Mighty is the power of the pen. Words bewitch. They weave magic. They shape the minds of our young. Children are like sponges. In my house, there's no reading at the table. Yet I brought your book to breakfast. Instead of flossing, I . . ."

These hospital beds were like cages. Jacob couldn't find the release button for the railings. He half fell out.

Berry's eyes bulged. "Bring me the head of Harry Potter!"

THE MERMAID THAT CAME BETWEEN THEM

Jacob reached the car just as lightning struck a shed next to the house. In the dust kicked up by a sudden series of chassis-shaking muffler backfires, the house shimmered as if it couldn't hold its place. Two hours to the Ark, time enough to reflect. One little eight year old has his finger on the pulse. Anybody up there listening? I've always thought not. But if You are, whatever You bottled for the kid, make mine a double. Find my First Love, return my Second, send conflict to the bottom of the deep blue sea, and help me work my writer's muscles.

Jacob seldom scratched.

Years of shaving religiously once a day, his follicles futilely dreamed the dream of ancient mosses, of how they would gather en masse and roll over the cities of man.

Unshaven, he didn't stop.

One hand on the wheel, the other on his cheeks like a fleabitten cat at the post.

In the time it takes to say, Mmmm, ummm, a little to the right, up more, more, under the nose, stop there, harder, faster—wouldn't you know it?—with his focus on nothing but alleviating the damn itch brought on by hairs pushing up through pores like prairie dogs, a particularly knotty problem on a topic preoccupying him for months solved itself. One-two-three. Suddenly, he knew why Cheryl divorced him. Grabbing the car phone, he dialed home. The real one. His temporary quarters around the corner was only a dwelling.

Overjoyed when Cheryl picked up, he stated the obvious. "You didn't go away with whats-his-face."

"Scott passed a remark. Considering how I went at his male organ, I probably had it coming. But when you've lived with a Prince as long as I have . . . to make a long story short, the crack he made wasn't to my liking."

"You'll always be a Princess to me."

"I deluged him with profanity. The closest I ever came to sewer mouth. I called him a doofus and a frogface."

He heard the buzzer. She went to see who it was.

Returning, she announced Scott was on his way up.

He hit the speedbutton. "I've stumbled across the elusive missing piece of the mystery puzzle. Years of exposure to the wild exploits of Cassidy, the sexual escapades, the colorful language, the one-after-another cliff-hangers, it's *life* imitating *art*. You divorced me in a state of literary inebriation which is still not out of your system. Divorce is your way of indulging your literary tastes. See what I'm saying? It's the nature of fiction to engage emotions. The totally alien life you're leading, you lifted right off the pages of my books. You're spellbound."

"I'm no young impressionable mind," she yelled. "Fuck your theory."

The phone thudded like a sawed-off tree.

Subsequent calls got him nowhere. Turning the car around, he pointed it toward the city.

Day lowered the blinds. The full moon, low in the sky, was a decal on his windshield.

Trying again, he reached Cheryl's machine. "Jacob, I'm following your lead with Finkle. Don't call me. I'll call you at the Arkhouse."

He pulled over on the shoulder, or more precisely, he drove up on the shoulder, intending to stop but somehow just kept on going. If not for the siren and the red light, he'd still be at it.

His wallet was already out when the officer said, "License." All thumbs, the contents fell out. On the way down, he bumped his head on the wheel. The license was nowhere to be found. The patrolman suggested between the seat cushions. It was right where he said. Nerves rattled, Jacob couldn't button his lips. "My ex-wife is in a crisis. I pulled off the road to think. Part of me wants to hurry back. Part says no. She's in therapy."

The officer gave the license a cursory glance.

"Reality check: What's worse? Cancer or divorce? Senility or divorce? Blindness, deafness, muteness, or divorce? Global war or divorce? Takeover by fanatics or divorce? Nuclear winter or divorce? Loss of the rain forest or divorce? Have your health, how bad can things be? Got all your teeth? Most of your hair? Heart in mint condition? Legs holding up? Count yourself lucky if you're *able* to get it up."

Able?

Able?

What's with the able?

"Perfect performance record," Jacob pleaded. "Never a blemish."

"Beat it before I change my mind."

Jacob wouldn't change his. How bad is bad? Bad is in the eyes of the beholder. You know you got it bad when you drive straight into the sea, throw the gears in reverse, drive out, drive in, drive out and stay out even though you've got your eye on in.

The engine flooded. Waves lapped the tires like nipping pups. Jacob stood on the roof of the car.

The canvas masts of the Arkhouse began flapping, as they sometimes did even on nights as calm as this. If a vessel can be said to have a heart and vital signs, this one almost seemed organic, as if the planks of wood still retained memories of a living, breathing forest. On a roll, the Ark could give a whole tribe of gulls competition. He had to shout to be heard above the racket.

"These were the words of your prayer. I say them now in the hopes you will show yourselves: Oh Still-Waters-Running-Deep, wise and ancient waters of life, do not forsake your Daughters of the Sea. May this be the day we spawn."

The Ark went into its flipped-out bagpipe mode. Since Grandpa Marshall's death, when the living room ceiling came down on his skull like a hammer, the floor of the Ark aiding and abetting, the Arkhouse couldn't go a month without mouthing off—a design flaw Jacob thought prudent to just let be. Treat the Arkhouse like the family heirloom it was, the Ark wouldn't dispose of you till, like Grandpa, you were good and ready to go.

He bellowed. "I have the utmost reverence for the biological imperative. But was I no more than a convenient piece of meat, a breeder to be milked for sperm and beached? You Daughters of the Sea, the waves you made are rippling still. There is no statute of limitations on Firsts. First Wakenings will never be water under the bridge."

He opened his fly, holding himself with both hands. He didn't need a mirror to tell him his face was crimson.

"Ready, willing, and able. Like you never had it before. Every boy has a First Love and you are mine. I am the hungry heart. My still waters run wide and deep. Tap in. You won't be sorry."

The Ark finally quieted. With no neighbors to the immediate right or left, the house wasn't breaking any ordinances. Jacob dropped to a regular speaking voice.

"The seas of life are stormy. My native waters offer shelter from the storm. Years from now, you'll tell your grandchildren this was a First for you. A man who wasn't just a boy toy, somebody you really got to know. Let me show you how the other half lives. Why spawn like a cold fish when you can spawn with all the romantic trimmings? It's no sea yarn. Jacob Koleman's an all-around nice guy. I cast no hidden nets. Based on one meeting more than forty some odd years ago, I'm hardly an authority. The three I met could've been exceptions to the rule. Today's mermaid, for all I know, could be on the fast track to a career. Look, I'll make this easy. Liveliness appeals to me. You should be somewhat uninhibited. First time out there were goosebumps. I sensed adventure. I definitely didn't feel like a Mama's boy. One of us doesn't like what he/she sees . . . well, as the saying goes, there are plenty of other fish in the sea. It couldn't hurt to meet. No strings. What do you say?"

A mile out, he spotted thrashing. Clouds ambushed the moon. He angled for a better look.

"Jacob, that you?"

Caught off guard, he looked away. A fraction of a second, if that. He turned back.

Too late.

Where the creature's tail had been, the sea was flatline.

Harris Lester scaled the roof of the car with a rock climber's ease. The great outdoors was stamped all over him. Weathered by the elements, he wore his grooves and craggy lines with grace. Where others would appear aged, his brand of rugged leanness was timeless. The sea was Harris's place of worship. Born of man, he lived only to behold the mysteries of the deep.

"Should you have any desire to justify marinating tires in saltwater when there's a perfectly good gravel driveway not four feet away, kindly resist the impulse. Ditto for your loins. Do not, I repeat, do not edify. No secrets out of the bag. Your penis is nobody's business but your own."

Jacob quickly put his pee-pee back though it stood absolutely no chance of becoming a conversation piece. Hell would freeze over first. Harris didn't operate on the same plane as the rest of the world.

"Difficult day at the Foundation?"

A volley of sighs. "This month's issue of *Oceanography* correctly refers to the Foundation as the School of Alternative Marine Biology. We've never been skewered in quite such complimentary terms."

Distracted by what he thought was another sighting, Jacob said, "Sorry, you were saying?" Just waves, and phantom fins.

"I'm imposing, I'll go."

"*Oceanography,* I got that far."

"They were sniping about our grant money. If the Foundation were dedicated to safeguarding the virgin soil of planets, we'd have universal backing. The sea's our Mona Lisa. Her beauty's in the mystery of her smile. All the establishment's interested in is strip searching, finding out what makes the ocean tick. When exploration traffics in commerce, the whole process is corrupted."

The Foundation had Jacob's financial support, a modest three-digit contribution in Marshall's name. The old guy would've loved Harris. "You're one of the few people—if not the only one—on the face of the Earth, I can depend on to keep secrets. The least obtrusive, the most respectful of parameters. The Arkhouse could do a song and dance—who am I kidding? You've caught the ship in the act—but you've never said so. Your self-discipline puts the rest of us to shame."

Here it was, two years into their friendship and Harris never once inquired after Grandpa who was something of a local legend, having refused to evacuate through the nastiest hurricanes. And every now and then, up to his seventy-fifth year, he'd take the Ark out of drydock for a "spin" around the block. Invited inside the Ark numerous times, Harris always turned down the invitation. "The Ark reeks of mystery, I couldn't possibly intrude," he would explain.

"I'm not spilling any beans by saying this," began Jacob tentatively, ready to stop in midsyllable if he were asked to. "The bond between Grandpa and the Ark was so strong, he'd talk to her. She was the woman in his life, he had a real thing going with her."

"Your grandfather was a mystic after my own heart."

They sat in companionable silence till Jacob broke it. "Come across any evidence of mermaids? You'd tell me, wouldn't you?"

Harris gave the same answer he always did when Jacob brought the subject up. "Surely you jest," he said.

Grandpa Marshall's ingenuity had squeezed a house out of a ship but the ship prevailed. There were portals, a galley, a captain's cabin and wheel, instruments galore. Carved into the bed in the captain's quarters were biblical depictions of the Arkhouse's namesake, the Ark that had held life and limb together for forty days and forty nights when all the world was overrun by flood—Noah's Ark.

More than a little of Grandpa's anthropomorphizing had been passed on to Jacob. The rocking of the Ark was unceasing and gentle. Cradles came to mind, maternal rhythms to soothe a furrowed brow. A far cry from the infamous bucking which took Grandpa Marshall's life. After that debacle, the ship gave only smooth rides. She didn't list to excess and anthropomorphically speaking, the "babbling" cost him less in sleep than a neighbor blasting the TV late at night.

Before Jacob called it a night, he raided the well-stocked galley. The late dinner, his only meal of the day, held him till well past eleven the next day. When he woke, it was to thick fog, not the most ideal conditions for surveying the coastline. But for surveying one's interior, you couldn't ask for better.

He put his feet up on the butcher block counter. A smokestack of steam rose from his coffee mug, super ambiance for a one on one.

Was the fictional Cassidy really Cheryl's puppetmaster? Harry Potter had a foothold with the Berry kid. Potter was throwing his weight around. Could Cassidy? Was Cheryl asking for it? Just how latent was she? Just how latentless was he? That was some spiel he gave Kate. Her money was on Freud, subconscious drives, the cooking cauldron and all that. Didn't work-in-progress work better with an open mind? Revision was salvation. Since when was the kidnapping of a child the basis for sound convictions, sound anything? Was being lovesick for First Love sick, sick, sick? A symptom of what? Just how dense was he? Sweep a latent under the rug, it will come back to haunt you, he thought.

Phone rang. He would continue this internal monologue later. Pushing the steamy mug aside, he raced to get it.

✿

"I'll be brief." Cheryl didn't even say hello. "Finkle and I had quite the session on your Young Impressionable Mind Theory. Taken literally, it's a stinging indictment. The target's bigger than me, maybe as big as all of literature, movies, and music put together."

Leave it to Finkle to make a simple thing complicated, he thought. "Anyone can be influenced by anything, myself included. What counts is degree."

"Do you or don't you want to purge literature, movies, music?"

"No purge."

"Smut is or isn't your current crusade?"

"That's what was discussed? I'm on a crusade?"

"Fact of life: Princes with high principles throw gauntlets from their high horses."

"I come in peace. Don't look for conflict where there is none. There's nothing to be gained from you and me fighting."

"God, the world could use a few mil like you. What a mensch. My Peacekeeper."

Her sudden cease-fire made him more uneasy. "Is Scott still in the picture?"

"New York's nothing but a collection of neighborhoods, each populated by wagging tongues. You were bound to find out anyway. Last night, I sucked him."

"A pact. I want to hear it from your lips: You will in no way involve Mac. In our family we keep pacts. Never has there been a broken pact. Pacts are written in blood."

"A pact it is. With the last breath left in me, I will abide. I love you, Jacob. More with each passing day. Even sitting on your high horse throwing gauntlets, you are the least mean-spirited man in the universe."

The catch in her voice was like that of a wounded animal.

"Going down on Scott, slowly working my way around to the main attraction, I almost blurted out words of endearment. To date, it's the closest call I've had with a connubial state of mind. As if I couldn't blow somebody just for the hell of it. As if blowing for the hell of it isn't reward enough. Certainly if Scott blew me off, it wouldn't be a low blow. Not at all. Not. Not. Not if the blow job was given in the spirit it was received. Which was . . . *a good time was had by all."*

He wasn't quite rendered speechless. The proof of that was he said good-bye. Ably.

Able?

Able?

We'll see who's able.

Dressed in nothing but pajamas, he ran—competently through the fog toward the sea.

Plunging in, he swam as if he had his foot on the gas pedal.

Her lips on Scott's pecker. Foreign matter in her mouth. An affair not of the heart. Use of foul language unbecoming to a lady of breeding. Lewd sexual acts. Gauntlets on the brain. Argumentative. Not the woman he'd married.

He saw a clearing in the fog, a spot without smudge marks as if someone had rubbed in stain remover. He parked there. His feet touched solid ground.

"Attention to any and all mermaids. I've come to let you off the hook. Whenever I've talked of myself, it's been in the most glowing terms. Always trying to reel you in. You must get a lot of that. Attractive as the bait is, it's still bait. But mating calls are probably all in a day's work for you, so let's hear it for the anti-mating call. The one that says, nothing doing. Cold water right in the kisser. Clear light of day. The fog's lifted. After a lifetime, I finally get it. From day one, you saw through the Prince to the puny, spineless jellyfish underneath."

Unable to push buttons after his are pushed.

Unable to break character.

Unable to scream bloody murder.

"Going to take anything away with you, take this: If your tastes run to spice, Jacob Koleman's inedible. Enjoy living on the edge? Fat chance. Crave a nightlife, anything past ten o'clock I'm a drip."

The tears rolled down his face.

"Kids need a diaper change, I'm abler than most. You need a hand bathing or feeding them, potty training, checking under the bed for night monsters, you-know-who's at your service. Need stud service, I'm no slouch."

He shivered. "I seem to have misplaced the shore, would you be so kind as to point the way?"

The ground swelled, lifting him clear out of the water. He would have tumbled off but his legs were held fast. Looking down from his perch, he saw a well-developed set of arms, strong shoulders, an obscene amount of sunkissed golden hair as if a spinning wheel were inside the scalp churning it out. Leaning forward to get a better look, he spied a pair that could have launched a couple of thousand ships. Any wet T-shirt contest in any dive in any part of the world, hers would walk away with the grand prize. Taking measurements like an interior decorator, the mental tape was off and running. Thirty-four C, full cup, taut, no fallen chins on those knockers. He stretched down . . . To do what? . . . Shake hands with a female's anatomy?

"Not so fast," she said. His fingers froze, as she continued. "Oh Still-Waters-Running-Deep, wise and ancient waters of life, how many more before I get a sign? He's older than the three who went before. I've got more meat on my bones than he does and just what am I to think of a man who doesn't make himself out to be the biggest fish in the pond? They all want me—I can feel their body heat, anyone of them would do for Raget—but which is the Egg Snatcher and which the Defender?"

Her nipples turned burning-coal red.

A man laid a hand on that, he might lose it.

Jacob hoped God in his heaven would forgive him for addressing another deity. He had always thought God make-believe. God help him, if that wasn't so. Whatever the punishment for blasphemy, God have mercy on his soul. "Oh Still-Waters-Running-Deep," he began, "Oh wise and ancient waters of life, I propose a pact, and the custom in my family is to uphold pacts. They cannot be broken. I hereby declare myself Defender. On the surface, a spineless jellyfish, the list of unables longer than my arm and after the ten o'clock news, a drip. But all this fresh air does something to a man's spirits. I'm ready for First Dibs. Grant me a sea-change. Turn my tides. Let this mark an era of prosperity and happiness. A change of life for the better."

He was lowered from her shoulders and placed squarely in front of her. The laws of physics were apparently different for mermaids than for the human race. She stood on her tail atop the water, and didn't sink. He had such a thing going with her breasts—inside his pajamas, his pee-pee was a cheerleader rooting for the home team—that the remaining parts of her (face, tail) took a backseat. Her lips, however, were outstanding. Voluptuous and cushioned to kill, they were like mashed potatoes whipped to within an inch of their lives. He flashbacked to when he was a kid licking the bowl clean. Below the waist, she was seal blubber. There were scratch marks, like luggage with lots of mileage.

Suddenly she upped and bit him.

The pinprick sting didn't draw blood. His yelp was cut short by a tingling in his limbs, similar to legs going to sleep. His arms lost the power to move. He had no recourse but to stand there and watch.

It was no longer necessary for her to buoy him up. Physics be damned, he could stand rightside up without assistance. Pajama bottoms fell to his ankles, his boxer shorts were ripped off. Modesty prevented him from taking a good look at his manhood (which felt stiff as if a steel rod had been inserted).

"Coming along fine," she said of his expansion. "Eggs are everything. Lay them, bury them, hope they hatch before the Egg Snatchers get them. Prophecy spoke of fog. And from the fog comes Man. And from the man, a Defender of my eggs. And from my eggs, mermaids. And from mermaids, more eggs. Better dead than unbred. Biting you prepares the way. The Moha sets the mood. Moha saliva is for pain control, yours not mine. It's best to let the Raget approach without struggle. The Raget won't hold screaming against you."

His mouth felt like it had been shot full of Novocain. "Duneven know name."

"Claritha."

"Rag . . . whatchacallit?"

"Eggs are stored deep inside the Raget. You work your way in, bring them out, pierce their thin shell, deposit your birthing fluid. Together we hide the eggs from Snatchers. You stay awake. I hibernate, feeding off my blubber."

Fighting the wooziness, "Painkiller for big pain? Small or medium sized?"

"None but you spoke the words. Speak them again, pleasure me with your words."

He giggled. "Show me yours, I'll show you mine. More Moha."

She tipped him over on his side. The water was firm. She lay beside him, separated by a good ten inches. "You've had enough Moha. Oh Still-Waters, hear my words. As his tide is turned, so too turn mine."

He wasn't a writer for nothing. He went with the tide turning theme. "Change of life for the better," he smiled.

"From your mouth to Their ears. Bless this union. May the eggs roll right out of me. Free my trapped eggs. He must be the Chosen One. Are not his words almost identical to Yours? Claritha is in her change of life. Sea-changes are at hand."

Processing was slow, but he finally got it: Eggs stuck? Trapped? Ovulation kaput? By any other name, Claritha is menopausal.

The green of her eyes was brighter, more phosphorescent than Irish clover. Her gaze dropped.

He followed their trek down . . .

"Loosen my eggs," she said.

. . . to her slit. Hundreds of tentacles emerged, tips rounded, curved like pygmy satellite dishes and padded like hooves. They swam through the air toward his boner (by length and width, a record breaker). Mob frenzy. They clamped his shaft with considerably more pressure than he had ever endured.

What they lacked in beauty, they more than made up in technique.

Like a crew of handmaidens, they took his bloated schlong in hand and gave it mouth to mouth.

Before blacking out, he begged to come. "I'll do anything you say, just let me finish. Stopper me up, I'll go belly up. Come on, be a good sport, come, come, come, come, just a teenie come. One a piece. One for you, one for me. We'll share. Tell you what I'll do, split the come right down the middle, even steven."

Losing consciousness, he heard himself, or Claritha, he couldn't tell which, saying "Wind me up and watch me go."

The wild man in his dreams mounted her, brutally pushing in, a rutting bull.

Take that.

Take that.

Take that.

Three

*In which Jacob and Claritha come up for air, consult with a
marine biologist, hear the diagnosis, relocate to Jacob's place
in the City, explore their mutual appreciation of Marilyn
Monroe, Claritha picks a fight, Jacob splits, Claritha stews,
Jacob raids department stores on behalf of Claritha, and the
sound of a chirp is the shot heard round the world.*

He woke up in the Arkhouse. Finding himself naked in bed with a
mermaid on top of him, he did what came naturally. "Tell me more
about yourself," he said.

Claritha kissed him. Her tongue bounced off the walls of his cheeks
like a tossed coin that just keeps on going. When she lifted her mouth
off him he moved his jaw side to side, checking to see if anything had
been dislocated. The tumble of her cascading hair blocked his view. He
detected movement on the part of her arms. Their whereabouts, however, were shrouded in hair. Sitting up, he'd have a better view. But if she
thought he were monitoring her every move, then she might restrict her
movements. And then, spontaneity would fizzle. It could spell the end
of getting kissed like someone was branding him. Her Raget reeds burst
out, reaching for his face like tentacles, cutting his scream short by placing a live, squiggly oyster on his tongue. Spitting was not possible.
Claritha's Raget reeds had the coordination of fingers. His mouth was
simply outnumbered. She shoved the creature down. Another followed,

and yet another. By the end, he was snorting oysters like burrito chips. Such tasty morsels. Such pee-pee poppers.

He plugged her.

His pee-pee drew blood.

The Raget wept pink.

"Where are my eggs? Where are my eggs?"

Moved by her plaintive cries to be a mommy, Prince Jacob came to the rescue. "We aren't calling it quits. Any eggs in there, I'll find 'em."

She reined in the Raget restraints. Then like a pig at the slop, he dove headfirst into a bucket full of squealing oysters. For foreplay, he took a bushful of Raget in both hands and swung them like kids in a schoolyard playing jump rope.

"Do-overs," he said.

His pee-pee—fueled by oysters, motivated by empathy, driven by a sense of destiny—was the most substantial it had ever been. Straddling her slick bottom half, he slid in. He pummeled her walls like a wrecking crew. It wasn't his style to debate a subject like female identity while his pee-pee was expanding like a sponge in water. But he ached to console her. "Birth is a miracle, a noble motive. But I also reserve the right to look at the whole person, who you are in the big picture, apart from maternal instinct."

"With the help of the Still Waters, a Man to turn my tides, a Man to make me fertile beyond my wildest dreams."

"The whole person, as I see it, is more than an egg factory. Not that I'm putting parenthood down. I'm a father. I practically raised my son single-handed. Perhaps I could interest you in making love by flickering candlelight? If that doesn't curl your tail, we could share intimacies. Mac's eighteen years old. My sun rises and sets on him. The major relationship of my life was Mac's mother. Give or take, thirty-three blissful years. She divorced me. Out with the old bathwater, in with the new."

Spoken so nonchalantly—what manner of man can just wipe the slate? Of course, it wasn't a clean break. But all baby steps are Firsts. The mermaid in his bed was a tide yanker, now if he could just return the favor. "And you, any significant others in your life?"

"The Still Waters brought us together. They commanded me to go forth. Multiply. Breed. From my Raget, a nation of mermaids."

"They said all that? In the same breath They said you were in your change of life, They said you'd seed a nation of mermaids? You heard it loud and clear?"

The Rageteers coiled and squeezed. His Thing was suctioned so deep, it was nearly pulled out of its socket. Jacob put his hands in the air, exactly what you see the bad guys on TV do. But to his surprise, he didn't stop thrusting.

"The Still Waters don't explain every little thing. All the seas, lakes, inlets, and Man—Man the polluter, Man the despoiler, Man the poisoner—to concentrate Their thoughts on, a lowly mermaid is not uppermost in Their minds. The black-eyed Feeble Ones drove me off so that I would go forth, multiply, and breed. They were doing the will of the Still Waters."

Daring-do coursed through him. Win her eggs, win her love. Restore her dwindling egg supply, throw everything you've got at her. What a difference a day makes! But at the same time, he cautioned himself: Don't be so foolhardy, you miss the curveball. "Feeble Ones? Are they feeble in mind? Weak in body? Spirit? Both?" His next statement, he surmised, might hit a Raget nerve. "Feebleminded would seem to imply dullness."

"My eggs are jammed, dammit. It is by the will of the Still Waters, I am here. I don't put words in Their mouths, They put them in mine. Ordered by the Still Waters, the Feeble Ones chased me. Though I would have gone on my own."

He kissed each of her breasts. The nipples bit his lip. Able? Able? He didn't flinch. "Think of us as the currents of the ocean. Push, pull. We may not always see eye to eye. Crosscurrents, undercurrents, bracing currents, blindsided by currents, currents merging into one consuming mother of all currents, the bond between currents strong enough to survive differences of opinion. We can even agree to disagree. The sparks between our currents are electrifying. A female acquaintance of mine, Kate Vestor, was speaking pearls of wisdom on this very subject. I didn't catch on till now. We can make beautiful currents together."

"I've lived amongst oysters. If I had an egg for every phony pearl of wisdom, I wouldn't be the last of my kind." The Raget strands fell away, floundering and flopping like landlocked fish.

The what? Last . . . as in no other in the whole of creation? With the swiftness of a dagger, his pee-pee whacked away.

She came before he did.

"Where is my egg? Where is my egg?" Shredding the sheets with her teeth, pogo-jumping out of bed, pacing the room, her tail strong as a ballerina balancing en pointe, blubber flesh compressing and expanding like a Slinky toy, breasts ding-donging, hair doing a Yondle. Finally she halted at the foot of the bed. "The black ink of squid drools out of the mouths of Feeble Ones. Their faces are wrinkled, their eyes are blank. They have holes where their teeth used to be. Their minds wander. Before I go feeble, cut me open. If you do find eggs, bathe them in semen water and keep them from harm. On your life, swear it . . . make a pact of it . . . do not let me live into my feeble old age."

Kill, gut, split her open—yeah, like he could ever. "I swear on my mother's grave."

First lie.

In the name of First Love, is there nothing a man won't do?

On the afternoon of their second day ashore, Claritha fell into a heavy slumber, all her linguini Raget strands were retracted. He tiptoed out of bed to make a phone call. "Harris," he said, "I won't take no for an answer. I need you to be a gynecologist for a mermaid."

Silence.

"I hope that's not just shocked silence, and you're thinking it over. You've got to help. She's ill, she could be losing her faculties."

Silence.

"Stay right where you are," Jacob warned.

Harris never broke his silence, not even to say good-bye.

In Jacob's absence, the bedcovers had been pierced. Hundreds of holes of every size. Raget strings were creeping crablike on the bed. At his approach, they slingshot out. Three feet away they had him. He didn't resist. Copulation resumed. Claritha slept through it. Twenty minutes of furious banging. No eggs. Forty-five minutes. Eggless. One hour of screwing, he didn't have an egg to show for it.

It was discouraging.

For a human female, the cessation of eggs isn't the end of the world. Life goes on, women pursue their interests. Whatever else menopause is, the onset doesn't do a job on teeth and hair. Mental faculties can be affected—Cheryl's bout with fuzziness lasted till hormone therapy kicked in. If Claritha's mind were slipping, the Prophecy itself must be called into question. A man to change her life for the better, to make her fertile beyond her wildest dreams. Life-affirming words. Spoken by the Still Waters exactly as reported? Or wishful thinking? And who's to say the Still Waters aren't themselves out to lunch? Think lead paint poisoning. What with the severity of ocean pollution, none of the native life is safe.

The Raget propped Claritha up. She was still dead to the world. The strands slid her on his lap.

For all his skepticism, he had ample reason to rejoice. She was every-thing he'd hoped for and more: the spice he'd been waiting for all his life. His sea-change didn't end with his pee-pee's astounding display of sta-mina and brawn. Coining that phrase, "beautiful currents together," demonstrated just how far he'd come: No wuss am I. I can face off. I can sound off. No stopping the Prince now.

She woke, dark circles under her eyes. He sat on his enlarged organ, holding it hostage while he pumped her for information. Harris would expect a detailed case history. Forcing Claritha to flesh out the Feeble Ones hadn't been easy. A genuine tug-of-war spar. He had badgered her, challenged her, incurred her wrath without hyperventilating. The Sparring Prince.

"If I'm to change your life, I need to know more of what I'm up against. So far we've only scratched the surface."

The Raget strands grabbed his horn and had sex with it.

Afterward, in her grief, she killed a pillow.

"Where are my eggs? Where are my eggs?"

Answering a question with a question, "Know of any freak-of-nature mermaids? It's been my experience, Nature doesn't always go by the book. Rules are made to be broken. Among your people, has any mermaid ever escaped being feeble? Is there no one without eggs, or less of an egg maker, anyone who didn't walk in lockstep and lived to tell the tale?"

Her mouth was puffy from beating the crap out of the pillow. "A man to change my life, to make me fertile beyond my wildest dreams and all we ever do is talk." A deft blow from her tail, the mattress was minus a corner. "In my childhood, I heard of such a one. Eggless all her life till she laid the golden egg. Before pollution, our mermen were dol-phins and sea lions. They can't be trusted anymore. But when they could, it's said they lined up to see the golden egg. The ocean floor was covered. Closely guarded as it was, a Snatcher seized the golden prize.

The mermaid found him. She ate him. I really don't see how this is of any use. She was one of a kind. Where is my egg? Where is my egg?"

He couldn't put it off any longer. "I'm not you, but if I were, I'd take a different tack. Let me show you. Be right back." He left, returning with a bolt of surplus sailcloth and his sewing kit. "For starters, I'd slip on a sundress. Then I'd make tracks."

She didn't ask where to. "I'm not what I used to be. Hot flashes make it hard to keep track of the Still Water's main camp. But it can be done."

"I'd make tracks to my friend Harris. He's sort of a sea doctor. He'll need to examine you, peer into the Raget, see what he can see." She didn't do what he expected. Nothing in the room got roughed up. She merely sat passively on the bed as if waiting for him to proceed. So he spread the fabric and he cut. It wasn't till he nicked himself with the sewing needle, drawing blood, that he found out about Claritha's extracurricular activities.

"Men. The ones I've known were all thumbs." Taking over, she finished stitching. Not bad for a beginner.

"Off season, when no one's around," she said, "between the birthing and the hibernation, I come ashore to watch soap operas on TV. By all means, take me to your doctor. I'll drive. You're to watch the doctor's every move. Some Snatchers are born. Some are made on the spot. Just the sight of an egg gets teeth clicking." Stabbing the pincushion. "Anyone even looks sideways at my stuck eggs, I'll tear him limb from limb."

The muslin dress looked like a potato sack, concealing all but the tip of her tail. Two bounces and she was in the driver's seat, turning the ignition on before he had even opened the door on the passenger side. Her seatbelt twisted. The third time she pulled, it snapped off. There was no putting it together again. A government tested seatbelt, subjected to hundreds of tests, bites the dust. Regardless of Claritha's heart-rendering, touching plight, she was no delicate flower.

A straight route, one beachfront property to another, two miles tops. She was a speed demon. While trying to wrestle the wheel from her, he was poked in the ribs. He let go.

Then out of nowhere, "A mermaid isn't a cold fish. We feel affection for our mates. It is with the deepest affection, I say to you, mermaids go through everyone—men especially—like water. Our First Love is Still Waters. First Love is also the eggs." Taking her eyes off the road, the car swerved. "You haven't actually said so face to face, but going by what you said the previous night, before you said you were a drip, I'm your First Love. So if you love me as much as you say you do, leave the driving to me." Straightening the wheel. "And if you love me—now that we're face to face, you could say it. Yet you *don't* and why you don't reminds me of something out of a soap opera. Anyway, don't do it. Just agree with me. Abandon the push, pull, crosscurrents, undercurrents, blindsiding currents. This is who I am: a fish. Unbred is dead. Bred is not dead. It would be a lie to say, 'I want to make love by candlelight.' Restore me to the prime of my life and earn my undying gratitude. My Raget welcomes you with open arms. Jacob Koleman, the Defender. Jacob Koleman, Egg Retriever. Had I not spoken of these matters, they would be anchors around my neck. This pact is of my own making: You defend my eggs, and I'll defend you from false pearls of wisdom. In your defense, I will never lie to you. One more thing, I don't like making conversation."

Suddenly handing him the reins, she relinquished control of the wheel. Then she ripped the bottom of her dress, bunched it, crunched it, rolled it, stuck it in her mouth, and chewed. "I've never felt anything like this in my whole life. My head's swimming. Am I feeble? Am I at death's door? Is it pollution?" She spit out the cloth and kissed him.

Able? Able? Steering from the passenger seat, his tongue flamenco-danced hers.

"Oh snuggle me, cuddle me, Jacob Koleman. Wrap those strong arms around me. Crush me to your rock-hard chest."

Rock-hard chest? Not in this world. He silently gave thanks (with a caveat: This isn't a profession of religious faith). Somebody up there must like me, somebody in the wilds of the ocean is looking out for me, he thought. I'm on two Somebodies' good sides. Strong arms, rock-hard chest, not in this lifetime. She's speaking the language of love. Even if she's the last to know, three's not a crowd. She's into multiple First Loves: Still Waters, eggs, me. I'm in the In Crowd. She loves me. But crisscrossing currents confuse her. Notice how she kept dropping hints. She's counting the minutes till I say *I love you*.

He heard another inner voice, perhaps the same one that accosted him in the Ark. Just how latentless are you? Hey buddy, the day you deliver the eggs is the last you'll see of her. The moment they hatch, you'll have outlived your usefulness. On the other hand, the doc could blow up in your face. Harris finds no eggs, you're history.

He rebutted. Go back, go back where you came from. I am a Prince. I do not plot in secret.

She kissed the chicken skin up and down his arms. "Me too, I've got gooseflesh coming out my ears."

Chilled to the bone, it was he who had to be carried into Harris's home. Claritha pogo-jumped past the test tubes and beakers. She tenderly placed him on the examination table. Lifting Harris off the ground, she gave him a hard shake. "He dies, you're a dead man."

Harris peered into Jacob's eyes, and took his pulse, then spoke to Claritha in measured tones. "I'm going to listen to his heart. This is called a stethoscope. That box, an electrocardiogram. The purpose is—"

"Mermaids don't have shrimp for brains," she snapped. "I drive. I sew. I'm no stranger to the Soaps."

Jacob asked for a blanket. Stick with me Kid, said the voice inside him. Able? Able? You ain't seen nothing yet. Everybody's got a better half. I'm it. Do mermaids do sleepovers? Were their titties magnets? That was my doing. Call me Naughty Boy.

Minutes later, Harris said, "No disruption in cardio rhythm. Listen for yourself."

Claritha bent over him.

"I'm sorry," he whispered to Claritha. "You caught me at a bad time."

Blackness closed over him.

⁂

"Wake up and smell the sea leaves." The smell was pungent, Jacob had to cover his nose. "Drink." Claritha blew cooling breaths on the water and pushed the cup at him. "The doctor fainted soon after you. He's coming to." Her dress was soaked and in tatters. "I left in such a hurry—these leaves don't grow on trees—I was there and back before I remembered the dress. There will never be another like it—never!—sewn with your own two little hands. I merely put the finishing touches on. You put your whole heart into it." Pouring a cup for herself, swigging it down. "Sick. Sick. Sick. A mermaid doesn't shed tears over a dress. Round and round go the waters in my head. I need to lie down."

They exchanged places. Jacob held her hand.

Harris came and stood beside him. "The shock knocked the wind right out of me. I'm Foundation through and through, born and bred. No diving into Nature's waters with a scalpel, no exposés. Mine is a disciplined mind. Yet how sorely I'm tempted."

"Don't be so hard on yourself," Jacob said. "You lapsed, a moment of weakness. But you can hold your head high. Science and ethics battled it out inside you and ethics won."

"Well, I just feel that it would be unconscionable of me to prod or probe a child of Nature."

Claritha began keening. "Out of the fog, turn my tides, change my life for the better, make me fertile beyond my wildest dreams, loosen the eggs. When the hair goes and the teeth go, when I can't recall my own name, then gut me, gut me, gut me."

Harris sucked air as if any minute his supply would be cut short. He untucked and tucked his shirt. He squirreled through his hair. He swished his lips. The hands went on a wringing binge. "Beautiful lady of the sea, don't cry. I'll take thee as patient, to have and hold in sickness and health till death do us part. As your physician, I thee wed myself to your vital signs. No papers will be published, no notoriety. Hippocrates and nothing but. There is a tide in the life of every man. Miss it, you miss the boat."

Jacob updated him: The Raget, the eggs, the Feeble Ones, the Still Waters, the Prophecy, the freak-of-nature golden egg.

At the approach of the rolling cart, the metal instruments clanking on top, Claritha roared, "Death to Egg Snatchers."

Under Harris's guidance, it was Jacob who did the vaginal insertions, the brain scan, the bloodwork. Wheeling the cart away, Harris motioned Jacob to follow. They were overtaken by Claritha. "Is it crowded in there? What's the egg count? Any damaged? Why aren't they dropping? Would you know an egg if it fell on your head? Maybe you were expecting big, do I look like an ostrich? My eggs are sea-salt small, beluga's bigger. No snap decisions. Take all the time you need. The Still Waters are never stiller than when They must come to a decision. Far be it from me to rush you when you've hardly had time to think."

"When will the results be ready?" Jacob asked. To his untrained eye, no eggs were on the horizon. But if they were microscopic in size, the smears might prove positive.

"Return at seven, I'll leave the door open. Just walk in. Don't ask me to the Ark. Not today of all days. Two phenomena in one day—forgive the pun but I'm already shaken to my very foundation."

They saw themselves out. She stripped. She swam back; he went by car. Half an hour later, she walked in dripping. "The Still Waters are everywhere at once, in the smallest droplets of water. But They're not evenly distributed. Location is everything. You will fill the tub with seawater. I shall soak. My sense of direction isn't what it used to be. It will take some figuring out." Her eye fell on the tattered remains of the dress. She took it to the bath with her, spreading it out on the rim, petting it. "How long till seven?"

"Four hours," he said.

Back and forth with his bucket, he fetched seawater.

With an aching heart, he set up camp on the bathroom tiles. Sinatra on the cassette player, portable phone, hot chocolate (not the drink of choice for August, but a throwback to the comfort food of childhood). All except the tip of her tail was submerged. Every twenty minutes or so, air bubbles rose to the surface. Some built-in adapter in her lungs—he saw no external gills—accommodated themselves to land and sea. His writing implements—pen and yellow legal pad, along with *Cassidy and the Sea Witch*—were spread on the floor. He could no more abandon Mac than walk away from a manuscript. Books have lusty birthcries. Some authors can commit bookicide; he wasn't one of them. He had done deep revisions before. This baby was going back to the womb to be reborn as a tempest at sea, a love story with currents. Cassidy is the Sea Witch's ardent suitor. She has commitment issues. Tie it to cultural prohibitions—her people regard all men with suspicion. Love will have quite a time conquering all. Two trancelike hours later, he reread what he'd written. Page after page of Cassidy exhorting the Sea Witch to bear his young, Cassidy in psychic pain: Where is my son, where is my son?

He phoned Mac. His room may have been packed up, but moving day wasn't till the next day. The number wasn't disconnected.

"I was just thinking of you. How'd orientation go?"

"Socially or academically?"

Jacob laughed. The only A Mac didn't get was in Teens Talk to Teens.

"My two roommates are girls."

"Play it smart. Cadavers don't score. The romance of taxidermy is over most people's heads. Not mine or your mother's—we grasp it. Kinda. Making the dead come to life expresses a love of life."

"Maya thought of me as a full-fledged artist inventing a Creation Myth on my own terms."

"You two don't see each other anymore, do you?"

"Don't worry your pretty little head. Anybody who wants me and my dad isn't going to get either. For the record, my female roommates aren't going to break my loner streak. I'm never going to be Mr. Popularity. But I won't mention Marilyn, even if their walls are plastered with Matt Damon, I'll be discreet. Being a child of a recent divorce isn't making me more gunshy than usual so let's not go down that sinkhole. Mom's on her third hairstyle by the way. And I caught her smoking in the bathroom. I really gotta hand it to her. She's on the move."

"In the first place, no son of mine is a done deal. You've got your whole life ahead of you. A one-hundred-eighty's yours for the asking. In the second place, save some admiration for your dad. Even your old man can be blasted out of stale waters."

"Mom thinks not . . ."

Jacob perceived hesitancy. "Spit it out, Son."

"The two of you simultaneously on the move . . . Don't be a slow-poke on my account, but it *is* my freshman year."

"Message received. You'll need more fathering than usual." Jacob was truly the defender of his egg. "I'm on it. Night and day, there for you. You, you, you. When father and son are palsy-walsy, twosy-woosy, every day feels like Father's Day. The door's always open. The apple of each other's eye, the sweeteners in one another's coffee, the raisins in your cereal, as you are the raisins in mine."

"Get a life, Dad."

"But you just said—"

"Yes, but I won't be smothered."

Jacob let loose a torrent of I-love-yous. Mac gave up. "Drivel," he said and slammed the phone.

Water drizzled down. As Claritha erupted out of the tub, the water overflowed. Jacob scrambled to gather cassette player, papers, and phone, placing them on high ground.

"The time?" she asked.

"About ninety minutes," tipping his head from side to side, pulling on his ears like he had water in them. His alarm grew when he stood on his toes and in perfect imitation of Claritha, bounced up and down. "I'm not making fun of you, a wave just washed over me."

She kept apace with him, bathroom to bedroom. "Moha bites again. The original Moha makes it difficult to move. It sedates, it puts you in the mood and holds you there while Raget goes to work. Living under the same roof with a mermaid is a mental Moha. Some of me has soaked into you. You're feeling your unborn. Eggs are under your skin."

"Brainwashing?"

"The bouncing will pass, you'll see. It's been my experience Daddy Fever's temporary. Men munch on mermaid eggs like beer nuts. Hide the eggs, they dig them up. Distance does not deter. Men don't even have the decency to remember their deeds. Out of sight, out of mind."

"This Defender will never take the eggs and run."

"The Still Waters can think rings round any man. They don't say much, sometimes They're hard to follow. Last time I saw Them, They couldn't have been clearer: a man out of the fog—you, though they didn't name you by name—to turn my tides. By now, They might know more. The Hudson's Their destination. Near the rock you call New York City."

One and a half hours to go. Her eyes were faraway. Opening her mouth to sing opened all the faucets, the sound of running water, her chorus. "My fair mermaid girl, what will you be when you grow up? Trala, trala. A mom who drives a car? Trala, trala. A mom who sews on the side? Trala, trala. A mom who makes love by candlelight? Trala, trala."

Faucets snapped shut as Claritha jammed her fingers in her mouth, testing each tooth. From there, she went to her hair, counting strands.

"What stinking kettle of fish is this?" She was astonished. "More hair on my head than off. My teeth are steady. Yet I'm changing my tune. The sacred songs passed from generation to generation, words I've known by heart since I was a child, suddenly I'm making it up as I go along. I wouldn't wish the change of life on my worst enemy." Dropping down, she hammered the floor with her fists. "One more egg's all I ask. Still Waters, You'd tell me if You changed Your tune . . . for the sins of the mother, You wouldn't punish the Egg, would You? Know thy enemy, so I obeyed, swimming ashore to learn. I've watched their shows, I've worn their clothes. On land, I'm no fish out of water. But when this man spoke of candlelight, it was a song in my heart."

Floodgates opening at last? Jacob knelt. He whispered, "I love you too."

Hissing like a she-lion, she slapped his face. The Raget hit him below the belt, holding him down like a wrestler to the mat.

He cried uncle. "Okay, you don't love me. Love is only going one way, me to you, not vice versa. Satisfied? You're one hundred percent marine life. The fish gets laid, she doesn't cheat on the Still Waters." His temperature soared. The Daddy Fever returned with a vengeance. He took out Mr. Long Shanks. "Now let's make us a sister for Mac . . . He's a superkid . . . To know him is to want to know more of him. You two will hit it off, dinner at my place, the three of us celebrating Egg. It's his freshman year. He's not really in the swim, but soon as he is, I'll introduce you." He wriggled and jiggled inside her. "I'll knock you up, right to the rafters. Able? Able? This is the winning inning, the home run." He pulled out and stuck his hands in her, his fingers going deep into her fold.

He came out empty-handed.

Baying like a wolf, he rocked back and forth on his haunches. "Where is our egg? Where is our egg?"

Seven o'clock on the dot. He and Claritha were making their way through Harris's living room, a hub of computers and lab paraphernalia. Pioneering nonintrusive research, Harris never raided the sea. He examined only those specimens that had died of natural causes. Claritha's towel sarong elevated her cleavage to Wonderbra heights. She walked lightly on her tail—neither glass nor bosom went bumpity-bump.

Jacob was spent. Friction burns on his pee-pee, whiplashed thigh muscles, soreness in his fingers. Able? Able? He had been dynamite. If there were eggs in there that he couldn't shake free, they'd have to be impacted like a bad case of impacted teeth.

Bent over a slide, Harris's back was to them. His tall, thin frame gave no clue. Hearing them, he stood, six feet of sag. He turned, a rat's nest of hair, and an Adam's apple jumping up and down like it wanted out. The whites of his eyeballs were marbleized.

"There's good news and bad news." Harris rubbed his sweaty palms on his gray slacks. "The good news is no matter how negative the data is, I categorically refuse to draw conclusions. But the facts say menopause. Conception impossible. Eggs, nowhere to be found. That eliminates harvesting. Implantation isn't an option. I tried hormones they don't yet have names for, but they made the blood samples disintegrate." He gave Claritha a wan smile. "Fear not, pretty lady. You have

THE MERMAID THAT CAME BETWEEN THEM

no sexually transmitted diseases, pap smear's normal. The markers for life expectancy seem consistent with middle age. I'm no expert on the brain but my analysis reveals no gross irregularities. Unless there's empirical evidence to the contrary, I'd say right as rain." His eyes meandered to her chest. The valiant effort he was making not to ogle—frequent blinking and forays into the peripheral zone—triggered Jacob's pity. Harris was a solitary man, a man with no prospects. If ever a man needed nurturing, it was he.

With Claritha in tow, Jacob took Harris by the hand, sat down on a chair, and pulled Harris down on his knee. Able? Able? His lap spread was like a table with an extra leaf. Installing Claritha on the other knee, he said, "Daddy's going to make it all right."

Claritha was fish-eyed. Her glassy stare was like one of Mac's dead pets.

"I cower before mermaid mythology," Harris said. "The mystical isn't pretend. Mermaids call shots men haven't dreamed of." He had a tremor in his voice. "Woman, you're a mermaid. You don't *have* to face facts."

It thawed her out. "Even if you had attempted to snatch my hope, I wouldn't have wrung your neck. If anybody's neck should be wrung, it's mine. Pollution softened me up for the kill, it's got me by the tail. Give me a hard time on that, it will be your last. But a dying mermaid doesn't keep her teeth and hair. I'm bad off, but not so bad that I can't recognize a reverse Moha when I see one. Herein, nothing—and I mean nothing—gets past me." She pinched Jacob's cheek. Hard.

"What I do?"

"That's for candlelight."

She smacked him on his thigh.

"And that's for the hand-stitched dress."

A flip of her tail sent Harris rolling away. She toppled Jacob backward. "Consider yourself warned, Defender. The prophecy didn't identify you by name. Send me one more wave, and I'll be waving good-bye."

Harris made his farewells from a distance, staying clear of the flying beakers. Claritha left, her tail thumping like birch switch. "Don't think you have to keep in touch," called Harris. "I've served my purpose. A single dose of Mermaid fulfilled me. I wouldn't want to overdose. The Foundation has a protocol: staff minds its own business. But if I were a Q&A man, I'd ask, 'Which way to the nearest Stress Management Clinic?' For you as well as me."

Begging Claritha to wait up, Jacob couldn't proclaim total innocence. Deep down, the heart of man is a patchwork. Damn Kate Vestor for Moha-ing him.

Schmuck, screamed the voice he could not banish. Want a backup plan, Naughty Boy's your man.

They each drew up an itinerary. Claritha said she was headed for New York City.

He said, "So am I, I live there, let's drive in together."

She said, "When?"

He said, "Now."

She said, "Why not? Just watch what comes out of your mouth. Other than eggs, there are no other fish to fry, that clear?"

"Yes Ma'am," he said.

"Enough. How's this for buts? But for you, no man's ever made a deeper impression. Every human being was always water off the duck's back. Nowhere near the reverse Moha. Always Us and Them. Defeat Man by learning what makes him go—don't get involved." Her voice was shrill. "Until further notice, think before you speak." Then mostly to herself, "Is Jacob Koleman the true Defender? I'm not certain. The Still Waters will decide. My first and only loves are the Still Waters and Eggs. I dangle on Their hooks—hook, line, and sinker." She glared at him. "When you look at my eggs, you are looking at the whole fish. Romance ends now. I won't

THE MERMAID THAT CAME BETWEEN THEM

take the bait. Not for all the fish in the sea. I've had it, all right. Up to here. When a mermaid's sacs are at their emptiest—and so far nobody's seen the slightest speck—that's when a mermaid's had it. But why did the Still Waters single me out? Why isn't Nature running her course? What's in store for me? Give me eggs or give me death or give me . . . what?"

Able?

Able?

Naughty Boy was screaming bloody murder: You gotta hustle. By hook or crook, land the Big One. Make her love you.

"Don't stand there gawking," she said. "State your opinion. Are the Still Waters singing my tune after all? Might I be a freak of Nature, the bearer of the golden egg? This could be your golden opportunity."

"Happily ever after to us both," he said.

You don't run the show, he told Naughty Boy. We do this my way.

Packing up the car for the return trip, he was a furnace inside. Like water, he too had a boiling point.

Claritha was sprawled out on the backseat, tail hidden in a plastic green lawn bag. Jacob drove with obsessive attention to vehicular detail, observing speed limits, signaling to switch lanes, keeping a distance of at least two car lengths behind the car ahead of him. However much of a hurry she was in, Claritha didn't contest the leisurely pace. She was contraband. She'd seen enough TV to know the ropes. You don't screw with the men in blue.

They traveled in silence.

He was in no mood to violate the moratorium. First things first. Get a grip. Lose it now, and you might say things you'll regret for the rest of your life. I couldn't fight my way out of a paper bag when she found me. Look at me now. Lean, mean, ready-to-fight-for-your-love machine. Take it to the bank, heads will roll.

She requested windows down.

He downed them.

"Windows up," she said.

Up they went.

So wired, I could easily take the windows into my own hands, establishing cutoff points, according to my own air circulation comfort levels.

"Air conditioner," she said.

So short is my fuse, I don't care if we freeze our asses off.

"Lower," she said.

It fell on deaf ears.

"Have it your way," she said. "I made a pact to always be honest with you. And in all honesty, I liked you better when I first laid eyes on you."

He immediately lowered the windows, pulled in at a McDonald's drive-in, and ordered four fish-on-the bun for her. Nothing for himself. She washed it down with Coke. Despite all her worldliness, she mangled six straws. He patiently showed her how to sip.

"Honestly," she said, "what would I do without you?"

The lean, mean, make-her-love-me fighting machine said, "What in the world would I ever do without *you?*"

As they turned onto the last leg of the journey, he was debating whether or not to try detaining her. Up to now, nothing he'd heard of the Still Waters instilled confidence. They'd never approve a love match between Mermaid and Man.

Suddenly Claritha spoke one of the sweetest words in the English language. "Carsick," she said.

Double parking in front of the brownstone, he schlepped her up four flights of stairs, savoring the irony: Mermaid gets seasick on land. He fell exhausted beside her in bed, beset by contradictory currents. Love her/hate her. She's barren, a freak of nature. No golden egg/yes, golden egg. She needs me not just my pee-pee/putz, she only wants to get in your pants. Play your cards right, you can cohabitate/no matter what you do, she's a mermaid. The Still Waters will tell her to dump you/maybe not. Maybe the Still Waters who don't have a soft spot for Man will prophecy in my favor/what prophecy? If there ever was one, she could have misinterpreted it. The prophecy's not wishful thinking/is so. Without her, I'm fillet/you win, you are fillet.

Opposite the bed, the larger than life poster of Marilyn Monroe was illuminated by its own art gallery lighting.

It was where Claritha's eyes fell. And stayed.

Just as he always surmised: Monroe's appeal was universal. Marilyn hits the spot. Marilyn is a Goddess. In a moment of shared camaraderie they each paid tribute. He whistled.

She went hmmm. A sustained hmmm in the morning. Like she was hmmming and gargling at the same time. She wasn't bedridden. The hot water bottle pressed against her abdomen slurped as she pattered from room to room hmmming at the Marilyns. It occurred to him the hmmm was a form of meditative chanting similar to Ommm. Perhaps Claritha was doing her mental homework prior to consulting with the Still Waters. When Jacob positioned himself directly in front of the floor-to-ceiling living room poster of Marilyn in her renowned blowsy skirt pose, Claritha looked through him.

The prolonged hmmming was quickly becoming a nuisance noise. He put on a pair of earmuffs. He had barely settled into his favorite easy chair when she shooed him. Change of seats. Same routine. Shoo, shoo. Switch of rooms—there was no getting away from it—she wanted him out. He obliged. Under the earmuffs, a world of hurt. Dressed in roomy to-the-knee walking shorts, he tied a shirt around his waist to conceal the growth spurt his pee-pee had undergone. The three-sizes-too-big T-shirt helped.

"I'll be back in thirty minutes," he said.

He couldn't score a single nod. A novel current, this one. Ever since she'd locked eyes with Marilyn, she hadn't made eyes at him. He tried re-entering his apartment. She put a finger on his chest and jabbed. She slammed the door in his face. Going down the steps two at a time, he was psyched.

"She's asking for it, she's gonna get it," he thought.

"You and who else?" he thought back.

He didn't miss a beat. His answer to Naughty Boy: me and Kate Vestor.

⊛

Pacing Kate's living room, he waited his turn. The closed door of the Think Tank didn't stop voices from carrying.

Female client: Outside this one implacable problem tying me in knots, I'm the most laid-back woman in the world.

Kate: The orgasm you've expressed a desire for is the most elusive of all.

Female client: Is a conflict with the near impossible any less worthy than a conflict with the possible? If they can put a man on the moon, why can't I get my rocks off without the usual accouterments?

Kate: I love the concept . . . contractions catching you unawares, out of the blue, in a public place, nothing vaginally inserted. What woman wants to be on a first-name basis with all her orgasms?

Female client: It wouldn't have to stay an utter stranger. After the anonymous climax, some associative link could be established. Who or what did I come over?

Jacob was already anxious. Listening to women discussing orgasms elevated his levels even more. He had to vent or bust. The furniture was every-hair-in-place neat. Emulating Kate, he stacked. Light weights to begin with. One chair atop another. He took it down and started again. Heavy backbreaking tables. His body rebelled.

Have a heart. In bed you've got the stamina of a twenty year old. You don't conk out. Face it, furniture may not be your thing.

He missed Claritha. Say what you will of her, compared to women speculating on orgasms of unknown origins (a new one for him) his mermaid was just an old-fashioned girl.

And was he an old-fashioned boy? Dating from the time he'd met Claritha the changes in his life were dramatic. Able to lie—he said he'd gut her if she lost her mind, but he wouldn't. Able to have a five-second spar without feeling like the world was coming to an end. Able to be ballsy. Challenging her, cross-examining, playing the devil's advocate. Last time he looked, he hadn't given an inch. He was seeing her for who she was aside from her reproductive organs. She needed a good talking to, he was just the guy to do it. A lean, mean, fighting machine doesn't surrender. Not when so much is at stake. Protect the damsel in distress. If necessary save her from herself. Arrangements may not be to her liking but hey—act first (a first for him), ask questions later.

Yet . . . she hadn't made a totally new man of him.

His old-world values were still intact: meet, make nice, fall in love.

Between the second and third story of his brownstone, he heard Naughty Boy squawking, *Two heads are better than one.* The refrain was still going strong when he let himself into his apartment.

He was immediately set upon by an army of Raget filaments which bound him hand and foot. They delivered him like a parcel, placing him on the floor directly in front of the couch.

"I can no longer hold my silence," he said.

The Marilyn tape in the VCR was giving him vocal competition. Two large bowls of popcorn rested beside Claritha. Her crunching was pig-slopping loud.

"What's gotten into you? Granted Marilyn Monroe isn't just anybody. I didn't know her in the flesh. She's long dead. But even in death, the legend lives on and on. A woman for all seasons. The world will never know another like Marilyn Monroe. Beauty, talent, intelligence, sensuality. If ocean waves could part for mortal woman, they'd part for her. I'm definitely leaning toward forbidding you further contact. Your choice: Go straight to your room and stay there, or explain yourself."

In between fistfuls of popcorn, "Soon I will be well enough to see the Still Waters."

The Raget called in reinforcements. His hair was absentmindedly stroked. The touch did not seem like a prelude to sex. "I shall make an additional request of Them. Only once before have I made one. Always, the Daughter of the Sea prays, *May this be the day I spawn.* To that, I will add, *May I have Your ear?*"

His heart leapt. Yes. Yes. She intends to talk Their ears off: Jacob Koleman isn't water off the duck's back.

I will say, *"Here is a woman who calls to me like the sea. Here is the man who brought the woman who calls to me like the sea.* What freak of nature is this, that I cannot wash my hands of Marilyn Monroe?"

She pressed the volume button on the remote. Marilyn was singing, "Diamonds Are a Girl's Best Friend."

"Anything she's saying to you, you can tell me," he said in a fatherly manner.

She snapped her fingers. The Raget reeds looping his pee-pee drew it out. She rammed him to her, to the hilt.

Eyes only for Marilyn. "Where is our egg? Where is our egg?"

Egged on, he hightailed it back to Kate Vestor. She kept him cooling his heels in the living room. He picked up where he left off, building the stack higher and higher, a kindergartner at the blocks. He rested after his exertions. Nothing to sit on but floor.

Suddenly Kate was standing over him. He was flat on his back like he'd been decked. The sweat pouring down his shirt leaked to his socks. "Not bad for an amateur," she said. "Get anywhere, any epiphany?"

"Neck's stiff," he said.

She turned. He had rolled the carpet. Acoustically, the click of her heels was gunfire.

"Meet me in the Think Tank," she said.

He crawled in on all fours. The chair was manageable, its seat almost kissing ground. Soon as he was in, he threw his legs out like dice. Mopping his brow with his sleeves, his vision finally cleared enough to look. She had on a cranberry suit, the jacket was cropped and tight. He stared at her pussy. Blatantly. The type of stare that gets men slapped silly. He put his arms up in front of his face, apologizing from behind them.

"I wasn't making a pass. God, no. I'm a one-woman man. Currently I'm involved . . . a female. She's older. Her ovaries and yours are the difference between night and day. I was just having an ovarian reverie. I do not, however, want to . . . to do it with you."

"You fled barefoot from my boudoir. I've hunted down men for far less. To look at me, you'd never know I can be the wrath of God. I won't rest till I find out why you've been spared. Is it your age? When Maurice died in my arms, his corpse shriveling like tissue paper, his penis rallying like a parade float, he was no more than six years your senior. Though I didn't kill him, some days I'm guiltier than others. Am I a glutton for your particular brand of put-down? You've got something that stays my hand. Whatever the fuck it is, Jako, you can run but you can't hide. Identification, then closure. I live for the day. Live. Live. Live. The day cannot come soon enough. Kate Vestor doesn't take being disarmed sitting down." She got up, thumping her chest like Tarzan. "You piss me off, off, off."

"Let me give you a hypothetical: A female of considerable beauty, brains, and brawn, totally disinterested in clothes, makeup, politics, with an active heterosexual sex life, suddenly finds herself fixated on Marilyn Monroe—"

"The ovarian broad, day to my night? Say no more. Marilyn wouldn't be Marilyn if she didn't make men and women go weak at the knees. The timing of the fixation should clue you in. Are you so bovine? . . . Look who I'm asking. This was the guy who declared he wasn't latent. All the world is latentized, no exemptions. Latent. To the kazoo. Marilyn's definitely doing a number on your friend's latents."

"Could you be more specific?"

"Asking in that disarming way of yours when you know how pissed I am is extraordinarily disarming. Even my eyes are disarmed. I can't be seeing what I think I'm seeing." She grabbed his Thing. "Man oh man, Jako. You are a cuntteaser."

He split.

He hightailed it home.

Was latent going to save the day? Years from now, would he and Claritha have a good laugh at how everything latently came together at the very moment all seemed lost? (Kate's scolding and all the implications of groping him would have to wait for a more convenient time.) But latent isn't something you do consciously. Claritha was behaving like a latent dissenter. Her natural aptitude for sewing and driving (the VCR didn't turn itself on) might have less to do with infiltrating Man and keeping dossiers on him, and more to do with a latent desire to broaden her horizons. The Marilyn connection? A big broadening eye-opener. But to exactly what horizons? He'd have to keep tabs. The important thing was, Claritha was coming up in the world. Yesterday, she wasn't a people person. Today she's a . . . a groupie. Even the golden egg epitomized going against the grain.

A man's house is his castle, he may enter any old way: loudly, lumbering, snorting, burping, chuckling, whistling a happy tune, yammering, blowing smoke rings. He looked in on Claritha, *tenderly* as one who peers into a bassinet. He saw a fetching sight. Yards and yards of yellow silk bedspread, inherited from one of Grandpa Marshall's voyages around the world, were spread across her lap. A yardstick was in one hand, cutting shears in the other, his sewing kit nearby.

Claritha looked up for an instant, then returned to her work, softly singing, "She walks like the sea on a moonlit night. Her skin is pond water under the stars. She ripples me. Fathoms deep, I am a rushing stream."

He stood with hands clasped behind his back, something he imagined presidents do in the Oval Office while deciding, for the good of the entire nation, what is best for each individual. "A most fortuitous choice of words. Just what I wished to discuss. The topic is Fathom-Deep Thoughts. There are regions of our mind which are recessed. Recesses are like underwater caves. In these fathom-deep mental caves, wells and wells of thoughts. Round-as-egg thoughts. Our minds are hatcheries filled with eggs just waiting to spring to life. And everyone who is anyone—us for instance—is in labor, birthing herself and himself. I can help you crack out of your mental shell." None of the sewing pins pierced his flesh. "I can see you through your birth pangs. You: the egg. Me: the midwife. Marilyn, in the end: just a passing ripple."

As she started in on a different section of the cloth, she looked up for a moment. "It's like listening to a seashell. All foam, no substance. I've heard babbling brooks make more sense."

Sink or swim. "Think of yourself not as the last of your kind but the first. A mermaid for the millennium. The New Wave."

Pricking her finger with the needle, she sucked the wound. "Look what you made me do. Some help you are. Barging in here, telling me I'm not myself. It's hard to miss, isn't it? That's like telling the ocean it's wet. If I'm an egg—anyone with half a brain can see I'm not— I'd be rotten. Are you so waterlogged you can't tell?

Something spilled over in him. "Marilyn was *nobody's Mama*. Get my drift? She *bore no children*."

Weeds of Raget spread out over the yards and yards of material like a security fence. "I made a pact: Tell no lies. Never have I met anyone—man, woman, mermaid, merchild, dolphin—that I could not take my eyes off of. But even when I'm not looking I see her. She's something else isn't she? Now if you'll excuse me, I've got a dress to finish."

He could feel the veins in his throat pop. "You sit there calmly after what I've told you? Marilyn was *childless*. Reports differ. She might have tried to conceive, but she didn't try all that hard. Eventually she got over it. Her interests were far ranging. How does that ripple you? My brain's not so waterlogged that I can't visualize whose clothes you're trying to step into. When you see the Still Waters, give them that earful."

Then he dropped to his knees, sorry for . . . he-wasn't-sure-what. Probably for his lack of tact. A thousand pardons.

Her voice shook with fragility. "If you love me, you'll let me work in peace. Go."

He wasn't through yet. Insight was hitting him like a tsunami. "I understand you better than you understand yourself. For the first time in your life, you're trying not to put all your eggs in one basket."

Out of the Princely goodness of his heart, he left. Crucial for all eggs is the Incubation Period. Time to mature, time to understand that it's Marilyn's diversity she's attracted to, not Marilyn herself. Incubation is a time of reflection.

He desperately needed kisses and hugs, giving them as well as receiving them. He missed the company of his other love, a First Love on par with this one. Two First Loves.

Mac, my baby. Daddy's on his way.

In the cab, he slipped into something more comfortable—baggy jeans so relaxed in the crotch you couldn't tell how well hung he was.

The obstacle path to Mac's new quarters at New York University was swarming with the stop-and-start of traffic jams and gridlock. Parents, friends, friends of friends lugging cartons, carts, shopping bags, backpacks, and suitcases. Everyone was devil-may-care. Mac's floor smelled like a street festival of ethnic foods, mostly Chinese and Tex-Mex. The music was salsa. Mac's movers had been United Parcel Service, but unpacking was strictly a family affair.

Suite 703.

The girl scouring the communal kitchenette wore over-the-elbows rubber gloves. Her apron started at the neck and fell to her ankles. On her feet, rugged terrain boots. Not a stray hair slipped out from under the snug aviator's cap. The surgical face mask hid her features. Cyclops sunglasses shielded her eyes from kitchen mites.

He turned left to his son's room and put his ear to the door. Coast clear. In Cheryl's absence, perhaps father and son could hold a love fest. Kissing and hugging, opening their hearts. Filling the coffers of his empty womb.

The door swung open.

"So you're my heavy breather." Mac had on a striped polo. The large bars of blue made his puny chest even punier. They wallpapered him. The legs protruding from the shorts were cut from the same cloth as his torso, all frozen in a preadolescent time warp.

Jacob entered and closed the door.

Starting off on the right foot, he said, "The other day on the phone, I overstepped. My 'love yous' were too effusive. Your mother doesn't smother you, neither should I."

"I came on too strong too. Apology accepted."

They hugged. Blink, you missed it.

"The box cutter on the dresser's yours." Mac knelt over a half-opened container of juice. His mop of curls, corralled by a red bandanna, was infant downy. "Want some?" slurping it down, a line of orange drool meandering his chin like he was still in the high chair.

"Maybe later," Jacob horse-whinnied, a mare neighing for her colt, longing to nuzzle the flank of her newborn.

"Sinuses acting up?"

"Not sinuses." He began blathering. "Any pedestrian, especially a child, can't be too careful. A red light's nothing to some motorists. Gap between the subway platform and the train car—a hippo could fall through the cracks. Flu season's coming up; don't get your shot, germs will come gunning for you."

Mac slowly uncrouched, his hairless cheeks darkening with annoyance. His eyebrows, which had more hair than his armpits, clenched like a fist. He scowled. "Not Mr. Worrywart again? We have a pact. Signed, sealed, and delivered during junior high. Mr. Worrywart doesn't show his face unless there's an emergency. Even then, it would have to be life threatening. What's the deal?"

Leaping over the cartons, swiping an unauthorized hug. "I can still hear the patter of your little feet. Seems like only yesterday, you'd come running into my arms. Daddy would pick you up. My neck would be sopping with kisses. I know the clock can't be turned back. Time marches on. But my love for children remains undiminished. In full flower. Thumbs up to kids."

Mac squinted, perplexed. A shadow flickered across his face. "After all those lectures on birth control, did *you* slip up?"

Jacob sat on the cot, patting the spot next to him. The spot went unclaimed. The patting went on and on, finally dying out like horses hooves on the plain. "I didn't get anyone with child. You'll see when you're a father. Bringing up baby is a labor of love. The child is like First Love, a priority. I've always put First Love in the context of two consenting adults, but I stand corrected. My heart's big enough for multiple First Loves. Even if a woman were to come into my life—not just any woman but *the* woman—your position will be secure. First Love is the whole schmear, A to Z, Z to zippo. Both of you. With nil competition."

Mac sat down beside him. "Same here, Dad. Never second to anyone. You're right up there."

"Pact?"

They kissed on it, two pecks worth. Fraction of a second, it was over. Mac cuffed him on the arm. "Let's get to it."

"We've made a pact. Any woman with designs on us will never have the simultaneous pleasure of our company. Maya was old enough to be your mother. I have nothing against aging women. But a young man such as yourself may need a crash course in menopause."

". . . isn't the time or place."

"Menopause isn't something you sail past. The vacant womb is a stormy sea."

"Shelve it, Dad."

"Just for future reference, a woman in the trickle-down lean years of dwindling production wrestles with demons. She may fly in the face of logic. The currents of one's mind boggle just trying to keep up. If it's a fling you want, find someone without egg issues."

The bedroom door practically blasted off its hinges, and a laminated apron and aviator's cap bore down on him. Tearing off her surgical mask, Cheryl snarled, "What a poor excuse for a man you are, filling the child's head with bias. Screw menopause. Women aren't tied hand and foot to the womb. Hormones don't dictate policy, we do." She put her palm out. "Hand me that box cutter."

Like fruit-picking migrants working the field, Jacob stuck to his corner, she harvested cartons in another, her back to him. Mac divided his time, going from one to the other, hauling away the innards of disemboweled boxes. Cheryl's cap was off, her apron discarded. Jacob got a good look. Oxidized red hair. Some scissor-happy person couldn't tell a straight line from a zigzag. Replacing the signature elegant dress were white capris, second-skin tight. Her off the shoulder top was slit in back, showing spine and black bra. All the years seaside at the Ark, she had never worn a two-piece bathing suit. Her one-piece had been turtlenecked.

He couldn't arrive at a consensus. His currents were on overload. Tsk-tsking. Shame on you, tarting yourself up. Countercurrents admonished him. Cut her some slack, she's a work-in-progress. Takes one to know one. Her Naughty Girl's out on the town. Undercurrents of guilt pushed to the forefront. This the best you can do? Eye her from afar? Sling mud? Sling slack? How does this look to Mac? How do you look to him? Going to turn over the cart like you did Claritha's? If you had to tell her Marilyn was barren, did you have to use a barbed harpoon? Just how good at First Love are you?

He cleared his throat. "Cross words aren't the end of the world. While there's much to be said for harmony, I could quote an equal amount for the other side. In the words of my conflict counselor, Kate Vestor: Making beautiful conflict together is the gold ring."

Activity came to a standstill. It was as if he had started a campfire. They drew near, squatting down.

He went on. "Squabbles—in moderation—clear the air. They provide an adrenaline rush. Sparks fly. It's a trip. But in the interests of harmony—all for one, one for all—not another cross word. Agreed? Mac's moving day shouldn't be marred by petty differences."

Cheryl reached into her bra, took out her bubblegum, chewed. "Just when it was getting interest'n'. I coulda taken your nose 'n' Brillo'd it off. I was cook'n'. A box cutt'n' bitch. Got it down to a formula—do ya? Harmony/disharmony/moderation." Naughty Girl glint in her eye. "Let you in on a little secret. Uh-uh, not the one you think, still no definitive answer on why I divorced you." Glint gone. "The secret is, Scott and I did trial runs on your formula." The bubble she was blowing popped. She spat the gum into her hand, staring as though she couldn't remember where it came from. "Couldn't achieve beautiful conflict with myself, let alone anyone else."

Jacob commiserated. "Rough turf inside? I have my days too. Psyche is the City that never sleeps. Currents flow in our veins like blood, rumbling with the sounds of the subliminal."

Wrapping the gum in foil, she slipped it back inside her bra. "The line between fashion and fashion disaster is rice paper thin. I can't go to the beauty parlor without a close encounter with a line. You sound so nonchalant. I don't know how you do it. When I eavesdropped outside Mac's door, invading his privacy, I crossed the integrity line. Something's going on with me and lines . . ." She flung her shoulders back. "Don't dump that 'subliminal' line on me: Psyche is the City that never sleeps. It's the oldest line in the book."

"But in the interests of harmony—"

Her elbow grazed his. "I heard fighting words."

"On this day of all days, Mac's moving day, let's not—"

She cut him off. "Going by what you said, Mac might think menopause makes a woman batty. He might think I'm hostage to my hormones. Now it's you that's walking the thin line between misinformed and malicious mischief."

He threw it right back at her. "Mac didn't take it wrong. You're not his mouthpiece. He took it in the spirit it was meant." His nostrils flared. "You don't see me flying off the handle, do you?"

Mac whipped off his bandanna. "Nobody interrupt. I'll gag anybody that tries. If I didn't see it with my own eyes, I wouldn't believe it. So the honeymoon's finally over. It looks like the two of you can't be in the same room without fighting. Look, I couldn't stop you guys from divorcing. All I ask now is, behave like adults."

Cheryl stood, extremely agitated. Jacob shot up, manic. Pacing back and forth, opposite directions, glancing at each other, muttering Nevermind. The last go-by she said, "If you won't tell him, I will." He halted. She curled into Jacob's upper arm, and the crook closed around her. "On behalf of your father and mother," Cheryl said, "We will always treasure our first sparks."

He didn't contest her statement. Sparks had been present. He couldn't account for it. God help him, there had been chemistry. He charged the cartons, ruthlessly breaking open the remaining crates with his bare hands, quick as a cardshark, unloading the contents. When Cheryl and Mac couldn't keep pace, he took over placing everything where it belonged. He didn't have to look up to tell they were bewildered.

In making farewells to Mac, he said, "I love you. First and foremost." One and a half kisses from Mac, doled out like he was counting calories. To Cheryl, "Gotta go."

Lip smacking behind his back. He glanced over. The mother of his son planting kisses on Mac's cheek . . . Mac didn't push away.

Jealousy sparked . . . and died.

Mac and I have an ironclad pact which none can put asunder: Daddy is First Love.

Walking down the hall to his apartment, he leaned his forehead against the cool wall. Sparking with someone makes heat. Just how hot is hot? Divorced for mysterious reasons, it has to spark interest. That Cheryl should generate additional sparks should not lead to false assumptions. Not all sparks are created equal. Okay, Scott's cock had driven him to take to the sea on a foggy day. But no spark of jealousy existed now. Cheryl looked like a hot number. If your taste ran to tits, ass, and bubblegum, it might strike a spark. A man can lose a bucket of water just thinking of sparking with his ex. Blasphemy! Only a few feet from Claritha, he mustn't be irreverent. He squared his shoulders, then reached for the door.

Assorted scraps of Grandpa's bedspread speckled the room. Swatches hung from lampshades. Claritha's arms were crossed in front of her chest, green eyes boring in, teeth bared, canine growls. "Dr. Harris didn't find any eggs, but maybe he missed a spot. After all, he didn't think I was a lost cause. Marilyn's why you're holding back on the whomp and clonk. Did you think what you said this morning went in one ear, out the other? Marilyn this, Marilyn that. She's your leading lady. If only the Still Waters said your name. I would rather die than find out you really are the one for me but I wasn't the one for you because she got there first."

"You're right, my feelings for Marilyn are strong," Jacob admitted. "Aha."

"And wrong. You're Numero Uno."

"Tell it to the Soaps. Marilyn's the Other Woman. When you're with me, your mind's on her." Bouncing off the walls, her tail ricocheted her. Books tumbled from their shelves. They caught her eye. His publicity photo on the back of one cover fell nearest to her. "A writer, are you? Soaps are written by writers."

She loves, loves, loves me. Naughty to fan the flames, but I'd be crazy to put them out.

"It's OK for *you* to love the Still Waters *and* love the eggs," he explained. "One doesn't take away from the other. Multiple loves. I love you, I love Mac. Pardon the expression, but once you meet him, you'll take to him like a fish to water. I love Marilyn. Same principle: One doesn't take away from the other."

She pinned him against the wall, lifting him off his feet. "I'll see you at your best inside my Raget or for the rest of your life, you'll be looking over your shoulder. Don't underestimate me. Buy me some-thing—I haven't got a damn thing to wear! Hmmm. . . ." (An ordinary wheels-are-turning hmmm.) "I require a Marilyn dress." She rubbed her Raget. "And watchamacallit."

"Underwear? What for?"

She let him go. He dropped to the floor in a heap.

Hammering away at the wall with her fists, her tail was a tom-tom on the floor. "My rival's dead. She didn't bear young. Yet I ripple for her still."

"A passing ripple. Remember what we discussed? There are eggs fathom deep. Your mind is a hatchery. Thoughts new to you ripple up from your . . . water caves. It's all part of you getting in touch with yourself. You are the New Wave. The vanguard. You shouldn't put all your eggs in one basket."

"Hop to it before I tear the place apart."

The pile of manuscripts on Yondle's desk formed an impenetrable wall.

"Pull up a chair." Finch stayed behind the wall, talking through it rather like neighbors over a backyard fence. "I spoke to Berry."

"Really? Listen, Finch, I'm looking for Yondle."

"At lunch."

"Back when?"

"Shortly."

Ms. Gets-the-job-done, meets-her-deadlines, Yondle was his first pick for his personal shopping guide. "How long will she be?"

"Ten, twenty minutes. The lady who usually covers for her couldn't make it. Not that anybody fills Yondle's shoes. These submissions are peanuts to her."

Twenty stories below, they heard the screech of wheels. Finch paused, then continued. "Berry the book doctor put you in his infirmary. *Pirate Cassidy and the Sea Witch* didn't make the cut. Berry is going through a bad patch with his son Craig. Maybe his bedside manner was brusque. But did you have to burn rubber off my tires driving away from his place? Reckless endangerment of property, reckless endangerment of self—what were you thinking?" Jacob heard the snapping of pencils. "The report I got says your book's terminal. You will not make a mockery of my wing. When I take you under it, it's for life. Forsake the book if you must, but live to write another."

"I didn't catch the name of Yondle's restaurant."

Drawers were pulled out, forcefully shoved in. The wall of boxes shuddered.

"I have your best interests at heart. Line up another book project. Keep your mind engaged. Mine the mind."

"Yondle?"

"I wasn't always an agent. Caught the writing bug in college. Nobody mentored me like I mentor you. Nobody cared like I care. Nobody networked me like I network you."

"Tell me where she is or —"

"Like a thief in the night, you fled the infirmary. Lightning storm just above the house . . . odd doings . . . Berry reading at the table. Even odder, it's your book. He couldn't put it down . . . He'd like nothing better, but he can't. Did you have a father-and-son talk with his son?"

"I did not side with the son against the father. Nothing's more precious than the love of a father for his progeny. Harry Pottersville cast the spell, not I."

"Potter. Harry Potter."

"Yondle. Yondle Carr." Jacob dismantled a column of boxes, leaving nothing but air between them. "Where is she?"

"She who?" Finch played dumb.

"You won't wring a confession out of me because there's nothing to wring. Craig took me into his confidence, he wants to be a warlock.

Blame Harry Potter. I'm an innocent bystander. The speed of my driving was on the wild side of the street. (Seat belt's busted, send me the bill.) But I wasn't looking to crash. The future beckons. I'm not giving up on *Pirate Cassidy and the Sea Witch*—nothing doing. My books are children. I make no orphans. My life is turning a corner. I had an initial visit with a conflict counselor, one maybe two follow-ups to go. I'm semilatent. Not out and out latent. No lurid details. Abler than ever, getting abler by the minute. Mostly good egg. Lean, mean, fighting machine for a good cause." He inched the desk toward the window. "I confess that I'm losing my patience. Satisfied?"

"No."

He felt a thump on his rump.

"Unhand my desk. Don't let the soft bosom, the round hips, the luscious thighs, the cuddly bellyrolls, the Rapunzel braids, the Santa Claus eyes fool ya," growled Yondle. "I came up the hard way, through the ranks of women's groups."

"A word in private," Jacob said.

❀

They were in Bloomingdale's before he concluded what he was sure would be a bombshell. "It's not just that Claritha brings out the best. She elicits the spectrum: naughtiness, volatility, sexuality. I'm in the thick of it. Nothing craven. Nevertheless an edge is creeping around my borders."

What speed-reading is to the written word, Yondle was to women's apparel. She shucked the racks like oysters. "I'm shocked. You're actually dating a woman who's up there in years, no spring chickadee? Her menopause doesn't make you feel like a senior citizen?"

"She's my love, my aphrodisiac . . . and my pain in the ass. In other words, the greatest adventure of my life."

Yondle flitted from rack to rack, a bee checking out the flowers. "You're stranger than fiction." Her hair fell across her shoulders, oohing and ahhing like he was a celebrity. She hailed over a clutch of salesgirls, women who hadn't seen their twenties in a long, long time. "My friend's looking for a Marilyn Monroe dress and lingerie. Never was there a truer ally for the menopausal. Get this—his girlfriend's not young enough to be his daughter."

And from there it grew. By the time they reached Saks Fifth Avenue, he needed no introduction. Saleswomen modeled the goods, an exclusive fashion show usually reserved for VIPs. They shared true-life stories. They aroused his W spot. His writer's instincts were doing cartwheels over menopause. Theirs . . . their moms', aunts', cousins', grandmothers', godmothers', friends', neighbors'.

Yondle was like a manager on a campaign trail. "You're looking at the esteemed author, Jacob Koleman, who's going to write the guide for men on female menopause."

He would, too. By putting men inside the minds and bodies of mature women, he would do his brethren a good turn.

Gift-wrapped boxes were tucked securely under his arm, three dresses in all, sized differently, all styled alike. Clingy, luminescent, petal-soft pale lilac, weighing no more than a postage stamp, dipped in front, slit on the sides, even standing still they had pulse. Glitter, like fairy dust. You don't just look, you *lo and behold*. Claritha's Raget was a full package. The lace-trimmed panties he purchased were stretchies. Anxious to get home, he took Yondle by the elbow, propelling her past the handbags, the scarves, the costume jewelry, the street bazaar that is the main floor of most department stores, out the revolving doors, onto the sidewalk.

"In the acknowledgments of my next book, *Men in Menopause*, there'll be a prominent place for you." Jacob promised.

Yondle's hair extensions gripped his wrist. "The sparks of life you're throwing off bespeak of passion. Grand groundbreaking, groundshaking, epic passion. If you need an aficionado of passion to give you pointers, I'm your gal."

Using the hand that wasn't cuffed by the hair, he hailed a cab, and opened the door, bowing like a gallant. The coils unwound, releasing him from bondage.

"What beasts we be," Yondle said. "The Beast of Passion ignites the imagination." She licked her chops at him as if he were a tasty morsel.

He paid the driver in advance and sent her off alone.

※

Nonstop Marilyn, the Marilyn film marathon still going strong. The latest flick, *Some Like It Hot,* two men in drag, vying for the one and only Monroe. Claritha wasn't in front of the set. Steam bellowed out from the bathroom, the shower dishing out so much fog that when he knocked and walked in, his eyes had to adjust. He took it as an omen. The replay of their first time: from out of the fog, a man to turn her tides. Rattling the boxes, he invited her into the bedroom.

She spurned his offer.

The shower curtains were sealed.

"You won't come out, let me come in."

She declined his offer. Plain English, scram.

"I could scrub your back."

A slit in the curtains. One puffy red eye, pouchy underneath. The spark of jealousy reducing her to tears? He rushed to reassure her. "Making yourself into a Marilyn look-alike won't make me love you more. I've given Raget nothing less than my personal best."

The steam was making it difficult to breathe. She gasped and wobbled. He dropped the boxes, catching her as she went down. Over her protests, he dragged her to the sofa. Hastening to the kitchen for ice water and ice packs, he heard a sound he normally associated with more rural surroundings.

Do I have crickets?

Tracking it, he was led right back to the living room.

Pressed against the television screen, Claritha was rotating her pelvis.

The Raget chirped, like a flock of canaries in her crotch.

He put the ice pack on his head.

She belts it out for Marilyn while I get the silent treatment? he thought. Do my ears deceive me? Is that a mating call?

The Raget chirped in the affirmative.

The mermaid sings . . . she sings not for me.

Four

In which Jacob tries to fend off Marilyn Monroe with a short, pithy, three-word concept, Jacob gets physical with Kate Vestor, Jacob brings Yondle on board, and there's that damn chirpish racket again.

He kept telling himself she wasn't coming out of the closet. Wasn't. Wasn't. Wasn't.

Was she?

The ice pack on his head was on its second refill. The Raget was plugged and duct-taped, folded inside itself for insulation like a soft but durable eyeglass case, keeping the chirps, tweets, and warbles quarantined. Splayed across the sofa like a Victorian woman on her fainting couch, Claritha couldn't meet his eye.

"It's never needed shushing before. It's never vocalized. I know of no other Raget with sound effects. What a yakety-yak. How that woman loosens my tongue. I came ashore to spawn. Am I the spawn of Marilyn Monroe? By the will of the Still Waters? Marilyn's Moha? My own feeble mind?" Clinging to his proffered hand, she moaned, "To be honest, I'd like to wrap my tail around her. Arms as well. Closer and closer. Lips touching lips." Rolling off the couch, she spun toward the television. The power was off; a dishcloth covered the screen. "If I am indeed the spawn of Marilyn Monroe, then death to anyone who would snatch me away."

Jacob sat on her. He didn't have the heft to stop her. Even slowing her was iffy.

"Yes. No. Don't you dare," maneuvering herself out from under him, freeing his pee-pee and headlocking it. "Is it the drinking water? You people are fluoride-happy. I want her. This minute. Sex with Marilyn Monroe . . . find a way." Rubbing his pee-pee along her face. "Oh the indignity, how can anyone bear being at the mercy of chirps? I'll make it worth your while, help me."

Able?

Able?

Like a jilted lover, he ably cried foul. "All along, I warned you. Did you listen? It's the first day of the rest of your life. Let's hear it for chirps. Hail to the birth cry. No birth is ever complete with crying a river. Only a sick puppy would come quietly into this world. Twitches for Marilyn? Grow up. Marilyn Monroe's a force of nature. Take a number. If that's no help, try this one on for size—below the waist's not your only eggcase. The brain's inseminated with ideas. Marilyn procreated like crazy. That's why she's a Fertility Goddess, an inspiration to us all. You too can lay eggs left and right. *Mine your mind.* Create a body of work. The business of the brain is begetting."

Like the man said, given half a chance, the brain can't help but beget. He mindfucked her, with all his might, pushing in, unloading his seed, so she might go forth and multiply.

"It's a lot to take at once," he consoled, hands on her skull. "But with these words, I impregnate you: IDEAS ARE CHILDREN."

She bolted, locking the bathroom door while he was still picking himself off the floor. He knocked. He kicked. He scraped his knuckles banging. He took his shoes off and clomped away.

"Name one child you ever made with an idea."

"My books. They're the children of my mind."

"Have you lost your mind?"

"Books *are* children."

"Are *not,*" she shrieked, running water, until foggy steam billowed out the chinks in the door at the top and bottom.

Suddenly the blast of the street buzzer summoned him to the foyer wall. He hit the intercom so hard plaster flaked off. "Whatever you're selling, I don't want."

"Kate Vestor. Five minutes, I'll be on my way."

He was still able to think on his feet. Without a woman's touch, would there be Woman's Lib? As the sole male kicking off the Mermaid Liberation Movement, might not the opposite sex be of some service?

"Stay right where you are," he told Kate.

Barefoot, he ran like hell.

※

In profile, Kate Vestor's breasts were stuffed Christmas stockings. She didn't profile long. The second the lobby door opened a crack, she put her foot in, black pump with satin bow, ankle nicely turned out. Her lips looked dipped in a vat of gloss, moist and Vaseliney. Her black dress was air conditioned—peek-a-boo cutouts, just larger than grains of sand, revealed little, while promising much.

"I'm not thin-skinned." Kate, brittle and high-pitched, like a train whistle in need of a tune-up. "Conflict bombards me twenty-four hours a day, like UV rays. I can shrug off with the best of them. But until I determine how you came to have the run of the place—me waiting for you to return from the bathroom when you never did, you waltzing in a few days later, staring at my unexposed vaggie, you picking my brain, man oh man, you're stacked between the legs, thicker than a side of beef. Here I go again, blabbering away. Damn you, how do you do what you do?"

"Claritha's incommunicado in the bathroom. Quick . . . what more can I say to convince a woman of her worth? I've already declared my love. I've cited brainpower. The mental field's always fertile when one puts one's mind to it, wouldn't you say so? Previously, I've touched on topics like latent and making conflict together . . . currents . . . I call them making beautiful currents. See, everything you said was fodder. You've made no small impact on me. Currently, my currents are a mixed bag: up with women's lib, down with gumchewing exes; up with ex-wives who don't chew, down with the ex chopping off her hair, down with same-sex orgasms, down with any orgasm of unknown origin. I couldn't help but overhear you and your client discuss climaxing at random, a subject I could never in a million years conceive of. Up with the traditional, down with women who would alienate sons from fathers, down with mystery divorces, down with water torture." He opened the door wide, pulled her in, and shoved her hard against the mailboxes. "Give me what you've got on starting up talks after they've been blocked by a bathroom door."

The gloss on her mouth plopped like candlewax. Her blinks were rapid heartbeats. She fingered the peek-a-boo cut-outs nearest her collarbone, ripping them to get more ventilation.

"Negotiation is a process by which two or more people talk with each other in order to reach agreement. Mediation is different from negotiation in that the people having the conflict agree to let another person come in as helper. The helper doesn't take sides or tell people how to settle the conflict."

"Third party. Got it."

Banging herself against the metal mailboxes, three sharp clangs. "Distinct from mediation is binding arbitration. In binding arbitration a neutral party hears both sides and *imposes* a solution. *Neutral* is key, an objective person listening impartially to both sides." Her eyes were manhole wide. "The shove you gave me really had umph. Rough stuff per se isn't disarming. Nevertheless, I'm taken aback."

He put her out the door. The tiniest push. You couldn't get salt out of a shaker with a tap that inconsequential.

She was incensed. "I'm not putty in your hands. I refuse to go that route. Mark your calendar, you're not getting away unscathed. I should live so long."

She opened her shoulder bag, pulled out a tissue, blotted what was left of her gloss, reached in again, produced an eyelet jacket, put it on, buttoned it, and tied her hair back into a bun. "The consummate professional doesn't allow personal feelings to conflict with mediation skills. Getting the ball rolling is the cornerstone of my life's work."

"I'll take it from here."

"In practice, it's a lot harder than it sounds. Many third party shysters hang their shingles as if they were neutral, impartial, objective. But they're not."

Precisely what he wanted. A candidate who would rally around him, someone he wouldn't have to win approval ratings from.

Gently closing the door, he turned his back on Kate Vestor, his heart set on Yondle Carr. When selecting a "neutral" mediator, it's only human nature to want an ace in the hole.

🐚

The shower was running harder than ever. He turned the knob. Still locked. "I can hardly see my own hand," he called through the door. "It's the perfect setting for us to start fresh. A man to change your life, turn your tides. This fog, like the one at sea, is our chance . . . can't we begin again?"

"Ideas are children. Ideas are children. Ideas are children," she sobbed. "I say it, I think it. Yet no eggs roll out of me. My ears are barren, my mouth is sterile. Take me to the Still Waters."

"Meet a woman friend of mine. Her name's Yondle."

"No more women. Marilyn's more than I can handle."

"Yondle's well-versed in Marilyn Monroe. Haven't heard the woman's angle, you're just scratching the surface."

"Take me to the Still Waters."

"Yondle's a sister under the skin. It was Yondle I took shopping with me. She's resourceful, no project's too big, no detail's too tiny. A job to do, she gets it done. She's caring. From out of the fog—an Earth mother."

"I will if you will."

"Deal . . . after Yondle, the Still Waters." He'd get Yondle to corroborate ideas as children, the brain as ovary, cranial kids. For a mermaid, a revolutionary frame of mind. How pleased the Still Waters would be. Claritha, the egghead, the mental procreator. The mother of invention. Mission accomplished. The Still Waters should give him a medal. They should break out the champagne. They should shake hands all around. Any thoughts to the contrary, he pushed aside. His brain balked. What if the Still Waters were enfeebled? Toxic? Polluted?

Feeling his way to the phone, he dialed zero. The operator connected him. Hell or high water, he was going to bring these babies home.

Yondle on the other end was like Yondle in person—very there, even her hair. A persona.

"Claritha and I need a favor. Women's issues are coming up. Dinner's on me, how soon could you be here?"

"*The New York Times* didn't scoop us, we scooped *The Times*. Menopause is topically hot. Tomorrow's health issue: MENOPAUSE IS OBSOLETE, FACT OR FICTION? Bring Claritha."

"She's indisposed."

"For the sake of your book, *Men in Menopause,* you ought to be here."

"Your plans following the meeting?"

"Where you go, I go," hanging up with a kittenish purr.

He threw kisses through the bathroom door. He said he was going to get Yondle, but there would be a delay. Her woman's group was in session.

Fog puffed like no tomorrow.

"In session?"

"Talking, listening to each other with all their hearts, exchanging . . ." He let her figure it out for herself: Women hatch ideas.

The fog went ballistic.

Yondle lived in a walk-up apartment in a rent stabilized building. Four large sunny rooms, cluttered with hand-me-down cherubs. At her thirty-eighth birthday party, which he attended months ago, her woman friends outnumbered the men three-to-one. He worried he'd have to fend them off, but it didn't go down that way. Instead, they shared. A congenial, cooperative, communal group.

Now, the door ajar, he walked in.

"Scumbags." Kicking over her chair—not Yondle's familiar face but a face he recalled from the party. She addressed the circle of seated women, stopping when she got to him, his sports jacket hung neatly over his arm like a shower curtain on the rod, positioned strategically in front of his Mr. Big, his size a side effect of all the sexual sparks between himself and Claritha. She smiled at him. "Marcy Pestillo. You helped me carry the punch bowl." Pleasantly spoken, the same mouth that had twisted with *scumbags*. Her lipstick was smeared, slanting precariously toward her chin; the mascara meant to thicken her eyelashes clumped on the tips of her bangs.

He broke off eye contact, stepping sideways to a vacant seat.

Marcy stripped to her bra. "Tampering's what you'd do with a radiator. Turn up the heat, lower the heat. Let them stay the fuck away from my pipes. I've barely settled into menopause, now I'm being evicted. Some wise guy inventor learns how to put eggs on ice in near perpetuity, and I'm supposed to take it lying down? Can't even buy a bra anymore without selecting from a menu: underwire, wireless, lycra, lace, cotton, see-through, front snaps, back hooks, sports, formal evening, workaday, strapless, strapped—thin straps, how thin? thick straps, how thick?—rounded bosom, conical, au natural, cleavage, padded, black, "nude," name your color, custom-made, off the rack, matching panties, hidden compartments, wired for sound. Screw the options for conceiving."

Twenty of them, one of him. Yondle, five seats to his right.

"My honeypot isn't Barbie-dollish, it loves being on the cutting edge." He slumped down as the new speaker took over for Marcy. If memory served, that would be Racine, six feet of great bones, editor-at-large, *Vogue* magazine. "My filly's fully photogenic. A valentine shaped trim, the best dye job money can buy. I do vaginal isometrics. My toned little nooker has her own personal trainer. I apply creams for a soft dewy complexion, same as I do with my face. Menopause is a menace. I'd sell my soul to stop the biological clock."

A small slip of a girl with features as delicate as the work of a calligrapher, said, "Racine doesn't speak for me. I recently lost a sister to menopause. She didn't die of it. She set up an incense shrine in its honor: menopause, the rite of passage, menopause, the point of departure, menopause, the new you. There's no ending without a beginning."

"Wrong." Racine again. "Psychobabble. Rite of passage crapola. Propaganda. You heard Yondle's news. Her name's going to be in the acknowledgments of *Men in Menopause*. Let her name not be in vain. Periods stop, can death be far behind? Menopause makes you think of where you are in the food chain."

Yondle rose, marched to the center of the circle, and sat cross-legged on the floor. Her pantaloons looked like something out of

Arabian Nights.

"The beasts of passion are loose tonight, I feel it in my bones. The hunter and prey. The stalker and the stalked. The wild and woolie. The beasts want to romp, who will romp with the beasts of passion? We're all women here, and just one man. While the beasts of passion lick their lips, beat their mighty chests, and pop breath fresheners, what does just-one-man say?"

All eyes on Jacob.

"*Men in Menopause* is not just a book deal." He was so tinny, it was like a can of tuna talking. "Claritha is my girlfriend, my love, my heart's desire, the flower of my manhood. She lives, eats, and breathes menopause. She's stuck on the baby treadmill." He dropped to his knees, palms pressed prayerfully together. "In front of this entire assembly, I implore Yondle to accompany me. A woman's eggbearing days are never over if she keeps her imagination fertile. Ideas are children. Boil me in oil, I used Marilyn Monroe to drive the lesson home: Creativity is a gold mine of eggs. Mommyhood's a head trip. No rotten apples here. My beast of passion is a gentle giant."

Yondle uncrossed her legs. "Your tinkering might not look like the worm-in-the-apple now, but it's hardly open and shut. Some of my best friends are mental over having kids. Whisk me away but give me time to regroup." After a minute, she stood. "You want to know what else I feel in my bones?"

He asked that she save it for the cab.

⁂

He gave the driver their destination. He buckled up, he waited for Yondle to do the same. Getting into the cab felt like a getaway. "For what I am about to divulge, no less than a pact will do. On a stack, swear what I'm about to say will never leave this taxi."

"May I rot in hell, sworn on a stack."

He said, "Claritha's a mermaid."

She said, "Want to know what else I feel in my bones?"

He said, "Claritha's a mermaid."

She said, "It came to me unbidden. I did no foreplanning."

He said, "You'd think me telling you Claritha was a mermaid would not go unremarked on."

"In my bones, something to do with you registered with me. It hadn't registered before and that is why I made like a soothsayer, to empower myself. It was a rip-off. The Beasts of Passion are always around. Every night's their night to party. I want to bare my bones to you, will you let me?"

"Claritha's a mermaid."

"Shopping's a passion. The pocketbook's where it should hurt, not the heart. Taking you into the stores showed me what I've been missing. I've always been a solitary shopper. Maybe it's because I'm not a perfect size anything. Is it better to have a shopping spree with a man for someone else than never to have spreed at all?"

He nodded, "I'd be glad to discuss it at a later date. After *this* is resolved. Can you hold off till then . . . will you try? Claritha is my First Love."

"I too had a First Love. With but a glance, my First Love put me under his spell. The lengths I went to, the scheming. My feminine wiles fell flat. So through his window I crept. Naked into his bed I crawled. Musk of elk and ether, pressed against his nose. Two inhalations, he was out. While he slumbered, I helped myself. On my tongue, joystick juice. Fingers, jam sticky with his nectar. The one-eyed cock crowed. It hurled, it curled, it righted itself. We ended up in the woods. Under the stars, I confessed my love. Any beast will tell you, tenderness is the enemy. The curse of First Love isn't that the stars are in your eyes, it's that passion isn't the beast it's made out to be. He didn't love me.

Forcing myself on him wasn't an act of love. I went home alone. I cried myself to sleep." The tiny chimes braided into her hair pinged like cut crystal. "I've been bitten by the shopping spree bug—the beast! But I can still roll my sleeves up to help you. Beast!"

He wasn't sure how to take it. "You calling me or the shopping bug a beast?"

"Don't you feel it in your bones? The beast is in the bone marrow."

He paid the driver off. She ordered him to walk ahead of her on the stairs. The stairs were cramped. Her hips needed the leg room. No central air, and the stairwell windows were nailed shut. They paused to catch their breath.

"Claritha and Marilyn Monroe are tight. Ignore the sexual innuendo. Make every word count. Focus on Marilyn's creative niche: Ideas are children. Post-menopause isn't the kiss of death, it's a golden age, abundant in golden nuggets." He gripped the banister. "One more flight, ready?"

They made the summit.

They proceeded down the hall.

Chirps and whistles, a barnyard coming from his apartment. "You hear what I hear?" he asked. She steadied his hand, otherwise the key would never have made it into the lock. Entering ahead of her, his arm automatically shot out, barring the way.

His son's ass was in a holding pattern. Below the airspace where Mac's butt hovered, Claritha's Raget weeds stared up at the boy's loins, very much like a crowd mesmerized by a spectacle. The dick, rock-hard, with a three-day stubble, still looked babyfaced.

"Mac," he said, "put your clothes on."

Five

In which Jacob participates in Group, Jacob meets the Still Waters, Jacob gets egg on his face, Jacob battles a beast, Jacob and Mac have a father/son talk on a subject more delicate than sexual intercourse, and the mother of his child, Jacob's former spouse, critiques his performance in bed.

Like a Red Cross relief worker, Yondle tended to the disaster victims sprawled across the living room rug. She draped blankets across their shoulders. They sat speechless. She disappeared into the kitchen, reappearing with hot mugs of coffee. She dragged four dinette chairs into the living room and arranged them. She assigned places: Mac here, Jacob there, Claritha between them, opposite her. Claritha's tail was drawn up, much the way people with legs curl up. She hunched under her blanket. Walking with zombie stiffness, Mac and Jacob took seats, their skin tones slightly bluish like patients in intensive care. Yondle introduced herself to Claritha. "One cannot help but notice you are bipedally challenged. Like anyone with a handicap to overcome, you probably don't have all your transportation problems licked. While the floor's convenient, chairs in a circle work better for group communication, going all the way back to quilting circles, and King Arthur's Round Table. I'm Yondle Carr. Just ask, I'll be your crutch."

Claritha pulled her dress down. The Raget, hoarse from chirp overkill, was stone-cold silent. She looked as if she were scarcely breathing.

Yondle continued. "Most everything I know of mermaids, I learned at Disney's knee. Mermaids are waiflike, romantic creatures. Innocent of the ways of man, they may make faux pas. First time around, no one gets it right. We all goof. Jacob briefed me. Your self-esteem is low. Menopause makes you feel like a has-been, If you're not up to getting to a chair on your own speed, I can assist. One way or another, your place is here in the family. Families feud. It wouldn't be a family without disputes. But whatever the problem, the bosom of the family softens the blow."

Claritha's tail scraped as she went, as if its springs were worn. The hundreds of lilac beads on her Marilyn Monroe dress rubbed each other, sounding like the splat of raindrops.

The circle was closed.

"I'll be your group leader. I hereby declare this group in session."

Where is fog when you need it? Fog to conceal what your eyes cannot bear. Where is the cloak of fog to render the daggers in your heart invisible? Where is the absence of a clear, irrefutable visible record? Where is an easy out? Where is the claim of optical illusion? You only *thought* you saw what you saw, the pea soup *distorted* it all, your First Love *wasn't* screwing your First Love. Where the hell is the bathroom steam? Where's lights out? Does every goddamn light in the house have to be on? Where's the sand to bury your head? The loyalty of a son to the father, what drain did that go down? The Pact—where's that? No time-sharing of mates, sharing in the same time period is verboten. Where's the father's monkey wrench? How to separate the star-crossed lovers? Star-crossed what? Star-crossed nothing. The blitzed-out look on his son's face as his ass hovered was Moha induced. Mac let himself in, she pounced, poorlittleoldme, I am but a damsel in distress. Where is the drug that will obliterate the father's memory? Where is the judgment of Jehovah? (Jehovah, don't let my lack of faith hold You back.) She used you, Mac. She used your daddy. That's no mermaid . . . that's a snatcher. A cradlerobber. Daddy's baby. Daddy's egg. Where is eye-for-eye? Tooth-for-tooth? Piss on star-crossed. Do not even entertain the thought. The far, far-fetched, nonsensical thought. Mac's no Romeo. She's no Juliet. But I *am* a cuckold.

Jacob cried out like a man who's lost his way, "Where is up? Where is down?"

Mac raised his hand like he was in the classroom. Yondle grabbed the floor right out from under him. "Families bicker. Behaving like a dysfunctional family group is to be expected. The ground rules are this: Disagree all you want, gang up verbally, get down 'n' dirty. But take a swing at anyone, and you'll have me to answer to."

"I love my father. He's second to none. First in my heart. I'd lay down my life, donate my organs. I'll go away, into exile. He'll never have to lay eyes on me again."

"No," Jacob wept.

"No," Claritha echoed.

Staring at Mac, Yondle's arch brows quivered. "Something's afoot. Don't try to hoodwink my beast of passion. Out with it, Boy."

"I love her," Mac yowled.

"Puppy love," Jacob spat.

"First Love," Mac countered. "On first sight. End-all, be-all. All-encompassing."

"She drugged you, a bite on your arm, your limbs drooped."

"Lies," Claritha's tail flicked. "A man was prophesied: from out of the fog. Then through the shower's steam came a Manchild. What was I to do, defy prophecy? Still Waters, forgive this Daughter of the Sea. I didn't

lay a single tooth on him. I didn't immediately open the Raget. Mac and
I spent most of the time talking . . . getting to know each other. The
actions of a feeble mind? A scatterbrain? Or, mindful of all that Jacob
said, was an idea taking shape, one weighing so heavily on my mind, I
thought, how can it be anything but an egg? I've already done a thorough
body search. Fingers in my ears, down my throat, high and low. Nothing.
Nothing. And yet the egg's there, born of thought. I just wish the egg
would hurry up and fall out. My headache's the size of a killer whale."

Yondle was all gee whiz. "You expect to see, in concrete form, an
egg? In the flesh? Fresh from the intellect? You've got balls, I'll say that
much for you. You're sitting on a stick of dynamite—the center of a love
triangle. Father's beast, son's beast, both bug-eyed over you. Disney
would kick you out of the theme park. Not that there's anything wrong
with two-timing." In her most haughty voice, Yondle said, "Gentlemen,
are you mice or men?"

"I saw her first," Jacob thundered. "My insides will never recover. She
makes waves. Latents, currents . . . my whirlpools are tornadoes. Before
her, my interior had no local color. I won't give her up." He didn't have
a jaw that jutted. He had to lean forward, artificially simulating the jut.
"I'm asking real nice—stay back, Mac. Love is a multiple. May your next
First Love understand the difference between fact and fiction. The ear
isn't a chute, babies don't slide down the ear tubes or out the windpipes."

Mac moved his chair closer to Claritha. "Choose me. He lacks faith.
I'm a true believer. Ideas are children. For real."

Jacob lunged. But when Yondle hooped him with her arms, Claritha
got upset.

"Hands off my man," Claritha barked, as she picked up her
wooden chair, put her mouth to it, and took a chunk out. "You don't
want to tangle with me."

Yondle released him.

Claritha embraced the father and son. "This is the thought that carries me through. Never have I had such a thought: I'm pregnant with love. In believing this thought, I've set myself apart from every mermaid that ever was. I love the father. I love the son. In all the time I've loved the Still Waters and the eggs of the Raget, it's never entered my head I could give birth from a thought. And what a thought it is. Love's a pain in the neck. And the skull. But I am pregnant with love. The three of us can raise the brainchild together. Come, let's make a pact of it."

Yondle stood on her chair. "Love *rules?* Would that it could. It's no small matter to loose the Beast of Passion. Any corner of any street, any crack in any sidewalk, any room of any house, any bank, any library, any place people can be found (age is no factor), day or night, the beast of passion walks around like it owns the place. Checks and balances, however, do exist. Just being in the same room with you three, I'm all hot and bothered. But in check."

Claritha was rubbing her forehead. "I can see the whole thing in my head. The living room rug will do just fine. Me in the middle, flanked by Jacob and Mac. We'll consummate. We three. Afterward, on to the Still Waters. But They might not give Their blessing. It's more than my poor head can bear. Such pressure inside, like the top's flying off. Two human First Loves. Yet I chirp for neither one. Just Marilyn. Why is that?"

"I'm no mind reader," said Yondle. "But I bet the farm we're going to pull an all-nighter." Reaching into the pocket of her pantaloons, she pulled out a cell phone. "Chinese anyone?"

Yondle set up the snack trays. Just as the silence was turning awkward, the food arrived. Assorted jewels of the sea, a veritable banquet: shrimp, prawns, salmon, halibut, trout, tuna, swordfish, bass, lobster, sole, squid, scallops, little neck clams, crabmeat, and one order of steamed dumplings.

Claritha dug in. "Excuse me while I eat for two."

Jacob pecked, chewing the same bite-sized piece. His throat constricted. It all tasted like gristle.

He marveled at his son's hearty appetite.

Mac packed it away, opening wide like a baby bird in the nest, as Claritha parceled over care packages from her plate. His son wiped the corners of Claritha's mouth, then using the same napkin wiped his own.

Jesus Christ. Jacob was beginning to feel like a third party. Then Claritha placed his hand on her lap. Atop that, she covered his hand with Mac's. Skin against skin. Blood still thicker than water?

"You had gone to fetch Yondle," she began to explain reminiscing, her voice dreamy. "The room was steamy, I was just out of the shower, stretched in front of the television. I heard a key in the door. The next thing I knew, Mac was cradling me in his arms. At first, we spoke exclusively of you, of your kindness, your goodness, your honesty, your generosity. How much fun I had driving with you, talking. Frustrating as it was to come up empty each time we mated, our time together was and always will be . . . loving. Once before, I nearly took your head off for suggesting I could love you. On this occasion, soon as Mac explained love to me, I was seized, swept off my tail. How could I *not love you*? How could I *not* love Mac who loves you and loved me on sight? As water takes the shape of any container, I became love's vessel. Where is our egg? Where is our egg? The answer is, the egg's inside my head. What egg is this? What egg is this? The answer is, the egg's a love child. What can three do better than two? What can three do better than two? The answer is . . ."

The pile of hands was abruptly enlarged by one more.

Yondle plunked her hand down on the pile, talking rapidly. "Goes to show you, group dynamics isn't a science. Everything was pointing to somebody ripping out somebody's throat. Who ever heard of a love triangle getting a clean bill of health? But here in the heart of the Upper

West Side, a mere stone's throw from Lincoln Center, I'd like for the threesome to be a foursome. Condoms won't be a problem, will they? We can order in. I can feel it in my bones. It's not group sex. It's possibly Disneyesque."

Gently as a ring bearer balancing his precious cargo on a velvet pillow, Mac inclined his head and lifted Jacob's hand to his lips. Jacob was in tableaux heaven. Ten, twenty, fifty kisses, with promises of more to come.

Mac fell against his father's chest. Jacob burped him. "You'll always be my baby."

Yondle and Claritha conferred. Footsteps and tail thumps to the front door. Claritha returned alone.

"Yondle?" Jacob asked.

"On an errand, I sent her for pickles and ice cream. We have an understanding. She doesn't watch us loosen the brainchild in my head, and I let her keep her head."

Claritha undid their pants. They worked her dress free. They all dropped to the floor like petals. "Yondle made me promise to say these words: May all our beasts be benevolent." Claritha opened her mouth. Raget stalks shot out of her gullet, swimming through the air. As father and son held hands, she slipped their pee-pees into her mouth, each one in its own private groove.

She gave head.

The Raget stalks jived like a jazz joint during Prohibition. Jacob gyrated like a belly dancer, slithering, undulating. The act seemed newly invented, as if Claritha had just thought it up on the spot. Free-for-alling, the Rageteers came out of the woodwork, no squishing them down like you do with carry-on luggage. His pee-pee gave the performance of its life.

Improv times two. Mac the musical genius, as if banging on piano keys, harmonized with Dad.

Father and son, front and center, first-row seats, like patrons of the theater, watching the action. Claritha's mouth suddenly becoming as transparent as a fishbowl. Agape at their motor coordination, they were in awe of their pee-pees (which did not touch, for that would be incestuously taboo).

At last they rested from their labors.

Claritha said, "Sure as eggs are eggs, I love you." No mistaking her meaning: *You* wasn't singular. "Right now, I'm thinking up Theirs. If They doubt the power of love, up Theirs, up Theirs, up Theirs. Just imagine what the Still Waters will say to me? Can you imagine? Up Theirs."

The buzzer.

Like executives holding a conference call, all three were on the intercom. Yondle yessing as Jacob and Mac suggested postponing the Still Waters.

"Up yours," Claritha said. "There will be no postponement. Perish the thought."

Following Jacob's instructions, Yondle turned right around. In addition to renting a car, she was to see to diving equipment. For one.

"Who died and made you boss?" Mac frantically pulling on his pants, was halfway out the door when Claritha tackled him.

"We Daughters of the Sea believe the Still Waters to be the great-great-great-great-grandparents of our ancestors. They are guardians of all the sea's creatures. The Still Waters are dispersed. Approach a puddle, there They'll be, yet They become stronger when concentrated in one geographical place. Words cannot adequately explain. What has been passed from generation to generation, is how They communicate: a drop at a time, rather than a spill. Their Prophecy—*Out of the fog, Claritha will meet a man to change her life, and from the change of life, a child*—was such a mouthful, coming all at once. I was blessed. They levitated me. I stood on water. Not in a million years could I have arranged such a thing for myself. Your father will accompany me. Man the polluter, Man the scourge. This man, however, is the original First Love. The son no less treasured. Equally first, but oh so young. It is said that you can take the mermaid out of the water, but you can't take the maternal instinct out of the mermaid. I'd die if you were snatched from your mother's arms. I've never been an egg snatcher, and I'm not about to start now. Death to all egg snatchers!"

Held fast by his ankles, Mac appealed to Jacob. "You laid the groundwork: Ideas are children, but talk is cheap. If not for me, she wouldn't be pregnant with love." Angrily pulling his legs free. "Look, you may be the world's best dad. I love you with all my heart. They don't come any better. But this was First Love bursting me at the seams! I couldn't stand on ceremony. I couldn't let the Pact keep me away." His face softened, radiating an inner light, as if he had swallowed a candle. "I impregnated her by willing myself to make the leap of faith with her. A child's in *my* head too. Mind over matter. *I'm* as pregnant with love as *she* is."

Mac, the best man? The Prince, the runner-up? Not for love or money. But what tack to take? Mmm. A Prince would be noble.

"If you want a fight, you're not going to get it. I'm going to turn the other cheek. My love for you is unconditional, undying, eternal, infinite, nonjudgmental. You think I would've consented to a three-way *anything,* if I weren't zippo over you. Ideas are children. In that sense I'm a babymaker too. And for the sake of your kid," he lied through his teeth, "you should remain on land with Yondle."

Mac burst into tears. "I'm not fit to lick your boots. When I grow up, I want to be just like you. No hard feelings?"

"None."

"Really."

"No grudges?"

"Slate clean," he said.

Rageteers sprouted like vines. They were under her armpits, in her nose and dorsal. "My vestal veil," Claritha said. "It's a miracle, the Raget's everywhere, in virgin places. Anybody who would drive a wedge between us, up theirs."

A white sheet was placed under her, like a chaste bride on her wedding night.

They took her slowly, no footprints on sand. An hour, making baby breath love.

Seeing the bloodied sheet, Yondle fussed. "Don't think me beastly. I'm happy about Claritha's hymeneal blood. Count me in for babysitting the kid in her head—Mac's too, yea!—I'm a terrific godmother. But for now a simple hug would go a long way. Diving shops don't do a bustling business at two A.M. Avis was no breeze either."

They dressed. Claritha, in her Monroe sheath, nibbled the pickles and ice cream Yondle had purchased for her, while Mac pulled on his jeans, and Jacob the diving suit. Then they surrounded Yondle, and showed their gratitude.

And as Jacob quickly ushered his little group out, down the steps and into the car, he continued placating Yondle with pats to the rear. Very versatile, that arm of his. Able to wipe the slate clean between Mac and him, able to kiss ass.

Stopping along the Hudson River route opposite Jersey, Claritha pogo-jumped to the water's edge, listening and sniffing. At the tenth spot, she said, "This is it."

They weren't in the middle of nowhere. The Chelsea piers in daylight were used for recreation. People fished off them, they strolled the wharves. A mile off was a sports center.

With hair flying in the windless night, Yondle brought the loot over to the gathering. Strapping oxygen tanks on Jacob, shodding him in froggy flippers, goggles for his eyes, she contemplated the rest of the equipment, then hooked him up till he looked like a space astronaut.

"You're wired for visual and two-way audio. Activation's automatic. What you see, we'll see. Same for audio." Yondle seemed to switch gears. "Now you know me, I'm the quickest read in town. This group's gone metaphysical. Claritha and Mac, pregnant with love, are like expectant parents, but real kids are a stretch for me. Even a fertile imagination isn't the stretch real kids are. So kudos to you for bursting no bubbles. You've renewed my faith in tender mercies. I'm stimulated like nobody's business by your spiritual journey." Then she faltered, her chipmunk cheeks caved in. "Take this last chance to back out. The sea isn't all that hospitable. Divers can get the bends, they can fail to come up for air. The Still Waters could be a Bermuda Triangle."

Mac didn't need the light thrown off by the lamppost. He was lit internally. "My faith in my father is unshakable. Whether he goes or not, he's got my unequivocal support. Look at me. Not only am I pregnant with love, I'm basking in his. So he's short on faith, so he scoffs in secret at the child I'm carrying, so he'd deny it if I called him on it, so he's bluffing, so he's a hypocrite. All that pales before his unconditional, nonjudgmental, undying, eternal, infinite love. He's in for the long, long haul."

Could he have rubbed it in any more? Sons like this, who needs enemies? Jacob thought. Now, in the eyes of the world (with Yondle and Claritha witnessing) the son had stood up for the father's love. He had no real out. "Get the worried look off your faces," though worry lines sliced his like he was a pizza fresh from the oven, a buck a slice. "In catching First Love, we've all caught the Big Wave."

A running leap off the pier and he was over the side. The last word his. "Don't *up yours* to anybody," he said to Claritha. "It might be hazardous to our health."

It wasn't free fall that delivered them to the mouth of a cave—suction determined their path. He held Claritha's hand, his left arm braced against the cave's stony entrance. The contraption fastened around his forehead was similar to a miner's light. Although it had functioned perfectly on the way down, the light suddenly clicked off. Dark caves were not his forte. He hung back, fueled by visions of cavedwelling eels feasting on his carcass. Claritha's anchoring tail restricted him from a full galloping retreat.

"Enter," announced a male of unknown origin, "at your own risk."

Perhaps it was the acoustics. The voice sounded imperial. Jacob's fingers burrowed into the crevices at the opening. Claritha pried him off. Once inside, the cave's torches lit up with motion-detector efficiency. The sand beneath Jacob crunched with a walk-through-the-woods sound, closer to dead, fallen leaves than moist grit. There was no trace of water anywhere. Removing the breathing apparatus from his mouth, he sampled the air, drawing one breath, then another. He found it satisfactory. Dozens of emaciated, balding mermaids filed in, dead space in their eyes, their tongues purple.

"It is as You prophesied," Claritha declaimed, head low to the ground. Jacob automatically followed suit, lips brushing sand. "A man to change my life for the better, to turn my tides, to make me fertile." Only on the upswing did he actually see the Still Waters. The old man lounging on the beach chair was a composite of Father Neptune and Grandpa Marshall— belly round, legs spindly, a crown of gold, shoulder-length white hair. The bold blue eyes were icy. Against them, the rest was backdrop.

"May I proceed?" Claritha bowed again, head scraping bottom. Jacob made obeisance too.

The old man in the beach chair wagged a bony finger. "Tch. Tch." To Jacob it didn't have the ring of green light. Keeping respectfully low, he slowly crawled backward.

An obstinate Claritha inquired again, "May I proceed?"

Jacob rose and tried to hustle her out.

"May I proceed?" Claritha stood her ground.

The *tch, tch* shook the walls. A fresh line of mermaids trooped in, barring their way. They were armed with sharp jagged shells. A hag stepped forward, crusted over with algae. "We're feeble. We'd sell our own mothers for eggs. But word travels fast. We're not so far gone we can't tell a whopper when we hear one."

Claritha was undeterred. "The Prophecy *was so* Theirs: man, fog, eggs. Eggs galore."

"Tch. Tch." The old man in the chair heckled.

"Up . . ."

Jacob clamped her mouth. "Ladies," he said. "With all due respect, any event, even one plain as the nose on your face, is open to interpretation. The way perception works, what holds true today may not hold true later the same day, or the next. Perception comes from the Latin . . . er . . . I'll look it up for you . . . be on the lookout for a message in a bottle, OK?"

Gaunt, with wizened breasts, they looked like twigs. Their cackling was not the comfortable log-burning-in-the-hearth kind.

Claritha bit his clamped hand, breaking his grip, not skin. It wasn't a Moha sting. "You want eggs, I'll tell you how to get them. Give me your word, you won't use those shells."

"Word."

"Word."

"Word."

The cave was filled with echoes: word, word, word.

Which counts for nothing, Jacob thought, as Claritha made her case. They'll demand to see an egg. When they don't, they'll cut us.

"We're no better off than salmon. All our lives, we've lived like fish. See where *that's* gotten us. It's high time we stopped putting all our eggs in one basket. From the neck up, we have an egg case. Ideas Are Children." She strutted up and down, parading in front of them. Jacob stayed on her tail, whispering to put a lid on it. "I'm pregnant with love. Not one, but two First Loves. Jacob Koleman, you've all met him. If not for this man, I wouldn't have an inkling." She clapped her hands with glee, hopping like she was putting out a fire. "Imagine a love so dear, it inspires you. His son is but a boy, a slip of a child. Yet the strength of Mac's love gave me the courage to make a leap of faith."

The old man in the beach chair sucked air through his teeth, then thundered like the God Thor. "How dare you? We are eons. Man is merely years, still wet behind the ears."

The mermaids deployed, crouching cats ready to spring. So many bubbles welled up from the ground, it was like water boiling.

Claritha was motionless. Jacob prostrated himself. "Everyone knows at my age there's more chance of being eaten by a shark than finding true love. When I told Claritha that ideas are children, I was intoxicated, drunk on love. Spare her. Unduly influenced by the blabbering of a befuddled man, she knows not what she says." Availing himself of one of the shells, he sliced his wet suit in the groin area. "Can I interest any of you in getting laid? How long since you had any?" Out it came, like a boxer defending the title. "Undefeated champion, no erectile dysfunction in my family tree. Just let Claritha go. My son Mac's completely pro-life. He gives death the finger by stuffing dead animals. He'll lobby on behalf of the welfare of the ocean. It could become his cause célèbre. He loves Claritha. Without her, he'd never recover."

Claritha chimed in, "Mac's also pregnant with love."

"Don't hold that against him," Jacob implored. "The kid's first time in love, he's not lucid."

Claritha swallowed hard. "My due date's soon."

"Give it a rest!" Jacob was in her face.

"Pregnant with love," Claritha shouted. The bubbles trailing up from the ground started popping.

Jacob put a mouth to her ear. "Do I have to draw you a picture? My pecker buys you freedom. You and Mac carry on without me, thriving on love, lovebirds, insanely in love. In a nutshell, go at it like rabbits, dance on my grave, take First Love to heights hitherto unknown."

She opened her mouth. Aagh was all that came out. Wracked by spasms, she flopped like a fish. Her eyes locked on his. Her mouth widened, farther and farther. The mandible loosened, dropping her jaw to her collarbone. She discharged a mustardy mucus. A wad landed on his nose, sliding down. He saw her lips rip. She cupped her hands.

The old man in the beach chair (aka the Still Waters) called for silence. The mermaids took a collective breath and held it.

Then tumbling into her hands he saw . . . a golden egg.

Mute from her wound, she gestured toward his pee-pee. His erection outdid itself. Some smart cookie she is. . . . You go, girl. Mac too, hatching an egg from scratch. The golden couple with a golden child.

Taking aim, he was poised for consecration. Bim, bam, bang against the membrane. Oh the whipping boy he made of himself.

Crinkling like cellophane, the starch went out of his Mr. Able-Bodied. The egg went sunny-side up, thin and watery.

Claritha's mouth, sliced and gashed, struggled for words. She grimaced. "Egg snatcher, defiler of eggs." She died in his arms.

Barnacles the color of coconut shells covered her like a shroud. The mermaids dispersed, blowing out the torches one by one.

His flop-eared good-for-nothing half-dead pee-pee lolled like the tongue of a hound on a hot summer day . . . unable to breathe normally.

The old man in the chair yawned. "Begone."

Excised. An insect, flicked. Topside, he floundered in the water. Yondle frantically tossed life jackets. Mac stripped to his skivvies. Jacob couldn't have Mac diving in—the Still Waters were tough cookies. Reaching up, grabbing on, Mac and Yondle dragging him, he was on solid ground . . . with no strength left to flee interrogation.

Jacob had some fast talking to do. Questions hit like attack dogs. "Where is she? What went wrong? We have more supplies in the trunk—need oxygen, a harpoon, a revolver? What egg? What snatcher? Who's the defiler? We tried contacting you on the two-way, but got nothing but static. Whatever ruined the audio got the footage too. Everything's garbled, except for 'egg defiling snatcher.' Who's the defiler? Who snatched what? Who? Who? Who? Where's Claritha? Where is she? Where? Where? Where?"

The pier's planks were uneven. Jacob felt like he was sitting on a bed of nails. He clutched Mac, pulling him close. "Her body just gave out. She's gone."

Mac took a swing at him. "Go back and bring her up. If you won't I will."

Jacob caught him by the wrist. "The Still Waters are tyrants. They've got eyes in the back of Their heads. Navy Seals wouldn't get through. I'm not losing you too."

Mac stared at Jacob like a specimen under a microscope. "Being pregnant in love agreed with her. Her spirits were never higher. You don't drop dead for no good reason."

"I did the best I could," Jacob panted.

Yondle said she was taking him to the emergency room. Jacob said she would do no such thing.

"What about the egg?" Mac mewed. "Who's the egg snatcher?"

"Give Mac closure, don't hold back," Yondle urged.

"I didn't get a look at his face, the snatcher was too fast." Like a man lost in a blizzard, he thought, get-me-outta-here. Evasiveness dogged his voice. The shadow of suspicion mousetrapped him. Big, big shadow. Little, little flailing fists. "It was a golden egg. The lovechild of her brain . . . just as you imagined it." He could bear no more. Somehow he got himself to the car, stumbling into the backseat.

Yondle and Mac followed, climbing in front, fighting over the keys, slapping hands, breaking nails.

"Nobody's going anywhere," Mac shouted, as he grabbed the keys, put them down his pants, and faced Jacob. "Tell me again how the golden egg got snatched."

Yondle smacked the wheel, opened the door, stepped out, stepped back in, and slammed the door hard. A lighter, smaller car would've dropped a bumper. Copycatting Mac, she turned to Jacob. Her hair, pressed against the roof of the car, resisted flattening. Her face was as stern as her hair. "It's like you're taking the Fifth. You should hear yourself."

Summoning righteous indignation, Jacob defended himself. "The Fifth's for hiding behind, and I've got nothing to hide. Frankly Yondle, butt out. This is between Mac and me."

Her eyes said, *You'll live to regret that.* He could hear the sharpening of blades. "When the beast of rivalry walks in, it comes on fanged feet," Yondle announced.

Mac was staggered.

"My gut tells me your father's latents have his ear," Yondle declared.

Jacob's beloved Mac, the-sun-rises-and-sets-on-him Mac, First Love Mac, child-of-his-loins Mac, kissy-kissy (non-incestuously, no taboos broken) flesh-of-his-flesh, seed-of-his-seed Mac. That very Mac looked accusingly and growled, "You're the egg snatcher."

"No, wrong, innocent," Jacob sobbed. "I didn't kill her. I wish it were me instead. I may not believe in God, but it doesn't make me ungodly. May God finish me off, I *welcomed* you into the mermaid family. *I* got your foot in the door. Ideas are children was *my idea.* I have no hidden agenda. The beast didn't unleash. When it's First Love, it's a cold father who leaves his son out in the cold." He kissed his own hand. "Your mouth smooched me in that very spot. Indelible, unwashable. I'll carry it to the grave. Would an arch rival be such a sentimental fool?"

After reaching into his pants, Mac tossed the keys at Yondle. "Drive," he said.

As soon as they began moving, Jacob began plotting. A plausible story, something that would exonerate him. Anything but . . .

"I didn't know the pee-pee was unloaded."

"An unloaded penis? That's your alibi?" Mac and Yondle chorused.

Crack of dawn, camped out on the front stoop of Jacob's building. Jacob's wet suit started to heat up from the early rays of the sun, a taste of hell's fires to come.

"Why then?" Mac bleated. "Competition eating away at you?"

"To what do you attribute your piece going AWOL?" The remnant of Yondle's makeup was a veil of fine soot.

"I did no wrong. I walk with the Princes, the devout, the boys next door," Jacob insisted.

Mac and Yondle, standing shoulder to shoulder, looked down on him.

He badly wanted to skip this part and go directly to tearing his hair out with grief. "Pregnant with love, she delivered a golden egg. Via the mouth. An oral birth. The egg was the size of an ostrich egg. Maybe there were underlying complications, breech birth, something internal. She needed me for the final touches. I took out my pee-pee . . . I went at it. Ingrained in me—from the get-go—is awe for the act of creation."

His son's expression said, You let the team down.

"Intimidation played no minor role. The Still Waters, in the guise of old man Neptune in a beach chair, were antagonistic. They conceded no prophecy. The Still Waters are eons old. The sea itself could be menopausal, suffering from memory deficit and depression. The mermaids threatened us, our lives were in the balance. I had butterflies but I was no saboteur. I begrudge no one an egg by whatever means— artificial insemination, surrogate storks. Without any hesitation, I would mount a goat. I tried my utmost to penetrate the egg."

"I can feel it in my bones," accused Yondle. "The green beast ate your boner." She gave his pee-pee a disparaging look.

"No. No." Jacob reached for Mac as Yondle sheltered him with her body. "Do not forsake me," Jacob cried. "I love you." He tripped on the stoop. Anyone passing by would have seen two skinny arms, darting from behind a fleshy woman, catching a distraught man. Righted, he wouldn't let go.

"Leave me be." Mac screamed. "I'm still pregnant with love for her. I've got an unborn child to protect."

Claritha dead, Mac nuts, legs rubbery, it was too much. Jacob collapsed on the sidewalk, his pecker panting.

I'm not the snatcher, I'm not the defiler, I'm the protector, thought Jacob. Why don't they understand?

He took the sheet to bed. The sheet was clumped in more than a dozen spots. Stained and scabbed over with the blood of a virgin. Those Raget stalks that had never been seen before, spilling out of her nostrils, her ears, her armpits, had been like intact hymens. He peeled off his wetsuit. The air instantly turned his skin clammy. The drop in temperature chilled him; his body craved warmth.

He had made his bed. Now he would have to lie in it.

The roughness of her dried virgin blood hurt. The scabs pricked his stomach. They were scratchier than a hairshirt. But in certain select sites—the loin neighborhood—he tingled. He should have been incapacitated, out of commission, too pooped to pop. Just coming off a colossal penile flop which had left a mother and child dead, he should have been in limbo.

But one by one he had sex with the scabs of her dried blood, his pee-pee bleeding semen like a vein pried open. The sheet ran red.

I am not the culprit. No cock is clockwork. No cock's that cocky.

❧

Shock waves . . .

Somebody was using his front door for a landing strip, driving his fists to the funny farm with knockout punches. Wearing only his boxers, he got up to see who. Jacob noted the time: quarter past four in the afternoon. The assault to the door grew more violent: Open up, don't delay, no time to look through the peephole, it's urgent we speak. He looked anyway. Jacob Koleman, mermaid killer (alleged), egg killer (alleged), wicked, thug father (absolutely not). His good name in the gutter, sullied. He must see to his own safety, keep a wary eye out for muggers demanding access. Just surviving is not enough. Starting now, he would live to restore his rep and save his fucked-up pregnant son from a fate worse than death.

One of Cheryl's sea-green eyes, identifiable as a fingerprint, was pressed up against the peephole. His boxer shorts would have to do. He opened up and backed up.

Her footsteps resonated, shoes pommeling like they were lined with steel plates. Her hair was shaved close at the sides, the stuck-up part in the center was peroxide white and porcupine quilled.

"I came straight from the dorms. I told myself it was to keep abreast of divorce backlash. It's not as though one can end a marriage and not leave loose ends. The truth is I was hoping to run into you again." She took a cigarette out from behind her ear. Lighting up she nearly singed her nose. "You portrayed me as a victim of my menopausal hormones. Menopause isn't just a dot on the map, even though it isn't what it was in my mother's day. You ticked me off, I flared up. Hardly the first time I've been flammable. Scott's cucumber in my mouth works me into a froth. The novelty hasn't worn off. He doesn't ask me out on a regular basis, which is a bone of contention. But making beautiful conflict together . . ." stubbing her cigarette out on her shoe, dropping the butt, grounding it into the carpet, ". . . for thirty-three years you were my Prince, my shoulder to lean on, my houseboy, my steady supplier of orgasms, a living monument to kindness, goodness, thoughtfulness, every creature comfort I could ever want, and *now* you start in? Menopause provoked the skirmish. We didn't fight like cats and dogs. We sparked."

The carpet, where the ashes had landed, began smoking. A small bush fire. She casually opened her bag. The perfume bottle was canteen-large. She dumped the contents.

"Mac all right?" He wouldn't play along, he would not be piqued, no sparks would travel between them. "He say anything unusual? I wouldn't want you to betray a confidence. If you did, I wouldn't tell."

"Exploiting one's son for a spark is reprehensible. If I sparked over giving away his secrets, I'd carry it with me for the rest of my life. Mother of God, can't we just talk?" Without waiting for an answer, she went on. "He's snooping. Mac wants the dirt on your dickie-pooh. Ever go soft? fall short? bend in the middle? That sort of thing."

In light of yesterday's events, perfectly reasonable. The kid was launching his own independent investigation, fleshing out the pee-pee's bio to see what kind of character it was.

Motormouth continued. "He won't name names, but I suspect he had a tryst which ended badly, prompting him to check up on the stock he came from, assess the family resemblance, the inherited traits, the weight, the contours of your tool. Duration wasn't the only topic. We also got technical. I was clinical and graphic, but I wasn't prurient."

"And you, as a woman of the world, assured him any man can run into difficulties, even one with a clean record, decline and fall, no underlying reason required. Pee-pees don't clock in."

She spread her legs. The material of her tube dress showed the clear outlines of her womanhood. "As a veteran of several close calls a day, crossing lines I used to run from, who am I to make light of my son's brush with peril?" She batted her eyes at him.

He didn't return the bat. "Even a sex machine has his down time."

"How can you?" Cheryl accused. "Trivializing his close call? Denying him the thrill of the high wire? What kind of motherfucking monster are you?"

Screeching like a car taking a turn on two wheels, "All men have their moments and those moments don't always come with hidden baggage. You go back and tell Mac I can't go on forever."

"His first bout of impotence? Mac's entitled to make a big, big deal."

"Shame on you," he shot back, taking the offensive.

She swung her purse at him, catching him in the ribs. "It wasn't blind rage, it was sparks I saw. Did you see them too?"

Pushing her out the door, all one hundred and two pounds of her pushing back. "Your zucchini is panting for me. You like when I get physical. Want Mama to spank you?"

The psst from his pee-pee was like the opening of an airtight jar of spaghetti sauce, only ongoing and louder.

He finally locked the door.

Her parting words: "We've had a close call, you and I."

His parting words: "Don't hold your breath."

On trial for murder. Witness for the prosecution: the mother of his child, her testimony unequivocal. "Your father doesn't know from spongy."

Second witness: Jacob Koleman incriminating himself: Claritha's changed my life. After all my talk of hatching her, she hatched me. Now I'm multilayered, more complex, a richer brew. Naughty Boy's my alter ego, alternating with who knows how many others.

Pulling his polo over his head. Inside out, but hey, what's vanity when your only child reviles you? Lean-mean-seething-fighting machine, good egg, honorable intentions. I drink from the cup of loving-kindness. But can I eat off my floors? Am I totally bereft of dirty dishes?

Stepping into his loafers—right foot, left shoe/left foot, right shoe. Pants zipped backward.

Buffeted by scheduling conflicts. I'd like to die of grief, but obligations to my son take precedence.

Buffeted by conflicts between able and unable. Able to masturbate on a sheet, able to let rip with quarts of semen, but unable to squeeze out one lousy drop for the two people I love most in the world. Squeamish in front of an audience? A bad-ass miser? A flaw in the pecker itself? *Or the harborer of secret grievances?*

Opening the door to his apartment, checking the corridor.

Buffeted by conflicts of irony. Ironic how the sparks between myself and Cheryl are still registering. Less than fireworks, more than a matchstick. Why's Naughty Boy giving Naughty Girl the eye when all I'm looking forward to (after rescuing my nutsy son) is dropping into the bowels of the earth?

Downstairs, he collared a cab.

Till I'm convicted by a jury of my peers, I'm not a fugitive from justice, but if I were, where would I go? What safe harbor? Who amongst my friends and acquaintances to talk me through my conflicts?

He told the driver to take him to the East Side. Kate Vestor, are you as good as you say?

🐚

Flannel nightie, long and flowy. Felix the Cat slippers, chewed as if a puppy had been at them. Kate tried to raise her head off the couch cushion; it fell back, paperweight heavy. He hurried to the kitchen, returning with an ice pack. She crowned herself with it.

Jacob asked if she were still dizzy.

She dispelled any notion of a dizzy spell.

"This afternoon, while applying lipliner, I had a flashback: me, sitting ass backward on Maurice Cohen's humongous erection. He keeled over on the fifth thrust. On or about the fifth day of every month, I'm overwhelmed by inner conflict. Did I or did I not hasten his death? Only a closed mind would not admit to a dark side. Maurice Cohen left me a bundle."

Answering as he himself would like to be answered, "At your core, you drink from the cup of loving-kindness."

"My poor clitty was in the wrong place at the wrong time. Maurice was a sick, sick man. The defect was in his heart. Till the big event, there were no early warning signs. It wasn't my fault. Most likely, I am what you said: a loving cup of kindness."

He brightened considerably. "Case dismissed, the defendant's free to go."

"Words, mere words. Actions speak louder. I humped hard enough to give him hairline fractures. The autopsy showed four such breaks. The shaft wasn't young. Solid on the outside. On the inside—dust to dust. In five strokes, I achieved the status of a femme fatale. The court of public opinion would never acquit. Maurice isn't the only skeleton in my closet. Others have concussed during sex. Scores have suffered nosebleeds. My college professor lost his hair overnight. So far, I've stayed my hand for only one man." Pausing dramatically. "*We* haven't been to bed. Somehow you've disarmed the warhead. I've never been this plain a Jane before. I'm so confused."

He clutched her Felix slippers. They honked like rubber duckies. "Claritha's dead. I don't want to lead you on. You and I were never meant to be. But could you—would you—might you—out of the loving-kindness of your heart, assist me in my tailspin?"

"From the bottom of my loving-kindness cup, I offer my condolences. How—?"

His tears plopped like lemmings off a cliff. "Like you with Maurice, on one level I was responsible even though I wasn't. At the crucial time, I couldn't get it up. The shock . . . well, you had to be there."

She sat, propping the pillow with her fists. "I fucked my brains out to become a femme fatale, but you became a lady killer by abstaining?"

"My cup of loving-kindness ran over and out. I didn't know my pee-pee wasn't loaded."

She bopped him with the ice pack. "Knock it off. We're both fatal attractions. Using diametrically, distinctly different approaches—I had sex, you didn't—we both gave our mates the heave-ho."

He bopped her back with the ice pack, hard enough to clank the cubes.

"Where have you been all my life?" she gasped.

He started toward the door. She got there ahead of him.

He panicked. "You're way out of my league," he said.

"Playing on my sympathy?"

"I have a prior engagement."

"Forty-eight hours is all you get. Clear your calendar. Nobody frustrates me. I'll get you before you get me." She stood aside.

He sprinted past.

A yellow cab carried him to a diving shop. The driver apologized: the back speaker was the only working one. "Say the word, I'll kill the sound."

The music wasn't deafening. The commercial break startled him . . . "Not-to-be-missed, soon-to-be-released, eagerly awaited, by the author of the Pirate Cassidy series: *Men in Menopause,* the story as it's never been told before."

Now the world was going to be looking over his shoulder. How would he keep the world at bay? Should he have the ads pulled? Did he want to get into it with Yondle? (Finch wasn't responsible. Finch always confers with authors. Finch would never put the cart before the horse.) Should he berate Yondle? The soon-to-be-released might never be. She should stop misleading the public. But then would Yondle take offense and go public with what she knows? Would he get investigated by the authorities? Didn't he have somewhere he had to be?

Kate's story about Maurice's hidden illness had given him a shot in the arm. Descend to the cave, bring the body up, put the corpse on ice, get Harris to do the autopsy. See if forensic evidence explains things. With any luck, it will prove that Claritha died of the most natural of all causes: menopause, the time bomb. Reach your change of life, it's all downhill from there.

Shouldn't dealing with Yondle's promo take a backseat to saving his son's life? Eventually he'd have dealings with Yondle . . . if things improved. If . . . ?

Six

In which Jacob confronts the Still Waters, sees a shrink (not Finkle), lands in the middle of a sidewalk scuffle, visits Mac, takes on Walt Disney, hightails it to Cheryl, rats his son out, and requests a body.

Full tank of gas, enough ice in the rented van to refrigerate a whale, diving gear piled next to him, he drove down the West Side Highway, hugging the embankment like troops near enemy fire. Just get it done, retrieve the body, deliver it to Harris, block out what Harris's scalpel will wreak, pray the cadaver turns up a nice, convenient excuse. He wasn't particular. The common cold would do, anything to take the heat off. A weak link in the aorta, something in the family of such and such. The mere sight of the body might cure Mac. Death was such an irreversible change of fortune that being pregnant with a lovechild in his head might lose its caché. In other words, facts were facts. The grisly remains would sober him up. He took the turn-off. No curb to park against. Less than a quarter of a mile away, highrise steel potholed the sky. He was reconciled to several hours of waiting around. Grave robbing during daylight hours bought jail time. The pier was idyllic, people chasing breezes like butterfly collectors. He didn't expect the Still Waters to put out the welcome mat. No one likes poachers.

He would have to negotiate.

Doubtless, the phrase "returning to the scene of the crime" would come up. Damn, how it ran through the mind (like a mouse who knows the ins and outs of your house better than you do). Criminal, was it not, how he had renounced *ideas are children,* calling it the ploy of a man drunk on love? A criminal offense. And when his pee-pee failed to follow through? Criminal negligence? Would he go to his death with his good name restored?

First, sift through the data till it yields.

If the Still Waters don't give me the body, I'll make a stink. For the love of my boy, I will not disappear, he decided.

Well after midnight. The last stragglers were finally leaving, young revelers in wedding garb, the groom's best man herding them down the middle of the street. Jacob, in full gear, walked to the dock. Fumes of carefree laughter, strong as ammonia, stung his eyes. He leaned over. The thunder from down under said, *Get lost.*

"Claritha revered You, I revere You too," Jacob pleaded. "You've known eons, men have only years. *My* formative years were spent in Southampton. Maybe you heard of the Ark, practically a member of the family? Of all the ships built by my Grandpa Marshall, she was the one he went home to at night. I was born at sea, I'm a seafaring writer, the sea and I go way back."

A sharp retort, like a hundred wet towels slapping wood. He was knocked over by a wave higher than the pier.

"Mermaids are Daughters of the Sea," he continued, on all fours at the pier's edge. "Your wards, so to speak. Parenting has got to be one of the more difficult jobs in the world, always worrying: Am I doing too much, too little, too overbearing, too distant, too hardline, too soft, too hands-on, too hands-off, too laidback, too meddlesome, too shortsighted, too visionary, too . . ."

"Bug off," warned a towering wave.

"Much as You and I would like to handpick who our kids partner up with . . ."

A four-by-four section of water parted just like the biblical Red Sea. "Claritha quoted a prophecy We never made. She made up Our minds for Us. The Still Waters let no one speak for Them. She had to be vanquished. Then she succeeded, she changed Our minds. The Still Waters aren't wishing wells. Snap Our fingers and hope, that's the extent of it. Well, she struck gold, but gold wasn't the only thing she struck. She struck a nerve. A high water mark, a moment of moments. Now the dam has broken. The Still Waters aren't still. Suddenly We're gushy. Talking Our heads off. Blabbermouths."

Water sloshed. "But not for all the tea water in China would We trade places with Claritha. There's a gulf between mermaids and Us—she significantly reduced it. One can't get water from a stone, but somehow she spun water into gold. Fraternizing with Man, the daughter flourished, but in the end, she was way out of her depth. Now go before We start accusing you of pulling the plug."

"Not guilty," Jacob pleaded.

"Get lost."

"We may still be of some mutual benefit. Surely You've heard of the Foundation? The alternative school of oceanography—look-don't-touch, if you do, don't ravage? My friend, Harris, is the Founding Father. He'll do the post-mortem. You can't ask for better. He lives by the Hippocratic Oath: Do no harm. The data might be worth its weight in gold."

"We can't ask for better? Tch. Tch. We didn't ask for anything. And We've had enough of this conversation. It's time for you to go home."

"Go home? Go home? But I haven't finished explaining my intentions. You can't leave me here." Jacob tried to jump off the pier, but was bounced back on his ass.

"Don't call Us, We'll call you."

"When?"

"We are the eons, man is the years."

"I'm not asking for an end to the caste system. But mercy and empathy should rise above designations. Claritha was my beloved. She was Mac's beloved too. My son means the world to me. I keep the remains of his umbilical cord in a safe deposit box. He's convinced himself he's pregnant with love. I have every reason to believe he believes he's with child. It's up to me to set him straight. Claritha's body might be a start."

No answer. He wouldn't take silence for an answer. He backed up, a good thirty paces.

"My heart's broken. The mermaid was the love of my life. Come through on this, I'll commend her back to the deep as soon as the data's in." He took a running jump off the dock, trying to keep up the dialogue, but . . .

Flight aborted.

His arms were forced behind his back, metal cuffs slapped on his wrists. He screamed at his assailant. "The wallet's in the van, under the right front seat, inside the brown bag, between the Wonder Bread. Just don't hurt me." Whirling around, he confronted his mugger—New York's Finest.

"Take it easy, feller. Mermaid get you between the eyes? You're in good company. I'm gonna show you a place full of shipwrecks just like yourself."

Jacob demanded his badge number, his precinct. "By the time my lawyer finishes, there won't be enough left for the vultures."

The boy in blue didn't say, *Tell it to the judge.* He sang a different tune. "Off to Bellevue we go," he said. "On a fishing expedition."

The boy in blue was a big hit.

Standing unshackled in his wet suit, Jacob looked as out of place as the Easter Bunny. The triage nurse and the officer—Olasky was his name—had a head start on rapport. Before Olasky opened his mouth, she had begun nodding with her whole body.

"A bullet takes me out," Olasky said, "I'm gonna go with your name on my lips: Fatima, my black beauty. Fatima, my African-American princess."

She pulsated, head-to-toe harpstrings.

"Fatima, the Saint Jude of Bellevue, meet Jacob Koleman, a maimed and crippled soul, wounded in love, seconds away from throwing it all away on a . . ." big, conspiratorial wink, ". . . mermaid."

Fatima oooed like Jacob was a bouquet, a gift from an ardent admirer. The lashes on her almond eyes were long and thick. They fandanced her pleasure. Her uniform was snug. Waiting on a movie line going nowhere, the sight of her could take a load off your feet.

But with Bellevue's loony bin a few floors above, she was not a distraction. She was the Enemy, the Bureaucracy. Find anything good to say about officialdom, you really do have to have a few screws loose.

"I'm a published author. The scene at the dock was merely a discovery draft. The subject: mermaids. The setting: water. The writing wasn't going well. I was testing dialogue and wrestling with plot. We artistic types—anything for craft." Making a self-deprecating face, letting them know he was in on the joke. What writer isn't a bit off?

"The integrity of the piece is why I went to the pier, to give it authenticity. For an actor it's getting into character, committing to what's on paper. But it's the writer who has to do the preliminary paperwork. Often as not, that means legwork too."

Olasky, le chevalier, took his hat off. Olasky, le boy scout, pressed it against his chest. Le patriot, Olasky, hummed the first stanza of "America the Beautiful." Le opportunist, Olasky, reached over for Fatima's crucifix and kissed Jesus on the cross. Fatima's eyelashes fluttered like butterfly wings. The crucifix was stuck to his lower lip, giving his words a certain messianic weight. "My mother's third cousin was a writer. He was tortured, emotionally fraught. On a very, very, very, very, short, short, short string."

Did he think that would impress Jacob Koleman? "I'll sue, I swear. The hospital's liable, it's malpractice. You'll never eat lunch in this town again."

The crucifix swung free, clunking Fatima's top button. The button popped. Less constricted by the uniform, she took a breath and placed her fingers on the computer keyboard. "Time of incident?"

Olasky, le cop: "12:17 A.M."

"Motive?"

"Suspected suicide attempt, love affair gone sour."

"A scene from the manuscript," Jacob protested.

"Recommendation?"

"Don't answer that." The printer was slow. Jacob threw himself in front of it. "I'm as sane as you are."

"Every mental case who comes through those doors says those exact words," Fatima of the fluffy, bearskin eyelashes shot back. "If push comes to shove, I'll dope you. You'll be trussed like a turkey and you won't even know it."

"Book him," Olasky said. "Twenty-four-hour observation."

She went to get a signature. Jacob had been in some first-rate hotels where check-in took longer. Ten seconds later, she was back. His insurance card earned her goodwill. "You'll love the accommodations. Private room, bigger than my apartment."

An orderly took over, marching him single file. She was twentysomething, weighing no more than a sack of groceries. Fatima had given her a clipboard. He offered to carry it. Against regulations, she said. He could hear her lip-reading his chart, repeating the lines as if she were auditioning.

She tapped him on the shoulder. "The stairs are quicker." He didn't see how. One o' clock in the morning, shouldn't traffic be light? Each time they passed a stairwell—four in all—she said, Not that one. Ultimately, they stepped through an unmarked door. It was lit like a cheap motel. The red of the bulbs went with the satin red bedspread on the queen-size bed. She nudged him toward the bordello center-piece. "This job's just to put bread on the table. Waitressing pays better but Bellevue's a great place for contacts. Sooner or later, the entire world of film, theater, and television walks through these doors and says, *I'm as sane as you are.*" Her smile was camera ready. "Acting's my chosen field."

Sweet-talking like his life depended on it. "I thought so. Soon as I heard you read my chart, I said to myself, My people would jump at the chance to call your people."

She began undressing him.

He deflected her hand. "I would if I could. Any man would have to be crazy not to. The mechanism . . ." In a flash, he was cupping and squeezing himself, giving her a blow-by-blow on his worn and wilted pee-pee. "Curvature of the spine, a drooler, bad body odor, needs deodorant." He appalled himself. Defaming his own penis, slandering the lad, its darkest hour, putting the nail in its coffin . . . Really, he must be mad.

"Forget what I just said. I'm able. Try me. The setting can be any-where, fathoms deep, water isn't a deterrent, caves neither, nor specta-tors in caves. Able. High to the sky high achiever. I make hay. If pee-pees had honor rolls, mine would be Phi Beta Kappa. Able. Able." He panted from the effort to wake his manhood up.

She led him out, up two flights. She tucked him in. (Fatima didn't exaggerate, the private room was a beaut.) The orderly whispered con-solingly. "In your day, I bet you were a bruiser."

He laughed.

I laugh to laugh it off. I'm a man on a mission. This pee-pee's of no further use to me. It's not like I really want one more for the road. Once I bring the body up, prove dead is dead, abort Mac's pregnancy, and exonerate myself, fortune will smile. Harris will find out what did her in wasn't pee-pee—then I'll figure out the next chapter.

A prisoner's mentality: Take every test offered—endocrinological, neurological, gastro-intestinal, urogenital, cardiovascular—cooperate, earn time off for good behavior, maybe early parole. The staff was proprietary, walking in any old hour. Just to win friends and fans, he cracked jokes. *I'm so tired I could sleep standing up.* Ha. Ha.

His privates were another story.

He couldn't snow job *them.* Duck decoys were more lifelike.

When he next came to, he asked what day it was.

"We admitted you on Saturday, this is Monday." Extending his hand. "I haven't read you, but I've read your reviews."

"When can I go home?"

His visitor was gray. The hair, the suit, socks, shoes. He looked like a professional grown-up.

"I'm Milton Straffer, call me Milt."

"Can I go home, Milt?"

"Hospital policy requires psychological evaluation." Pensive panda eyes, you could almost hear the thoughtful munch of bamboo. "I'd like to help. Being something of a writer myself, I'm completely cognizant of the pressures. A piece doesn't work, it's doomsday."

An ally? The fellowship of authors usually transcends differences that would divide other people.

"Agitated as I was, suicide never once crossed my mind."

"Touchy business, publishing. Some writers go their whole lives never seeing print."

THE MERMAID THAT CAME BETWEEN THEM

Jacob had sat in on a few panels, attended conferences with writers disseminating to other writers . . . novices lingering afterwards to schmooze, putting their best foot forward, hoping for tips that would send them to the head of the class.

"So, do you work from an outline or do you just wing it?" Milt had no blubber to hide behind. Sliding to the edge of his seat, his butt pretty much said what was on his mind: *I'm plotzing with anticipation. Tell me how to break into print, don't leave me out here in the cold, cruel world of the unpublished.*

Looking around furtively, as if the walls had ears, Jacob confided. "Actually, the hottest property I'm working on is unrelated to the scenario at the pier."

Trained to pick up nuances, Milt needed no prodding. "It wouldn't be entered into the record. Nothing you say will leave this room. Theft of intellectual property is an egregious act. Consider yourself copyrighted. Gentleman's agreement. What established writer would ever take on an apprentice if there were no assurance of absolute confidentiality?" Butt doing a jig. I'm the pick of the litter. Panda eyes flagging him down.

Indecision. Pangs of conscience: A Prince doesn't play on the weaknesses of others. Yet the freshly minted Jacob Koleman—lean, mean, seething, fighting machine, man of more than one note, was a player. Bellevue wasn't going to incarcerate *him*.

"I'm just in the initial stages of a hot property, perhaps the hottest ever to come my way. The market's hot, hot, hot."

"My, my, my," Milton eyed him like he was the whole bamboo tree.

"What I intend is a road map for males, refine the male perspective, redefine attitude. Present company excepted, some men—flawed in their thinking—make complete fools of themselves when they get within two feet of menopause. The working title's *Men in Menopause,* you with me?"

"All the way."

Big fraternal smile. "I'm in the market for a collaborator, someone with medical know-how and a literary sensibility."

"In print?" Milt swallowed hard. "Seriously?"

"Just as preschoolers get reading readiness, I'd like to provide menopause readiness. Reports of its demise, I think, are premature. In any case, menopause/middle age, is still a viable syndrome, you follow?"

"To a т."

"Long before menopause/middle age sets in, it should be second nature to the mind—in the creative sense—to lay and hatch eggs. Sort of perpetual mental pregnancy. Ideas are children. The imagination is fertile. Incubation, gestation. Womb to tomb, the mother of all mothers is the mother of invention."

Milton amen'd. Jacob sat up in bed and swung his feet over, nearly knee to knee with Milt. Milt's eyes—in lieu of gorging on bamboo—ate up Jacob's anatomy. Head, shoulders, waist. Sharp dip below the waist. Jacob quickly retreated under the covers. x marking the spot? Imagination running away with him? Panda zinging, for what reason? Why were all roads leading to Groinsville?

"In all my twenty years of practicing in the community of males, I've never heard a patient put menopause and/or middle age so eloquently. You took my best lines. Not to worry, I'll percolate others. It's just so seldom that a man in menopause is so open." Milt opened the black satchel on the floor, pulled out a file this thick, took out his bifocals, placed them on his face, caught them as they slid down his nose, pushed them back up, held them in place. Landslide. One too many gestures at one too many angles. The papers scattered. Milt insisted on picking them up himself.

All Jacob wanted to do was pull the covers up, wrap them around him, make himself body-bag secure. Me menopausal? Milt needs a rewrite. I'm not menopausal. Menopause is for women only. Keep the men out of menopause. Women are ten times better at it. Menopause is more their speed. None of their roads lead to lukewarm erections. Women come together in groups. It's not forced, they're just natural congregators. They flock. They talk amongst themselves.

Milt opened his mouth to speak.

Jacob stopped him. "Spare me the pep talk. I'm the walking dead." Jacob could not still the quakes. His Death Valley panting wasn't the sound of music.

Nurses with giant syringes entered the room. They hadn't just dropped in. Milt must have hit the panic button. They lined up like recruits.

"Mr. Koleman?"

"Don't Koleman me. You saw my insurance, get me a second opinion."

"After all you said . . ."

"I said nothing of the kind," Jacob barked. "You're fired."

Where the panda eyes used to reside, two gleaming stones. "The results of your tests indicate a degree of severity. With proper medication, you should recover. Understand, nothing's a hundred percent. Viagra gets good results. But it's not a magic bullet. Psych factors can eat Viagra out of house and home. Whatever compelled you to the pier doesn't go away with a pill."

"You're off the case. I am not a nut case, I am not a psych case. You can't pin menopause on my psyche and make it stick. I'm not the author of my own impotency. The relationship I was in was not the instigator either. What kind of shrink are you, linking A to B, when there's a whole alphabet to choose from? A real writer doesn't settle for clichés. If an unloaded pee-pee does the bidding of its hormones, and the hormones act on their own volition, then everybody's doing what they do without the participation of—for the sake of argument—a Beast of Passion, and then—to sum up—He-Who-Can't-Get-It-Up *can't* be the culprit. You will not draw my latents into this."

The nurses cocked their syringes.

CAROL ANN SIMA

He made a mad dash for the door, only to be brought down by a barrage of needles.

Darkness closed in. "No relationship problems. Everyone relating to everyone, greatest dad in the world, treated her like a member of the family, love him like a son, since kindergarten, Jacob Koleman relates well to others."

Milt was at his ear. "Anyone we can call, friend or family to fetch you?"

Cottonmouth, Jacob said, "Finch Andrews, agent, in the book."

❧

He woke up trying to walk it off. Finch as his crutch, wedged into the armpit slot, holding him up, coordinating the walk (which wasn't like a walk at all, Jacob's legs sandbag-heavy, earth's gravity bullying him). His request to sit was refused.

"Doctor's orders," said Finch. "Milt phoned. Milt said to come. I do not get any of this, Jacob. Bellevue doesn't put you away for a dip in the ocean. Did you know Milt's assistant said you can be discharged in that diving suit? No law against it. He said Bellevue has sent patients home in space suits. I didn't think he was joking. The clothes in the duffel are for you, spares I keep in the office. Nothing in your size, but it's an improvement on the diving suit. And speaking of that dip in the ocean, whatever else you did, they aren't telling, and whatever you did to Yondle, she isn't telling. But you did do something. She's in another world. She stares into space, her hair's a swamp. Jesus, tell me. First I hear on the radio you're doing a menopause book, then my secretary/right-hand man/gal Friday/executive in charge of day-to-day operations offers her resignation for embezzling funds for radio ads she took it upon herself to authorize— well it's maddening. What kind of nut cases are you two?"

Finch dropped him. Jacob stayed down. He looked up. Finch's pants were sagging to his ankles. The blue shirt hung over his knees like a tablecloth.

"I'm going to my Doctor's office." Jacob was druggy enough not to feel embarrassed when he started crawling out.

Milt was not surprised to see him.

"The discharge papers are awaiting your signature. I've authorized prescriptions. Meanwhile the samples will hold you till you get a druggist."

"Hospital records?"

"Patient files can be obtained through Accounting. Now if you'll excuse me."

"What will it take to see a copy now?"

"Hospital procedure . . ."

"My literary agent's outside, I'll introduce you."

Milt opened his black satchel, rifled through, and produced a binder. "Second opinion, just like you wanted. You'll notice his and mine are virtually identical."

Visual focus was still fuzzy. "Summarize for me, please."

"Layman's terms: hormonal fluctuations, a particularly radical swing. Causative factors, unknown at this time. The usual lists of suspects."

Mac would never believe him innocent. "Relationship problems? That dead horse—surely you didn't include—say you didn't include personal problems between me and persons unknown?"

Milt's lip curled like early Elvis. "I did, corroborated by a second opinion."

"Okay, it's in print, right? The printed word can be altered, print isn't written in stone."

Milt pointed to the door. "Before RELATIONSHIP PROBLEMS get top billing, out."

The cab going home: A doggy bag of pills, and the two-page summary of his file, a short version, highlighting all the pertinent details.

Relationship problems had made the final cut. On Finch's lap, the duffel containing his diving suit and keys to the rented van.

Finch punched Jacob's arm. "You stun gun, you. Or should I say Beast? You'll devour the competition. This kind of publicity, money can't buy. *Men in Menopause,* written by a man in menopause? Ingenious! A giant among authors, you'll walk with the greatest self-promoters of all time: Dick Clark, Howard Stern, Martha Stewart. Leave everything to me. The least I can do is phone Avis for pick-up— late fees are on me. What's a few hundred dollars between friends? Don't ever, ever tell me how you did it, or who pulled what strings. If it should come to light, I wasn't part of the conspiracy to defraud the reading public. I know nothing of Yondle's conspiracy with my number one author. Like the average reading public, I don't move in certain circles with influence on certain exclusive hospital circles. Yondle's group probably goes all the way to the CIA . . . you coerced Bellevue, didn't you? . . . No, don't tell me."

Finch wouldn't hear of Jacob paying for the cab.

"Be on your guard. If I were a writer playing a role that landed me in Bellevue, I would wait till the contract was signed before I pulled myself together for cab fare. Leave the long road to recovery for the sequel."

Jacob couldn't stand it a minute more. At the next light, he bounded out. Finch called out the window, "Yondle's getting a raise. I'll send her . . ."

"Don't send her to me."

". . . your love."

He showered, the very tub *she* had showered in, the mermaid he was missing with all his heart, who had filled his life as never before. He found it difficult to stop, scrubbing himself long after the dirt had washed away. Parting the curtain, stepping out, towel drying, it all felt wrong. The same could be said of the mattress, the floor she walked on, the couch she honored with her presence—he just couldn't walk away. It was time to plan his next move. Damage control: present Mac with medical evidence. Compelling documentation: Jacob Koleman's been struck by natural disaster. Menopause is an act of God. Nobody blames a town for getting mowed down by a tornado. There's nothing psycho about hormonal fluctuations.

Play relationship problems down—who me? Play up the blood.

He cast his eyes down. His neck was too tired to hold up his head. He no longer looked like himself. His face was ratty, like the planet Earth before recorded time, a pockmarked tundra, meteors trying to knock it out of orbit. The meat between his legs was wilted lettuce. For all the important pitch to Mac (my hormonal dips precipitated the curl in my pee-pee) he wore a true-blue shade of navy.

He walked down the stoop, holding on for support.

Kung-Fuing herself out of the shadows of his brownstone's basement apartment where the garbage cans were kept along with several thriving plants (so the tenant would have a view of something besides overflowing plastic bags slit open by human scavengers), Kate Vestor blocked his path. "The match of our blues is too coincidental to be random." Straightening up from her semi-crouch, she ambled up to him. "We'll have lots to tell our grandchildren, beginning with how you played hard to get. The battle of the sexes is the sweetest conflict that ever was. You vex me. It's no coincidence that vex rhymes with sex. We are so two-of-a-kind-opposites-attracting. And killing our mates—you by frustrating her to death, me by bang-bang you're dead . . . it tremendously bonds us." Throwing her true-blue cape like a matador, she tossed it around his shoulders with mercurial speed. "You feel it too, the fatal attraction? Yet kill-or-be-killed can't be all we are. Our two cups of loving-kindness aren't just mantle pieces. We've internalized them. But no system of checks and balances is foolproof. You may one day be part of my body count as I may be of yours. Each skirmish, we die a thousand deaths. We don't quite though. Our hearts are bomb-ticking for each other."

"You're very kind to offer—"

She kicked him in the shins. "I dropped everything, I cleared my schedule. Now you want to thwart my driven impulse. I'd like to see you try." She held the drawstrings of the cape like they were reins. "Let the thwarting begin."

He wrestled the cape. It flew up, curtaining him, and when it fell, he saw Yondle exiting a cab, preceded by her hair, an unruly bush topped by a braid which looked like a unicorn horn.

Yondle walked directly up to Kate. "I am Yondle Carr, in the employ of Jacob's literary agent. Who might you be?"

"Jacob's conflict counselor, Kate Vestor."

"I need to talk to Jacob privately."

Kate slipped under the cape, coming up next to him.

Yondle tested the point of the braid's steeple like she was testing a blade. She sprayed it, primed it, then addressed Jacob. "Finch is already laughing all the way to the bank. But I know people who know people. Nobody pulls Bellevue's strings. I'm still digesting it. You really are up to your eyes in male menopause. You may not be the beast I took you for."

Kate looked disappointed. "This, I find out from a total stranger?"

"There's nothing Jacob doesn't tell me," Yondle declared.

"I didn't tell you I was in menopause," Jacob objected. "Finch told you. You found out through him." His neck chafed from the drawstrings of the cape. But having his laundry aired on the sidewalk chafed even more.

Yondle engaged Kate. "As you can see Jacob tells me a lot."

"Yet he didn't mention his conflict counselor, an indispensable, incontestable part of his life. The rock he leans on," Kate contended.

"My rock's bigger than yours," Yondle countered. "I was a witness to history. Claritha and Jacob weren't a twosome. He threesomed. I spreed store to store. With him. For her."

"See here—" Jacob was firm. "I don't like this leash around my neck. I don't like this conversation."

"Shut up," said Kate. "Yondle thinks my not being an eyewitness establishes me as an outsider. *She's* in the clique. *I'm* a nobody. Now the burden of proof is on me. How do I demonstrate my worth, when you don't deem me worthy of witnessing the threesome that wasn't a twosome?"

"If anyone's feathers should be ruffled, it's mine." He flung off the cape, Kate flung it back on. "I don't like you," he said to Kate. To Yondle, he said, "You, I like even less."

Yondle made a joyous sound, like she was unwrapping a present she had long waited for. "The beast's in heat, isn't he? I can feel a bad ass in my bones. It's your rutting season. My mama warned me about guys like you. Did yours warn you about girls like me? Like a flower that needs sunlight, I need to go slumming."

Kate balled her fists. "You've vexed the wrong woman. He's *my* cheap thrill."

Yondle pushed. Kate lost her balance. Jacob crawled out from under the cape.

"A catfight? Two women brawling over a guy?" Kate grinned. "This is so vintage. And when he likes neither one of us . . . so out there."

Kate took a swing. Yondle returned fire. They missed. They got him instead.

He howled, "You've declared your True Love. You've given your hearts away. You're willing to spill blood over me. Anything I say to discourage you will probably bounce off. It's the nature of true love that it is true blue. It goes on and on. Hardships don't chip away at it.

It endures. You'll love me even when I don't put out, when there's no sex, no conversation, when one minute in the same room with me feels like a year-and-a-day, even when there's no reason to love me, you'll love me without reservation because true love doesn't give up without a fight."

Shoving him away, Kate said, "He's yours."

Shoving him back, Yondle said, "I can think of a zillion places I'd rather be."

"And not one of them is here," Kate backed off.

As fast as their legs could carry them, they abandoned ship.

Jacob rushed to the corner, hand up hailing a taxi.

Striding into Mac's building, he was focused. Just get a dialogue going, milk all the angles: sympathy, pity, nostalgia. Remember third grade? It was me who let you stay up till eleven. . . . You accidentally busted my nose with a tennis racket, I didn't ground you. Sixty seconds is all I ask. You listen, I talk. We'll call it even.

Mac's doorman reacted swiftly to Jacob's name. "You're expected." He handed him the key.

"You must have me mixed up with somebody else." He spelled Koleman.

The doorman pulled out an index card and verified: "Give Jacob Koleman the key to my room."

"My son in?"

"Not that I know of."

"When do you think?"

"Don't know."

"I should just . . ."

"Looks that way."

With growing unease, Jacob took the elevator.

Once he let himself into the room, everything fell into place. It was a Disney takeover.

Sharing wall space with Marilyn were movie posters for *The Little Mermaid*. Mac's sheets, cover, and pillowcases: *Little Mermaid*. On top of his bureau, *The Little Mermaid,* the book, the doll, doll dishes, collectibles from the movie.

The world according to Disney: Mermaid falls in love. Mermaid trades tail for legs. Mermaid lives happily ever after. Death takes a holiday.

His baby . . . born again? A Disney fundamentalist cultist nut?

In the VCR was a tape. He pressed Power. He sat down on the bed. He watched the video.

Hating every minute of *The Little Mermaid*.

Loving every minute of *The Little Mermaid*.

He dreaded the Herculean task ahead: deprogramming his son. No ifs, ands, or buts, fairy tales don't come true.

❦

The boy had dropped weight. Missed meals, even a day's worth, immediately showed up on Mac. His gauntness made his skull look like an apple on a stick. One good gust, up and away.

"Mac, I love you."

Whatever else, Disney stands for family unity. Mac didn't reply in kind but he welcomed Jacob in a way that wouldn't bend Disney's nose out of joint. Mac took down a framed-in-glass *Mermaid* poster. "I want you to have this."

"Trade you," giving Mac his medical records.

Transfer complete, Jacob cut to the chase. "These past few days, I've been under the care of Dr. Milton Straffer, head psychiatrist at Bellevue. The report will bear me out. He said hormones had a field day with me. Men, as they get older, even the fittest, can't always have erections at their beck and call."

The manila folder in Mac's hand remained closed. Mac looked shamefaced. "When you and Claritha went off without me to the Still Waters, I wasn't on the right brainwave. The vibes I broadcast were negative. The Beast of Passion, consumed with jealousy, that was me. I was the obstruction."

Jacob was baffled. Why was Mac apologizing? Did he not understand who the real perpetrator was?

"The big, bad wolf is Male Menopause." Step one in his strategy: Get Mac to accept menopause, then haul the body up and see if what killed her really was Jacob Koleman's . . . touchy subject.

Mac ignored the file. "She chose you to make the dive with her. Secretly, I fumed. The Beast feeds on anger, and I gave it plenty to eat."

Jacob couldn't stand idly by while his son took the rap. "Your heart's pure, it's my heart that's mixed. Read the report. Menopause doesn't stand alone. Relationship problems plus menopause. The combination's lethal."

"I did more than my fair share. The biggest portion of the guilt is mine." Mac's ribs were like bones picked clean. "I'm so sorry."

"My Grandpa, your Great-Grandpa Marshall, roamed the sea in the Ark, like the ones from antiquity. The Ark's his legacy, to be passed on: Some voyages we choose, some choose us. But through it all, like the Ark, we endure."

Rubbing the *Mermaid* poster like a lucky rabbit's foot, Mac's complexion underwent a change. It was like looking at a religious painting when the sky opens, light pours out, and people have out-of-body experiences.

It scared the bejesus out of Jacob, but he didn't go straight for Disney's jugular. He warmed up with Harry Potter.

"God's honest truth, I know a kid named Craig who's into Harry Potter. The main protagonist's a wizard. Well, this kid Craig kinda diddles around with sorcery which is stunting his natural development."

Working his way up . . .

"Take George Lucas and *Star Wars: May the Force be with you.* In the movies anything's possible. In reality, it's all a computer-generated hoax."

He had Disney in his sights.

"Disney doesn't tell it like it is either. Disney softpedals. Disney's a distortion." Jacob frowned. It must be a trick of lighting—Mac was starting to look smug.

Mac said, "I've got seven words for you."

"Four for you," said Jacob.

"Claritha's coming back, she's THE LITTLE MERMAID," said Mac.

"Snap out of it," said Jacob.

Cheryl consented to see him.

Mermaid posters leaned up against Cheryl's walls. The rest of the living room was bare, except for two metal folding chairs. "All in storage," she sat, using the second chair for a footrest. "Where it will stay for years and years. I could no more bring myself to dump our stuff, than I could dump you from my heart." Her off-the-shoulder toga barely stayed on the designated shoulder. The ton of glitter in her purple punk hair alighted slowly, tinsel in free fall.

Where to begin? How does a father rat on his own son?

Mac was attempting to resurrect the dead, animate Claritha like she was a Disney cartoon. Mac was no longer of this world.

Betray the trust of his firstborn?

Yes.

"The name Claritha mean anything to you?"

Exasperated, she waved her arms. "The things we do for our kids. All mermaids go by Claritha. Coming from a child that named every animal he ever stuffed, I see no cause for alarm. Finkle's way ahead of you. He sees Mac's mermaids as a textbook case, a deepseated yearning for simpler times, the era of innocence, the other end of the spectrum from Marilyn Monroe, an idyllic retreat." She leaped to her feet and knocked on his head. "Hello? Mac quizzed me on your performance rating because his was lackluster. Perhaps so new at it, he climaxed instantaneously. The mermaid represents two steps backward for every step forward. But don't get your balls in an uproar."

As glitter flew like fireflies, she continued. "Finkle's OK with it, so am I. Mac will still wet dream. Living with a mermaid isn't a cloistered existence."

Picking flecks of glitter off his tongue, he disagreed. "I only wish it were that simple. Claritha isn't who you think she is. She is—was—a living being. God rest her soul, she's buried at sea. Mac fell hard for her. First Love isn't just something you walk away from. It's the love by which all other love is measured. Scars left by First Love are for all time."

Cheryl reached into her toga pocket, withdrawing papers. "Mac faxed your medical file. He has your best interests at heart. Clearly, you're flummoxed."

Informed on by his own son?—the tit-for-tat sneak.

"Hear me out. We've got to stop him from making the biggest mistake of his life. Claritha was *a real mermaid*. And now Mac's planning to raise the dead. Not pretend. It goes beyond embalming. He wants to bring her back to life, three dimensionally."

Her smile was not one of unqualified support. It didn't have the flash her glitter did.

"It wasn't so long ago you tried to pawn menopause off on me like I was its handmaiden. Fond as I am of the sparks you sent my way—hands off my boy." She kicked a chair over. "Menopause is making you crazed. You and Mac are the two constants in my life. Any day I don't drop by the dorm, delivering paper goods, assorted sundries, or pasta, I have the store send over a bag in my name. You too can be on my paper route. There are many fine, upstanding mental institutions within city limits. Commit yourself voluntarily, don't make me do it for you." Shaking her head, releasing a storm cloud of glitter. "Any more outbursts, I'll go to court and have you declared an unfit parent."

She'd do it too. Telling Cheryl I'm-as-sane-as-you-are would probably lose him the election. There is a time to fight. That time was not now. Better to take cover, mass his forces from a safe distance. "I'll be at the Ark," a user-friendly voice. "I hope you can find it in your heart to forgive me. Soon as I'm recuperated, the three of us will do lunch."

She glided to the door. "Get well fast, my love. We have so much to catch up on."

The poster of the Little Mermaid under his arm (Mac's gift to him), he set out for the pier—to leave his forwarding address and to find out Theirs.

She caught up with him on the stairs. "Scott's really starting to get on my nerves. I'm good enough to blow him, but I'm not good enough to date?"

"I'll give it some thought," he said.

Sprinkling pinches of glitter like holy water, "For luck, here's to a speedy recovery. If you don't have your wellness, you don't have anything."

Thirty-three years she was his Second Love, not the slightest clue she wasn't First in his heart. "Scott doesn't know what he's missing," he said.

❦

This time, his costume didn't draw undue attention: a fishing rod over his shoulder, the requisite tackle box. In it, rubber reproductions of worms. With his cap pulled low, pants rolled up, zinc oxide on his nose, and legs dangling off the pier, Jacob cast his line and spoke quickly. "Work with me on this. I'm worried sick over Mac. He thinks he can wish Claritha back to life. The body's Yours to keep. Just let me have her on loan for a couple of days. A picture's worth a thousand words. Harris's medical exam might explain the inexplicable. Mac needs to see there are no two ways about it. Dead is dead. Then he can get on with his life. What more can I say? He's not right in the head."

Twice, he honored her memory. "I love her. It cuts deep. I get so down. Death's courting me. But I've seen what death does. It hurts the ones you leave behind. I love love and I hate death."

"We are the eons, man is the years. Never in all the eons have the Still Waters been shallow. But now We say, long live the superficial, how it does take the mind off things. Water pressure weighs heavily. The weight of the dark deep is on Our shoulders. Big fish eat little fish. The sea's not a bed of roses." Hundreds of bubbles floated to the surface. "It's always the season for popping bubbles."

"I'd just tiptoe down, blink of an eye, in and out."

"Were We to give you another thought, you wouldn't get off so easy. Where were you when she needed you the most?"

"At stake is the life of my son."

"Do Not Disturb, the Still Waters are running Their bath."

He told Them where he could be reached, including the Ark's phone number. "And uh . . . once You decamp . . . where to? Will everyone be going?"

His fishing line was tugged. Reeling up, he beheld a piece of amber. Preserved in it, like a delicate dragonfly, was a teardrop, perfectly formed.

The mourning period had commenced.

"Dismissed," They barked.

Seven

In which Jacob solicits Harris's help, lunches with Mac,
returns with Harris to the "scene of the crime," hears from
Cheryl, eavesdrops on Mac, and Jacob could just die.

Lying on his stomach, head and shoulders sticking out of the pup tent like pushed-out toothpaste, he scanned Harris's house, zooming in with binoculars set on "see-every-pore." The tent was on loan.

Harris had been missing, four days, and still counting, but the Foundation obstinately refused to see his unexplained departure as a disappearance. After years of proximity to the Foundation, Jacob was just now finding out how loose the infrastructure was. There was no titular head; the departments were autonomous, dozens and dozens of them, each with its own receptionist and clerical staff. Nice people, not stand-offish at all. Drop by anytime—no time's inconvenient—you won't be making a nuisance of yourself—we don't have a corporate mentality—fluidity's a Foundation tradition—field personnel either surface or they don't, and sometimes they don't for months.

By now, the Still Waters could have pulled up stakes. Mourning Their dead, They could have taken Claritha's body with Them. He didn't have the luxury of waiting forever. Plan B was simple: get in good

with the Foundation, establish rapport, then hire the best. Ask the hireling to sign a confidentiality clause. (Word it in such a way that he would think twice before answering to his own name.)

Part of his nightly routine was dialing each receptionist at home. (The Ark, his calling card. Grandpa, his ambassador of goodwill. Donations, his way of saying thanks.)

Thirty calls later: Nobody knew anything.

The pup tent was insulated, hell would freeze over before he did. At 11:15 P.M. it wasn't the chill that finally drove him to kick in Harris's front door. He crawled along the floor, a shadow dressed in black, guided by beams of moonlight and flashlight, his paltry abdominal blubber scarcely a match for the hardwood floors, bruises spreading until his torso was stamp-padded in black and blue. He rose. He walked. He rifled drawers for clues to Harris's whereabouts.

Nothing.

Exhaustion set in.

He dragged the pup tent indoors, placing it near the entrance. Then, just as he had on the previous four nights, he phoned Mac . . . to tuck him in.

"Me again. Giving you a good-night hug. This is the longest we've ever gone not speaking to each other. Every minute seems like sixty. Explain the silence, that's all I ask. Don't cast me out till we talk. Your mother took your word over mine. You don't see me resentful, do you? Faxing my medical files to Cheryl was crafty. Not anything I'm holding against you. Outfoxed but not alienated. No more than you should hold my doubts on your mental stability against me. Breathe into the phone, one measly exhale. Is it because I told you to snap out of it? Because if that's it, I say again: *dead is dead*. Come on, Kiddo, for old time's sake, pick up. A son shouldn't stand on ceremony. A father's an elder, it's your filial duty to let yourself be tucked in."

Mac got on.

"No lectures, promise?"

"I'll try."

"Okay with you if I come for a talk? I could make the 12:40 tomorrow."

"Great—lunch?"

"After our swim."

"We'll discuss it over lunch, Mac."

"We swim out to the spot where you and Claritha met. We see what develops."

"Dead is dead."

"Channeling connects the living to the dead."

"For crying out loud."

"You may tuck me in now."

"With pleasure," Jacob sighed. "Sleep like an angel. Wake like a flower. Ride like the wind." He improvised. "Obey your daddy."

"See you tomorrow."

Still clutching the cell phone in his hand, Jacob closed his eyes and went beddy-bye.

❧

No room to sprawl, he toppled the pup tent in his sleep, then flipped on his side, one arm under him, the other flung up and out, nothing to impede its descent, nobody else in on the slumber party. Down, down . . .

Touchdown!

The arm which had fluttered out landed on a mass it couldn't identify, and gripped its prey like a hawk, then released the prey.

Harris rubbed his shoulder, as Jacob gently scolded, "You didn't leave word. Don't you check your messages? Something happens to you, I take it personally. It's not just neighborly interest . . . it's comrade in arms . . . it's being male, with male bonds." He helped Harris to his feet, an unusual occurrence. Foundation folk were fit. Even the receptionists were exceptionally spry. Harris didn't look unwell, but his tan had faded, as if he'd been indoors for an extended period. Nonetheless, his face was still chiseled and drawn, in his usual "beardless Abe Lincoln" reflective expression, a man of few words.

"I checked myself into a Stress Management Clinic. When you brought Claritha into my life, you brought acute stress. How I wanted to probe, to chat her up, to utter my innermost thoughts. Please don't talk apology nonsense—I know you meant well. I'm so out of practice. Am I talking your head off?"

"No."

"They prescribed talking to calm me down, but the mere sound of my voice doesn't soothe me. It's not like I could just talk to a wall. Would you say I'm being repetitive?"

"No."

"Boring? Putting you to sleep? Dull as watching corn grow?"

"No."

"Speaking in public isn't stress-free. How I come across is a source of constant anxiety. The Stress Management Clinic stressed the importance of a good friend. In silence you stood by me. Would you stand by me in conversation?"

"Yes."

"Then don't just stand there—start talking. How's Claritha, the mermaid lady, mysterious as the sea itself?"

Jacob was struck dumb. Alive, Claritha rattled Harris. Deceased, what would she do?

Harris put out his hand and slid two fingers under Jacob's chin, tilting it upwards. "I haven't lost my clinical eye. You just went pale. Your eyes are watering. Cheeks sinking, even as I speak. Out with it. The suspense is killing me."

"Claritha passed away. A week ago. Under the Chelsea piers in New York. Maybe age-related, ovary-related, related to a fungus of some kind—who knows what snatched her."

The corners of Harris's mouth twitched.

"The body needs retrieval. It's encased in a giant brown coffin of barnacles. She deserves a memorial service, a sacred ceremonial tribute. Can you get a permit for diving in New York City? Do you have the clout for a search at sea if the currents carried her out? It would be a two-man operation. You and me. Nothing leaks out."

Harris shook his head in disagreement. "May she rest in peace. May the sea watch over her. May she remain right where she is. May she not be removed from the sea in order to be commended to it."

The drip from Jacob's eyes could fill a sand bucket, as if work crews were inside the ducts pulling overtime.

Harris turned the collapsed pup tent into a picnic blanket, easing them both down. "We should talk. Stress is clouding your judgment. I admired her so. The courage she showed, her determination, she would've killed for eggs. All the things I wanted to say to her, I'll never get the chance. Beneath that tough exterior there was a womanly tenderness. Remember how she pinched you and said, 'that's for candlelight,' how she smacked you on the thigh and said, 'that's for the handstitched dress?' I recall quite distinctly thinking: lover's spat. She trusted you . . . she let you play doctor. How could I have failed to be touched? She called you Defender. Would you be mine too? She piqued my curiosity. Defend me from asking too many questions."

"I'll do my best."

Harris blushed. "Would you put up a vigorous defense for me if you knew I was attracted to her? In my own defense, I don't see myself as appealing, I don't have your way with words. She touched my social side. I need polishing up, so I don't trip over my own tongue."

"Teach you the conversational ropes—that's what you're asking?"

Harris gulped so hard, it sounded like a pit going down. "Guy talk—I'd love to do cars, sports. I don't even know how to ask for directions without really asking."

"How soon can you make arrangements for the dive?"

The pit in Harris's throat sounded like it was on the way up. "Eventually I'd like to speak to women without putting my foot in my mouth."

"The dive—how soon?" Jacob demanded.

"A day. Uncertain. Or two. I have no desire to add to your stress."

Jacob heaved himself up. "Mac's coming in on the 12:40. He took a shine to Claritha too. If you run into him, not a word. He mustn't find out that we're looking for the body."

Harris burrowed under a flap of pup tent.

Just as Jacob reached the door, Harris spoke. "I'm not dropping my objections to the dive. But if anyone else on earth (besides you and I) were to lay a hand on Claritha, I couldn't live with myself. What did you say about the nature of Mac's relationship with her?"

Not even bothering to turn around. "I didn't."

He didn't detour for a shower or a meal. He crossed the living room and pulled at the ladder leading to the attic. Roughing it in the pup tent, he had lived more like a camper than a sewer rat. He would have to make himself presentable for Mac, but after that, eating, hygiene, and laundry would be I'll-get-to-it-when-I-get-to-it. The steamer trunks in the attic were filled with memorabilia.

This time it wouldn't be Grandpa's nautical collections from around the world he'd be looking at. It would be the love letters. Once he got over the initial discomfort of reading someone's private correspondence, he would be transported back to the early years, a little boy watching Marshall at his writing desk, obviously made happy by his love for a ship, a love so strong that when he wasn't writing to the Ark, he'd stroke the walls and read to her. This trip down memory lane would refuel him for the travails ahead. Only after wrestling the body from the Still Waters, presenting Mac with irrefutable proof, dead is dead, would he be able to close the book on ruining his son's life, putting their relationship to a test that no father and no son should ever have to take.

He climbed the ladder, ignoring the Ark's persistent puppy-yipping creaks. Grandpa's final words, shouted while in flight to the ceiling of the Ark, assured Jacob that the Ark would be there for him too. Jacob, the child, was puzzled. Be there—how? The stallion-bucking Ark had tossed Grandpa out of his wheelchair. Be there to snap Jacob's neck too? Jacob, the adult, might like the Ark to do the honors . . . someday . . . but not today. Death hurts the ones you love.

Opening the brass-trimmed trunk, he jiggled a not-so-secret compartment concealed under the lid. He extracted the stack of ribboned letters. Also secreted away, blank parchment, quill pens, and airtight bottles filled with ink. Propping several goose down pillows against a wall, he moved the loot. He would have liked to give himself completely over to reading and writing. Alas, but for death, there's no escaping the burden of living (made even more burdensome by fresh guilt). He was now officially an exploiter of friendship. He didn't want to give anyone lessons in the art of conversation. He was Mr. Morose. Lose your true love, what's left to live for? (Hating death in the flesh, one can still wish oneself dead in the abstract.)

It's just too much to ask any lovesick, tortured soul to drop what he's doing and be a guy. He wouldn't know where to begin. Guy talk, indeed. Jacob Koleman was just like his Grandpa. Two romantics who caught the Big Wave.

Jacob suddenly averted his eyes from the papers on his lap. A sneeze coming on, you do it, it's done. But this was a fresh avalanche of tears. Not for Claritha . . . for Harris, the innocent. In the final analysis, Harris's inarticulateness seemed not much different from a toddler trying to master the mechanics of language. Who better to instruct a toddler than Jacob Koleman, the Da-Da with the underwear that reads World's Greatest Dad?

Later that day, he'd make a quick run to the bookstore, grab a few newspapers, bone up.

How hard could it be to get "guy literate?"

With the lifting of that burden, he returned to the letters, giving them his undivided attention. They all began the same way: *To the love of my life, dear Missy Ark.*

❧

"Filled out, half a size at least," Jacob teased Mac. The plaza near the docking area was congested. Mac took care not to accidentally brush against his father. They hadn't gotten around to a handshake either.

Mac didn't return the tease. "You've got grocery bags under your eyes. Sleep at all? Those shorts or a kilt?"

Jacob had made an effort, shaving and changing, an exercise in role modeling: if I can take the good with the bad, so can you. Going by Mac's appearance, the lesson had already taken . . . too well. Mac smelled of Dial soap. His hair was freshly shampooed. Jeans and T-shirt, spiffy as if he had just stepped into them. His sneakers were yellow, oozing sunniness. His shoulders were in the upright position. Anyone could see he was happy to be on his way, first passenger off the ferry, like the deck was greased. No sliding into Jacob, though. Flesh didn't touch flesh.

It isn't my place to demand, only to hope. I won't stalk him. Mac's mask slips, I'm here to pick up the pieces.

Jacob winked, giving Mac a quasi-phony smile. See my mask? I'll show you mine, you show me yours. Underneath is a daddy who needs a hug. Mac didn't reciprocate. It was unnerving. No kid who loses the love of his life should look this good. Channeling the dead isn't reality

. . . it's hocus-pocus. My boy is screwed and he doesn't know it. But how to reach him? Guy talk?

"I can eat you under the table, you watch. Jody's Café or the diner?"

"All the same to me. Can't you pick up the pace? Brainwaves can be broadcast at any hour, but I've never felt this close to the right brainwave. I'm trying to connect," Mac explained.

"You don't really think she's going to pop up from the sea?"

"Claritha's golden egg proved where there's a will, there's a way. No, I don't expect immediate success. I'm just tuning in till I'm fine-tuned," Mac insisted.

Walking faster, Jacob could feel his heart thumping. Parental worry thinned the air. "The constructs of Claritha's brain were unique. She had an evolutionary advantage. Under the auspices of that uniquely constructed brain, it was her love in tandem with her excitement and belief that ideas-are-children that produced the egg."

"Faith isn't a halfway thing. Either you have it or you don't. The woman I love turned out to be a mermaid, discovered in my father's house yet. A real in-the-flesh mermaid. Impregnated with love, she birthed a golden egg, from her mouth of all places, in front of the Still Waters. My understanding of Them is that They are an intelligent life form, maybe a higher power. All these impossibilities, how can you not believe?"

Out of the mouths of babes. Faith. Jacob subscribed to ideas-are-children; but he didn't sing hymns to it. The Ark intrigued him, but he wasn't committed. He could easily jump ship. Logic told him, she was just wood, whose noisemaking amounted to no more than acoustics.

But an anxious father can't bide his time forever. Keeping his voice nonconfrontational, "I can't get around dead. Dead is dead."

They were within sight of the Ark. One misstep, Mac might call lunch off, call off Jacob's reign as a father, call Jacob's whole life into question. He chose his next words with care.

"As a writer, I don't go around ruling things out. Writers are like vacuums. We take it all in."

"Then suck on this: We both share the blame for Claritha's death. My bad vibes, your psych angle. Why your hormones went awry isn't cut and dried. Today's the day we team up to send good vibes. We duplicate your steps: Ark to ocean, close as possible to the original sighting. Then we combine our psychic energy to transmit into realms unseen by the human eye."

In his own eyes, he'd never be exonerated from killing Claritha. Mac's indictment of himself sent chills through him. That was where the good doctor Harris came in. He'd examine the body. A cause of death would be established. Definitely not death-by-vibe.

"The unseen is right up a writer's alley," he said.

Both in bathing suits, they plunged in. Half a mile out, Jacob got his bearings, shifted northeast, picked a place, and declared it to be the point of origin. The sea was unusually hushed, like an audience waiting for the curtain to go up. Hearkening back to the original script, Jacob cried out. "Kids need a diaper change, I'm abler than most. If you need a hand bathing or feeding them, potty training, checking under the bed for night monsters, you-know-who's at your service. Need stud service? I'm no slouch. If you're going to take anything with you, take this: When your taste runs to spice, Jacob Koleman's inedible. Enjoy living on the edge? Fat chance. Crave a night life? Anything past ten o'clock, I'm a drip."

Mac, right on his heels, plaintively cried, "Where is our egg? Where is our egg?"

Swathed in bath towels, Mac stretched out on the floor of the Ark, Jacob next to him. Separated by two inches, Jacob shortened it by an inch. Mac lengthened it, penalizing Jacob, with an extra inch-and-a-half.

Jacob proceeded with extreme caution. "Think of all the unfortunates who go their whole lives without love. They live in a state of deprivation. You and I are way ahead. She lives on . . . in memory."

"Claritha's my whole life."

The last straw. Instinctively, he did what any father would do if a truck were bearing down on his child. Yanking him by the wrists—just look at those wrists, ever see a more beautiful pair?—Jacob dragged Mac to his feet. "She loved us both. Multiple First Loves. Fifty/fifty split down the middle is how it's done when it's done right. Without doing the math on the actual figures—who (if anyone) she might have loved more than the other—the operative word is multiple. Your second First Love's out there somewhere. Claritha's your whole life, but so is the one you've yet to meet."

They dressed in silence, Jacob going back to the same black sweats he'd slept in for the last few days.

Finally Mac spoke. "The diner . . . it's quicker."

Mac insisted on a booth near the front, all the easier to exit from. Mac ordered salads for two, all the easier to prepare.

Mac played with his fork. "Not twenty minutes ago, you were in the ocean with nobody but Claritha in mind. Then you bring up multiples. You say it like you mean it, but you don't look it."

Jacob masking his feelings was like a guy who never had on a top hat before. Each one he tries looks more and more forced.

"Which is which?" Mac asked. "Death warmed over, or snow job? Giving me a hard sell so I'll let go, or griefstricken? Do you really believe in a second First Love?"

The salads arrived, each one a twenty-bite meal, ten if you were in a hurry, three if you swallowed without chewing.

In his own way, Jacob was hardpressed for time. Make it snappy kid—take the bait. "Multiple Firsts," hoping his face wouldn't betray him. "Cast your net. The Second First Love is closer than you think."

"My path is faith. Death is a return trip. You take the fickle road, I'll take the yellow brick one."

Jacob, almost desperate: "Claritha wouldn't say two First Loves if she didn't mean it. She did mean it."

Asking for the check, Mac said, "I guess you're within your rights. But I don't have to like it."

Jacob allowed himself one brief internal victory hurrah. I got him thinking in multiples. Love can be a plural. Chalk one up for me. Disney messes with my kid, I mess with Disney.

The wait for the ferry was excruciatingly short. Determined to hold on to Mac a few minutes more, Jacob asked after Cheryl.

"Mom doesn't question your sanity anymore. I fixed it so your menopause doesn't sound like permanent derangement. Let's not squeal on each other again. It's not a good vibe."

"She still bringing the groceries?"

"Never stops."

"Her hair?"

"Glitter's gone, she's solid black."

"Does it worry you? her smoking, drinking, the hair chaos, the body imaging?"

"Baby-sitting the grandchildren will slow her up. Claritha and I want a large family."

Then, quick as you could say dead-is-dead and counter with keep-the-faith, the ferry was gone with Mac in it. The final second, Jacob almost went tearing off after Mac. Every cell in his body crying out, Hug, hug. I'm your Da-Da. Gimme some skin.

Parents strolling the plaza, tousling their kids' hair, taking them by the hand, sharing ice cream cones. Jacob ducked into the bookshop. The

THE MERMAID THAT CAME BETWEEN THEM

proprietress spotted him. The Hamptons were saturated with authors lobbying for shelf space. With Harris in mind, he asked for back issues of *The New York Times* (sports, auto, and biz sections).

"No charge," said the proprietress.

Do real guys do *The Times?* he thought. With the bookstore owner hovering over his shoulder, he loaded his basket with *Esquire, Auto Mechanic, Playboy,* and a new one on him, *Guy Dogs*. He didn't cruise the shelves where his *Pirate Cassidy* books were. Big Mistake. A writer ignoring his own shelf, now that was a red alert. Too late, he realized that he wouldn't be able to dodge her concern.

"Anything I can do? Tea and sympathy?"

He took a guy stance, feet apart, rolling his shoulders, a look of disgust on his face. Know what you can do with your tea and sympathy?

"Writer's block?"

He should knock the bifocals off her nose. He should break the pencil behind her ear. Bringing up writer's block is a bad, bad vibe. His scissored legs came together as if they were gummed. His shoulders were putty. Did he not have anything in that writer's noodle of his, some semblance of a story plot to fend her off, a slither of a thread so she wouldn't launch another vibe like, *Didn't I hear on the radio somewhere, something about a menopause book, completely out of your genre? Is that what's blocking you? You can't write in any genre other than pirates?*

"Father loves son. Father loves mermaid," he said. "Son loves mermaid. Mermaid dies. Son's convinced he can communicate with a dead mermaid, allegedly murdered by his father's . . . vibe. Pops could have had it in for her all along, on account of her affection for the son. He thinks not, ninety-nine percent not. But you never know what lurks latently. Father loves son, it bears repeating. Till the day he dies, he loves his son. The loving, caring, warm, generous Pops tries to snap the kid out of it. Dead is dead. The plot's subplotted. Pops is taking a crash course on guy talk cause he's that kind of guy, a loving, caring, warm, generous father figure to a bashful, stressed-out friend." He shrugged. "I don't have an ending yet."

"You're in good company. Hemingway always had trouble finishing. Didn't I hear on the radio somewhere, something about . . ."

He fessed up. "Menopause."

"That's the one. *Men in Menopause.*"

Like he was chomping down on a cigar. "Oh yeah." He didn't wait for oh-yeah-what? He pulled out a twenty, turned on his heel, and started off. Books are children. Here he was, railing every day against Death for taking his true love, and he was killing his book by being dismissive. He turned around again, got his change, and said. "The mermaid's tale's totally fictitious. Menopause is my calling."

She laughed. "Your secret's safe with me."

Again, "None of the mermaid's true. None. Menopause, all true."

"It won't leave this room. But just between us, the menopause book is not your cup of tea."

"Yes, well I prefer coffee," he yelled, wildly. People turned around to look. He started out. Along the plaza they moved out of the way for the sweaty, running man.

He compiled a list of topics for Harris: Volvo, the dream car, from *The Times;* the hairiest family on earth, from *Men's Health;* big shaggy dogs are a girl magnet, from *Guy Dog;* how you pick up dog doo-doo can be a turn-on, from *Guy Dog;* ugly is in, in *Esquire;* and skin care, from *Playboy.* Alternating with his reading, he went back and forth from bedroom to galley, reheating water for the hot water bottle. Like his heart, his pee-pee ached. Nowadays his formerly overgrown manroot was a pink piggy tail. Just before he dropped off to sleep, groggy as a student cramming for exams, he turned on the night light and the electric blanket. Heat on top of heat to keep pee-pee alive.

In his sleep, Jacob must have felt Harris sitting in a chair, watching.

"I don't care how you got in, just tell me, did you make the arrangements?" Pushing up on his elbows, he beckoned Harris over to sit bedside.

"My contacts called their contacts. We pick up the diving permit around three this afternoon. On paper, we're a film crew. The Foundation van has all the equipment we'll need."

The clock said three A.M.

"I came over early. She'd want for us to be together, wouldn't she? I'll never forget yesterday, when you told me. It's like it happened today. She wasn't just a patient. May she rest in peace. May no one disturb her peace. May no one lay a hand on her. But if somebody must, let it be us. Never in all my life have I felt such jolts of stress as I did when I met her and when she passed on. I could talk about her forever." He took Jacob's hand. "Defend me from monopolizing the conversation, from being long-winded, from chewing your ears off, from harping away, from running off at the mouth. The first time ever inside the Ark, I feel so defenseless. Who, when, where, why, how do I begin picking your brain?" Squeezing Jacob's hand, letting go, raising his arms to the ceiling. "Oh will the jolts never stop? Defend the Ark from me."

Harris looked like he'd bitten down on something sour.

"I'm so lonely," said Harris. "What I really want is a lady friend to talk to. And play doctor with."

"Zip it."

"But there are things I've saved up my whole life to say."

"The Defender says not now." Jacob was adamant. "Just like a toddler, you have to learn to crawl before you walk. Clear the guy hurdle, get comfortable with your own kind. Confidence begets confidence." Harris could benefit from the basics. Can't go wrong with cars . . . I taught Mac to drive . . . I've got cars in my pocket. He mentally accessed the data,

"Climb behind the wheels of a Volvo, want for nothing. Volvo's getting big PR from the press. Volvo's putting out its personal best. SCC stands for safety concept car. Among the SCC's numerous safety features are: an external air bag, which inflates to protect cyclists in a collision; the warning sensor alerts drivers when closing in on the car in front; a camera warns the driver when a car is veering out of its lane; heartbeat sensors detect strangers hiding inside the car; remote units identify a driver's fingerprints; rear seat cushions adjust to the size of passengers. Everybody's got their own take on a thrill ride. For me, security means the world. Anything happens, who doesn't want to walk away? The less serious your injuries are, the quicker the mend, the shorter the convalescence period. It's hazardous out there. Dangerous like you wouldn't believe." Suddenly he pulled the covers up to his chin and kept them there, shivering in the heat. "Don't you swallow the Volvo myth. The moment you hit the road, the highway of life is out to get you. Volvo's no perfect set of wheels. Volvo doesn't ride to the rescue. Volvo doesn't put the breaks on a broken heart. Volvo can't right a wrong turn. Volvo can't U-Turn in the "No U-Turn" zone of life. Volvo's not a guardian angel. Volvo's only a car."

Jacob's hand flew to Harris's hand, fingers squeezing like a hungry mouth. "I really would appreciate it if you tucked me in," he said.

❧

Afternoon. Time to get the diving permit. Jacob sat in the passenger seat, security blanket on his lap. The Foundation's minivan was stocked with hardware and a portable sub. Folded up, it looked like a laptop. "Stick with the mission," he urged. "Don't take your eyes off the road, don't pull off to the shoulder, above all, don't yap away. After the mission, expect verbal bedlam. Incoherence is par. And overlapping, the two of us talking at the same time . . . or maybe not at all. Lapses into silence would not be inappropriate. Grief garbles. Grief slurs. Grief shuts down the speech centers. Your clinic prescribed speech for stress? As I see it, forcing speech in times of sorrow increases stress. Listen and learn. It's my duty as Defender to prepare you for your immediate future. You may be approached by the Feeble Ones. Don't let their bare female chests throw you. They aren't really the opposite sex. If you must speak to them, nothing heavy. For the simpleminded, keep it simple. Opposition will come from the Still Waters. They'll have to be . . . handled. I'll talk you through every possible scenario, each word will be personally hand-crafted. Although I won't be down there with you, by the time we finish rehearsing, you'll never know the difference."

Harris stammered, "A . . . lone? Going a . . . lone? Can't a . . . lone."

Jacob smacked the dashboard, quickly rubbing off the sweat stains. "Look at it as an opportunity to develop your voice. The gift of gab is all in the training."

Harris continued shaking his head no.

Hiding trembling hands beneath the blanket, Jacob explained that he'd simply worn his welcome out, a misunderstanding. "No matter what They say, I'm no egg snatcher." He described the cave, the oxygen enriched environment where Harris could breathe naturally. He dictated every sentence. He covered every course of action open to Harris. He talked nonstop. While they were arriving in New York, while Harris parked, while Harris got out to see if he was too far away from the curb, while Harris reparked and reparked and reparked, while they abandoned the spot (New York City parking regulations, incomprehensible, even to the natives), while they pulled into a lot, even as they walked to the licensing bureau, even while they waited their turn, Jacob was a bottomless well of words.

While they picked up the permit and headed for the pier, Jacob paused a mere two times.

❀

Upon arriving, they fenced the perimeter of the pier with chicken coop wire, every few feet tacking on copies of the permit. Lights no taller than the average living room floor lamp illuminated the area, their rubber bases, shaped like toilet bowl plungers, adhered to the dock. Showbizzy cameras—props for their cover story—whirled away, shooting blanks. The lightweight submarine was wired for sound, as was Harris, his headgear so sensitive Jacob could hear him swallow.

Since agreeing to the deal with Jacob, Harris hadn't uttered a word.

"Say no more," said Jacob. "Classic case of stage fright. Any writer just starting out goes through it. It takes a while to find your own "voice," the style that suits you best. But down there, you'll be breaking your voice in. Use it or lose it. Break a leg, friend. The show must go on." He handed Harris a pair of flippers. "Want the last word? Go on, take it. The honor's all yours. It's not like I'm asking you for famous last words, just a little something to tide me over while I wait . . . in case the entire communication system blows . . . which it won't." Then, keeping his voice casual as if he just thought of it, he asked, "You were so set on not making the dive, now you're off and running—what really changed your mind?"

Like a horse out of the gate, Harris was over the side and into the sub. Minutes later, he made his first broadcast. "Testing one, two, three. This little piggy went weeee all the way home to the gift of gab."

Jacob instantly recognized the vibe: Happy-go-lucky. Chipper. Childish. Out of touch. Otherworldly. Too damn sure of himself. Same strain his son had been infected with. Kneeling over the dock, he was incensed. The slender wire mouthpiece curving out from his headset shook like a twig. "You will not trust in blind faith. I forbid it. Disney isn't your Defender, I am. You get your ass back here, that's a direct order. You're grounded. Pray I don't strangle you with my bare hands. Couldn't tell me to my face, couldya? Had to put your faith to the test, didya? Mark my words, faith will not carry the day. I never meant for you to read more into my words than I meant. The gift of gab's acquired slowly . . . one day at a time, over a stretch of time, a lengthy period, spanning seasons." He clenched his teeth, snarling. "Wake up and smell the danger you're in."

The line went dead. Something the Still Waters might do, but more likely it was Harris.

He paced.

The air grew chilly, he wrapped himself in the security blanket.

He walked in circles.

He mulled.

Calling 911 might be regarded as an act of war by the Still Waters. He frantically threw himself into the water. The water, treating him like a gate crasher, tossed him back.

He stewed.

He stomped.

He chased off a small band of spectators. He prostrated himself on the dock. He stayed there—he timed it—for forty-five minutes.

Does a man without faith dabble in prayer?

Oh God, God help me, why me? why? why? why? . . . why?

It began to rain, soaking the blanket. It seeped into his underwear. He stirred. He sat up. He fidgeted.

Another ninety minutes.

Water so black, the reflected lights looked like stills of flying saucers.

At last the sub popped up, but making so slight a disturbance that he leaned over and poked to see if it was there at all. He did the same to Harris. A poke. A welcoming whoop. Then a searching look.

"No sign of the Still Waters," he admitted. "It's like nothing I've ever seen, clearer down there than up here. If she were anywhere in the area, I would've spotted her. I'm sorry to disappoint you. May she rest in peace. May her bones lie undisturbed. If anyone lays a hand on her, may it be us. A word in private, may I?" Harris folded the sub and walked briskly to the van. Jacob, weighted down by soaked clothes, walked bent, as if he was carrying a heavy bookbag on his back. Harris spread a towel across the driver's seat. It was Jacob who squished when he got in.

"Faith demands I tell," whispered Harris. "By giving you the rest of the story, I am giving testimony to the very faith you tried to talk me out of. Four willful mermaids snared me in the cave, netting me like a butterfly. You predicted they would make lewd overtures and they did. They cowered before your words, which I repeated word for word: *ideas do not make children for everyone.* Their whimpering could make a stone weep." He wiped his eyes. "So I ad libbed. I could tell that the Feebles weren't the brightest lights in the sky, more gum in their toothless mouths than brains in their heads, but the things I said to them . . . I wouldn't say to my own mother." He bounced up and down in his seat like a jubilant child. "I flirted shamelessly. Hallelujah! I've got the pipes. The golden pipes."

Jacob smacked Harris's forehead. It wasn't a love tap. "Snap out of it!"

"Have faith."

Jacob advised Harris to sleep it off at a hotel, he'd reimburse him.

"Faith rocks," Harris exulted.

"Have your head examined."

After he watched Harris dismantle the fence, and pack up the cameras and lights, Jacob asked to be dropped off at his apartment.

"The night's still young," Harris was singing. His eyes were jeweled pendants. "Off to Starbucks I go, hi-ho, to set up playdates."

Every time they stopped at a light, Jacob opened the car door and slammed it, hoping the noise would bring Harris down. Jacob jumped out at his corner. He slammed the door with such force, a strip of paint peeled. Harris drove off, backed up, got out of the car, raced over to Jacob, threw his arms around him.

"Want me to tuck you in?"

❀

The ringing of the phone coincided with his arrival. Suspecting it was Harris, Jacob grabbed the receiver And barked. "What?"

Cheryl was highpitched and rushed. "Finkle's out of town, your cell phone must be dead, I've been trying the Ark for hours. I need you or the police. I'm at the dorm. Mac's locked himself in. He's been saying the most peculiar things: *The golden egg's in the nest. The It moment's at hand. I'm fine-tuned.*"

"Be right there."

However far gone Mac was, Da-da would fight tooth and claw. Like a lion.

❀

Cheryl puffed furiously on a cigar. Her pink skirt was a Southern belle large lampshade hoop. Made of taffeta, it had more than enough material for a wedding dress with train, but it was splattered with ashes. Her skinny-as-a-watchband-top showed midriff. Pink feathers protruded like potted plants from her navel. She related the day's events, fanning the smoke with something Jacob couldn't identify—it looked like part of a cookie tin.

"Shortly after another non-date with Scott, I dropped by with two shopping bags. I could not be more fed up. Blow job after blow job, and I still don't rate a date. Not even café au lait. No expense was spared on the shopping bags. Kleenex, Comet, Brillo, Lemon Pledge, Liquid Plummer, two-ply Charmin Toilet Paper, Bounty Quilted Paper Towels, Glade Air Freshener—all brand names. Mac paid scant attention. Date bait I'm not but I am a savvy mom. Mac's got kinks, but he's never given me any indication that I'm a lousy mom. So the connection between blowing Scott, getting nowhere in the café-au-lait department, and my son locking me out, was all in my head."

"You said he was fine-tuned to the It moment."

She opened her purse. She took out a silver flask. Tipping her head back, she knocked a few down. She made a face. "I've swallowed worse."

She wasn't sober. It was up to him now.

He pressed his mouth against the door slit. "Daddy's here to help. Probably, I sound faint and far away. I won't leave your side. Have your It moment. By all means, enjoy the rapture of your imagination leaping out of bounds. One piece of advice, if I may. Better minds than yours and mine would never go into an It moment without an exit. Do you have an escape route?"

Cheryl buzzed in his ear. "Déja vu! The coddling's so reminiscent. Me and you at Mozart's sipping café au lait from the same coddled straw."

"The safety net's out, Mac. Claritha will always be alive and well in your mind. In that vein—the insurance policy/contingency vein—there's really no such thing as a failed attempt to bring her back. Memory is a living memorial. So not seeing her in the flesh isn't reason enough to go blotto."

Cheryl monopolized his left ear. "The world of blow jobs, dyed hair, and bodice ripping looks glam from afar. But the inner child, the one who needs coddling, never forgets a face."

"Shush." He detected familiar sounds from the other side of the door.

She hung around his neck like a boa.

Jacob pushed the door with his shoulder. "I'd know those sounds anywhere. Forcing us to overhear you perform a sexual act on yourself isn't an It moment, it's a chemical imbalance. Let's talk guy talk. Open the door. We'll touch base, then you can go right back to it."

Mac's moaning rose and fell, bedsprings squeaked like cheerleaders, only seconds on the clock, make the point, score, score.

"If stimulation is what you want, you're not too old to spank. Unlock the door," Jacob yelling louder.

Unwinding from around his neck, Cheryl began sniffing the air. He feared it was his crotch she was whiffing. Did he smell of mold? "I'm picking up a second scent; fluids are mingling." She dug a nail file out of her bag. She stabbed the door, trying to carve a peephole. "The heavenly smell of secretions. My baby's copulating. He's doing the innie and out-tie. It's a she, isn't it a she? I smell bush. Well, nobody will ever be good enough for my little boy. I'm not leaving without laying eyes on her."

Jacob elbowed her out of the way, kicking the door, splintering wood, screaming that if Mac didn't let him in, he'd break both his arms and legs.

Cheryl grabbed him by the ankles. "Leave him to it. Coddlers come through for you, no matter what, coddlers indulge you. Thou shalt not steal thy son's thunder. Where oh where have all the coddlers gone?" She shouted into Mac's room. "Quit the chirping. Cheeping is for poultry. Jesus Christ, whoever your fine feathered friend is, this isn't an aviary."

The door finally gave way. He dragged Cheryl across the threshold.

The top of a giant golden egg had been sheared off. Glops of yolk stuck to the walls and ceiling. The splatter looked like a pie-throwing contest. Shards of coarse brown barnacles crunched under Jacob's feet. He rubbed his eyes like he was dreaming. He was looking at *her*.

Her breasts were sweet melons, baby-oil slick, the handiwork of Eros, nipples extended, way out in front like police motorcades. Her waist and hips were kissed by Cupid. Her crotch, with its golden locks, was as holy as the burning bush beheld by Moses. The legwork looked painted on by the Old Masters. She had the most arresting face, a face that drew you and kept you, a face you'd never tire of looking at. He didn't need to be introduced. He knew that face as well as his own.

A dead-ringer. The golden girl, Marilyn Monroe.

Cheryl would be lying there still if she hadn't helped herself up. The room's other occupants stood fixed like a Monday morning elevator crowd. She was delighted. "I'm the mother, he's the father. We love the two of you together. You have our blessing. Let's not be strangers. Dinner tomorrow night?"

His tongue, as flaccid as his pee-pee, had no muscle tone.

Could you . . . would you . . . let bygones be bygones? . . . Before there were ever bad times, there were good times . . . It isn't like me to go out of my way to snatch the happiness of others . . . Could you, would you, be my girl again?

"Already a child stirs inside me," Claritha/Marilyn cooed. "Mac and I are going to have a tribe."

His arms hung from his shoulders like one of those skinned chickens you see in the windows of butcher shops.

"I like that in a man . . . someone who finishes what he starts," said the golden girl.

He felt like swallowing his tongue whole.

Mac looked at Jacob. "I love you Dad, I always will. I don't mean to brag, but pregnant with love I brought her back. The cranial labor pains didn't get crippling till right before delivery. It was one wave after another. My water broke. Eyes, nose, mouth—I wet myself everywhere. But I wasn't getting anywhere. I did the mantra: Where's my egg? Where's my egg? All that squirting, still barren. And dehydrated as you can well imagine. So I drank some Pepsi."

Cheryl eyed the room with amazed bewilderment. "It's not your father's place or mine to question how you and your lady friend hooked up. It's good that you had the good sense to drink Pepsi. Love's a fever dream; Pepsi's a thirst quencher. How very mainstream apt."

"Mac and I are on the same wavelength," Claritha/Marilyn smiled. "No one can have it all. Nonetheless, we never gave up on faith."

Faith again? This was fast becoming a sore point. Was this how it ended, with faith and his rusty pipes getting the best of him?

He moved his jaw from side to side, then stopped. I'm not the jaws of death. Were you ever dead at all? Or merely suspended in a trans-formational, caterpillar-cocoonish, regenerative, resurrectional, hiber-nation simulation of a deathlike state? Put your faith in me, both of you. I deserve a fair share of the spoils. It was me who authored *ideas are children.* Now's the time for *both feet on the ground.* Earthbound. I'm your home, the home you run *to,* not *away* from. And while you're under *my* roof, no Disney gobbledygook.

At last the pipes were flushed out. His life, in the balance. To sweep her off her feet, he decided to go with a pinch of pirate, a dab of swag-ger, a splash of humor, a handful of throbbing manhood. He must not sound like he was asking permission. This was a daring daylight robbery!

"Lay down your arms, prepare to be boarded. You're about to be pirated away, and I'm just the buccaneer to do it. Get thee to my cabin, Wench!"

Cheryl said, "Drink anyone? This calls for a toast. Jacob, go get the glasses." He didn't move. Her taffeta skirt rustled. "Be right back," she said.

Claritha/Marilyn waited till she was out of earshot.

"When faith delivered me from death, it washed the hurt away. I've been healed by faith, mine and Mac's. His faith is as strong as mine. He didn't let go. He never doubted the power of love." Her Monroe eyes looked at him with pity. "You were the first to shake the fish scales from my eyes, I shall cherish you forever. I'm very fond of you. I love you like . . . a daughter-in-law."

His cutlass tongue turned to toothpaste. She loves me . . . like a daughter-in-law.

I could just die.

Eight

In which Jacob has a frank talk with the Ark,
Jacob hosts a surprise visitor, and Jacob makes a choice.

Invoking his Grandpa's name, Jacob asked that the Ark clunk him. "You don't have to knock the stuffing out of me, or the living daylights. I'm thinking something in the neighborhood of six-to-eight days out of this world, a mini-vacation from life. Tap me, bop me, jab me. Whack me over the head. Put me under. I'm ready to go. Not as far as Grandpa went. I could die from emotional distress. I could die from a stake in the heart. I could die from my true love breaking up with me. But I don't want to die on the spot. (Not that I have anything left to live for.) I just don't want to rush into any decision I can't live to regret." No cooperation from the Ark. After a night's sleep—hardly a sound one—when you've been truer to your true love than she's been to you, who can sleep?—he had another go at the Ark. He gave, in his opinion, a more than adequate rendering of a wounded, spurned, betrayed, tragic figure. Still, it didn't resonate with the Ark. In demeanor, she was steady-as-she-goes. Next attempt, he re-emphasized his themes: divorced by my Second Love, discovered, bedazzled, bedeviled by my First Love since childhood, a mermaid, rivaled by my son (my irrevocable unconditional First Love), jerked around by the

209

Still Waters, wracked by guilt—if I were the snatcher of the golden egg that would make me a beast and I should get what's coming to me, but I'm not the heavy, I'm somewhat hormonally challenged—laid low over Claritha's demise (the lowest point of my life), undone just yesterday by Claritha's rebirth (like the birth of my boy, one of the bright points of my life), struck dumb by who she looked like, shocked by seeing her with my boy together like *that,* but not so out of my head I can't take a moment to bask in my son's achievement, the kid's a genius, I defy anyone to say different, he's going places, let's hope it's not to more weirdness. The Ark was a sphinx. Just as Jacob initiated another go-around, he bolted straight up in bed and gave his head a thorough going over, searching for tender spots, bumps, sores, any evidence of clunking. Nada. Nowhere to be found. Yet something had to have hit him over the head. Suddenly, he wasn't asking the Ark to strike him. Suddenly, he asked the Ark not to. "The current's right in front of my face and I nearly missed it: A grandchild's on the way. My first. No less a First Love than my son, who loves me, always will. A grandchild whose mother may not love me like she loves my son but love me she does (like a daughter-in-law). My first grandchild's coming at me like a wave of the future past. I could die all right. Of not seeing the treeness of the tree." He closed his eyes and savored the moment. "Disney, hear me roar. Our young are our golden eggs. I am Jacob Koleman, grandson of Marshall Koleman, keeper of the quixotic, keeper of everyday nuts and bolts. As he did for me, so shall it be done: Ground the child, give the child wings to fly, teach him to think inside and outside the box."

The front door clicked open.

Jacob called out from bed, "That you, Harris? Don't take another step. I'm currently in seclusion."

The steps continued.

"I'm warning you," said Jacob. "There's enough on my plate."

Hasty footsteps coming closer.

"Me too, issues everywhere I look." Cheryl strode resolutely toward the bed. She took him by the hand, pulling his to stand. She met with resistance, pure reflex on his part. And then . . . she landed on top of him . . .

Where she stayed.

"I'm on the rebound from my first date in New York City. Just shoot me, I couldn't be by myself." Wriggling into his groin. "Dating is no laughing matter. To hell with dating."

He'd have to know more before making a determination, whether she was thinking in the box or out of the box. "So you're thinking of giving it up?"

"On *Seinfeld* it all looks so entertaining. I divorced you without knowing why. It could be anything . . . nothing even. The nondefinitive answer changes weekly. But not having a first date work out *really* makes me feel like I'm starting from scratch."

"People on the go don't have the luxury of looking before they leap from box to box. It's a box merry-go-round out there. Boxing with boxes is a metaphor for life . . . and dating's in a box all by itself. It tends to feel like the penalty box, does it not?"

"I dated Scott. He wore silk. I'm wearing what I wore to brunch: brown crepe, pearl buttons down the front, very French chic, one-strap pumps, medium heel. Bobbi Brown blush, just a hint of color. I'm not overdone, am I?"

Actually, she looked pretty. "Perfecto," he said.

"Scott thought so too. We were off to a good start."

"Till the walls of the box started closing in, how well I know that feeling." He patted her head. "From the inside of the box, how to think outside the box? That is the question."

"Scott looms so large in bed," she explained. "But out in public, he loses body mass, half of half, a quarter of the man he used to be."

"Scott weighs hundreds of pounds."

"At the brunch table, he was an eel. A skinny, slimy, one step up from a snake-in-the-grass eel. Did I cut him down to size? Do I harbor ill feelings? Does waiting forever to get a date out of someone you've been milking like a cow give rise to an eel? Is jumping into brunch on the first date high-risk behavior? Should I have met him for a quick drinkie? The restaurant ceiling was ballroom-high, the Greek pillars were tall, the windows were chapel-long. The chair he sat on was throne-wide. Was it the room that shrank him? Was it proportional? Natural attrition? Did the physical world shrink him or do I really think he's an eel in sheep's clothing? He was fun, I tell you the man had me in stitches. It's so paradoxical. A man is a good time and an eel? He looms large in bed, looms less in public, and still he makes me laugh? *You'd* tell me if you thought it was *me,* wouldn't you? I'd tell *you.* If I thought it was something you did or said which shrunk you before my very eyes, I would make you aware of it. I wouldn't let you diminish yourself, oblivious to your shrinkage. Some boxes can be seen, others we're the last to know. Those outside your box, looking in on yours from theirs, would be only too happy to pass you a box cutter."

He whimpered. She had shifted off Scott onto him. His heritage: keeper of the quixotic (spinner of stories, builder of whimsical castles in the sand) and keeper of everyday nuts and bolts, thinker inside the box/thinker outside the box was strictly between a Grandpa and his Grandchild. He didn't want to play in the big sandbox, where the grown-up boxes were. "I didn't ask you here."

"Indirectly you did. Yesterday you hit on your son's girlfriend. That, I cannot make heads or tails of. Claritha's a beauty. She was naked. But she was spoken for. Mac has property rights. She's bearing your son's child." Cheryl gave his ribcage a zinger. "You called her *wench,* you never called me *wench.* How come you never wenched me up? Am I not wenchy enough for you? Quite a line you laid on her. Of course, you said it to get a rise out of me, but by the same token, in context—two young lovers, child on the way—it diminished your stature. If you wanted to ask me out, all you had to do was ask. I'm here now. But use a less corny line, if you please, so I can keep a straight face."

His answer would die with him: not interested. You heard of gun-shy? I'm box-shy. (Size counts: Adult boxes are bigger.)

"A writer is only as good as his lines. I can't just lay any old line on you." I could die, he thought. Knock my lines, you knock me. I had to dig deep for the wench line. How else could it have been worded, but how I worded it? "More lines have been written about the art of the pick-up line than the first date. It's the one line that strikes dread in the heart of writers. Line 'em up, knock 'em out—what do you take me for, a hack for hire?" He turned on his side. She climbed off him. He listened for receding footsteps.

"Anything will do, just skip the wench."

If she keeps on putting down my line, I won't have a line left in me.

"Not so long ago, I remember sparks. Moving-in day, Mac's dorm, we had cross words. The exact wording escapes me; you were trashing older women so Mac wouldn't fall into their clutches. Sick lines, lined with lies. The conflict between *us* was beautiful." The tone of her voice said, Give us a chance.

Ever hear the one about the writer who lost his line of thought, couldn't walk a straight or crooked line? End of the line when you can't get your line up.

"And you haven't even asked about the kids."

Now she's trying to force-feed me lines.

"I haven't yet set a date for dinner. When we get together, I do not plan on bringing up the awkward way we met. I won't question the name coincidence either—same name Mac gave to his mermaids— what's in a name anyhow? I just hope her kinks mesh with his. Phone calls go back and forth. Claritha's going to enroll in Adult Ed, Environmental Studies. Mac's leaning toward Environmental Law. They haven't said when they're getting married, probably before she starts to show." She tugged at his sweats. "Why are you so soiled? When was the last time you had a bath?"

It didn't sound like an exit line. He didn't have a comeback. He didn't have a quip. What *did* he have? . . . Like a clunk on the head, a classic fell into his lap. "I'll drop you a line."

"E-mail dating?"

Would she be bought off with the cyberspace box, so much less boxy than face to face? "You could banter me, I could banter you back. But right now, my mind's a million miles away."

"An intriguing line if ever I heard one."

"Get going, before I change my mind."

"Not before you roll over, look me in the eye, and tell me how electrically charged the air between us is."

He rolled over, looked her in the eye, and said, "It's far from stale air. It's not recycled air. It's not secondhand."

"What else is it not?"

"I'm not going to play this game. Even though I stand firm by my lines—the air between us is not recycled or secondhand—so help me, leave now or I'll retract."

"Have it your way," she looked amused. "Spark me from afar. Hit those keys."

THE MERMAID THAT CAME BETWEEN THEM

The beat of his fingers on the keyboard was like a hard rain falling. Where are my lines? Where's the alignment? Got a line on life? I can easily dream of contesting Mac for Claritha. I can easily dream of following that pipe dream all the way to rat-trapped-in-a-box. Is there a book left in me? Do I spend the rest of my life dreaming of what might have been? He hit the keyboard like he was grinding stones. Dreaming of one day bumping into Harris, opening up a Pandora's box of loaded questions? What real evidence do I have that Claritha was ever dead? How sure am I there are no lucid mermaids out there looking for a Prince? Dreaming of someday asking the Still Waters to play matchmaker? Dreaming of a box with all the loose ends tied up. The closure box. Where are my lines? Where are lines that really deliver? His fingers hammered away. I could die. I could go anytime. Where are my lines? What's the punchline? So many boxes I can't write myself out of—the drive-yourself-batty box, the padded box—he stopped typing. He focused on a line he'd just written. It looked perfect on the page. He read it aloud. "Pretty please, can't I just write from the heart?"

✿

Four days later. Total page count: three hundred and twelve. Faxed daily to Finch. He stocked up on food. What I dream of most is nights under the stars. A box called getting-away-from-it-all—my ex-wife/my mermaid daughter-in-law (to be)/my son/my grandchild (could you just die, I'm going to be a grandfather). A change of scenery for the box-shy. The don't-fence-me-in, escapism box. He stood behind the Ark's steering wheel. "Take me away from all this before I die of complications. Just a guy, his boat, and his sixpacks. Footloose and fancy free. Disney, hear me loud and clear. I'm dreaming in real-world time. A seven-day cruise, extended in increments of two, and if I'm not better by then, extending the extensions. Do the math, Disney: any box bigger than a breadbox, I'm gun-shy.

✿

Laboring to release the Ark from confinement, he unclamped, unsnapped, unscrewed, unstrapped, and unplugged. The beltway ramps (devised by Grandpa) were for sliding on. They had reach, a mile out to sea. The wind was picking up. Through the open door, he heard the phone. The machine caught it.

"Yondle Carr, speaking. Don't talk, just listen. Before you, it was strictly ball, sometimes brawl, mostly kiss and make up. In my whole life, never a catfight. Just when you think you know your beasts, out comes Pussy with Claws. I'm working it—"

The machine clicked off. The phone rang. The machine pounced.

"—out in Group. No need to worry, your manuscript's safe with me. I'm still the consummate professional office manager/author advocate/die-hard fan. I really love what you did with *Men in Menopause,* so much heart: You made me, the woman reader, feel that you, the male writer, were my best friend, the big brother I never had. In the female part of the book (men looking at older women) you didn't just disseminate. You did for the egg what *Chicken Soup for the Soul* did for the soul. And in part two of the book—a man in menopause—you were a soup ladle for your sex. My crystal ball says literary pop star. Welcome to fame and fortune."

All the more reason to get out of town. Book tours, signings, readings, talk shows. The press of the people, many of them women. Women to go on picnics with. Boxed lunches, boxes of chocolates, unwrapping their boxes, getting into their boxes, looking for love in all the wrong boxes. He hurried inside, battening down the hatches, the ship beneath his feet, starting her voyage. She would have gone like a downhill skier if the Still Waters hadn't put on the brakes.

"That will be far enough," They said.

Blocking the way like a giant bridge troll, the Still Waters hosed up, rising from the sea, a water fountain with muscle behind it. There was, however, no spray. Standing on the prow, Jacob didn't get soaked. Nor did he have to shout to be heard. The water was shaped like it was coming through a nozzle; thousands and thousands of gallons, intimidating but not crushing.

"We're not charging you with every message in a bottle that comes down the pike. But you made a true believer out of Our Daughter of the Sea, blew her completely off course with *ideas are children*. We saw the golden egg. It wasn't sleight of hand. We saw her entombed. Then we turn our backs and the next thing we know, she's walking on two legs? She's going to go to school? Her face isn't hers? She's young? She's fertile? She's marrying your son? She's filled with faith and hope? Happily-ever-after is a message that travels like fire. Take a gamble, no matter what the price, go for it . . . As far as We're concerned, it all boils down to *juice*. 'Tis a bitter cup of water to live for the juice." The geyser curled down like a serpent hissing. "Jacob Koleman, We've had enough of your depth charges for now."

"I claim asylum. Spare some saltwater and sea air, the rest I'll do for myself. Stargazing, moongazing. Nothing taxing. I won't be contemplating the eternal questions: Who am I? Where am I going? How will I know when I get there?"

The Still Waters slowly lowered Themselves. They spread out, making Themselves into a palm. They cupped the Ark. The Ark glided out to sea. Eyes fixed on the shore, Jacob waved and waved. The gulls on the masts looked on in silence. No one to see him off. Nobody wishing him bon voyage. No turnout at all. It was enough to make a man think, I could die of homesickness. He flung his arms out, open to the world, gathering the world to him. A Noah on his Ark, wondering what was out there. Jacob's cry sent the gulls streaking across the sky. "And tomorrow . . . what will I die of tomorrow?"

The End

The coffee house of seventeenth-century England was a place of fellowship where ideas could be freely exchanged. The coffee house of 1950s America was a place of refuge and of tremendous literary energy. At the turn of our latest century, coffee house culture abounds at corner shops and on-line. We hope this spirit welcomes our readers into the pages of Coffee House Press books.

Good books are brewing at coffeehousepress.org